I've Got it Covered!

Rowland McGabhann

Also By
Rowland McGabhann

Come 'ere I've got an Idea

I've Got it Covered!

Rowland McGabhann

DoctorZed Publishing
www.doctorzed.com

This edition Published 2022 by DoctorZed Publishing.
www.doctorzed.com

Books may be ordered through booksellers or online:

ISBN: 978-0-6455072-8-7 (hc)
ISBN: 978-0-6455072-9-4 (sc)
ISBN: 978-0-6454665-0-8 (ebk)

Cataloguing-in-Publication entry can be found at the National Library of Australia.

This is a work of fiction. Names, characters, places, events, and dialogues are creations of the author or are used fictitiously. Any resemblance to any individuals, alive or dead, is purely coincidental. The views expressed in this work are solely those of the author and do not necessarily reflect the views of the publisher, and the publisher hereby disclaims any responsibility for them.

Cover image © Yelena Bushtarenko | Dreamstime.com
Cover design © Scott Zarcinas

Printed in Australia, UK & USA

rev. date: 25/05/2022

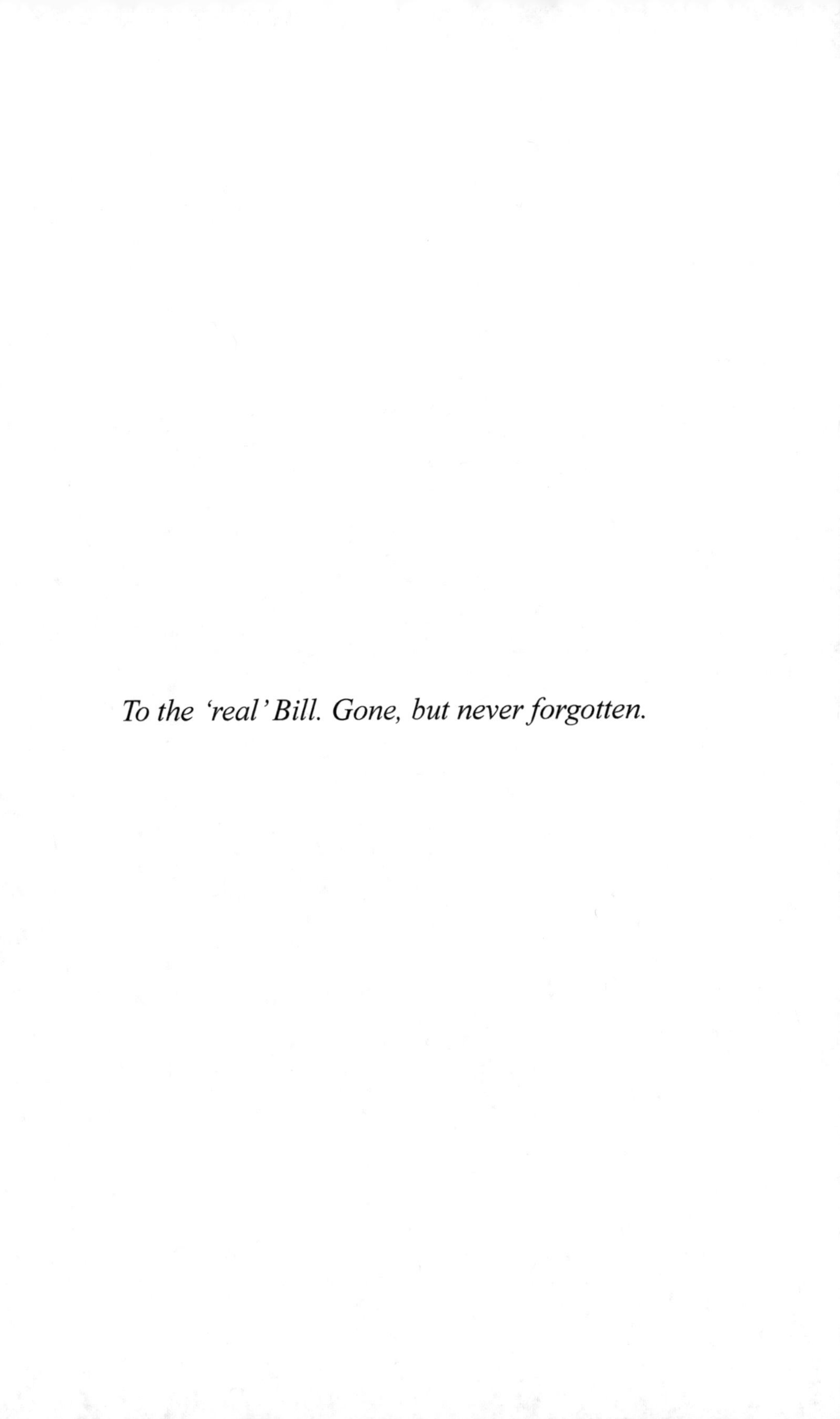

To the 'real' Bill. Gone, but never forgotten.

!

PROLOGUE

Something told me that opening my eyes would be a bad idea.

I was right.

Through the blurred haze of a really bad hangover, I tried to bring my eyes into focus, while at the same time the leprechaun in my head was doing his best to smash his way out with a hammer.

Massaging my head, I wondered why it was snowing, the sky was blue, and I felt quite warm?

I groaned, as I realised it wasn't snowing at all, it was just my drink-damaged brain deciding to punish me further by putting spots in front of my eyes.

With great difficulty, I struggled into a sitting position, as I leaned back, I could feel something hard and cold against my back.

I gently placed my head against the cool surface, while trying to calm that little fella with the hammer down, without much luck.

I turned around slowly, surveying my surroundings. Then I spotted Des.

He is my younger brother and the one largely responsible for my condition.

I could see him stretched out on the ground sleeping soundly with not a bother in the world, he looked as if he was lying comfortable in his own bed. I closed my eyes quickly as the pounding in my head threatened to push my eyeballs out on to my cheeks. The cool surface of what I was leaning against helped to calm my head enough to chance opening my eyes again. Glancing skyward I was greeted with the sight of the biggest blackbird I had ever seen. He was perched on the object I had found so cool a moment ago. We locked eyes and before I could react, to my horror he turned around and proceeded to shit on me!

I jumped up. 'Bastard,' I roared, which I instantly regretted as the man with the hammer resumed his work on my head. The bird tilted his head to fix one of his beady eyes on me. Then as if deciding I was not worth any more effort, took off, dropping one more shit on me as he passed over my head.

Now that I was standing, attempting to clean off his parting gift, I proceeded to take in where I had spent the night, I could not believe my eyes.

I was standing in the middle of a graveyard surrounded by headstones. My resting place from the night before belonged to the late *Juan Forteza*, apparently loved, and missed by his wife and six children since his passing sometime in the last century. I quickly stepped off his last resting place, although I was sure he was feeling a lot better than I was at this moment in time.

I sat down again, this time making sure that I was not sitting on anybody else. Putting my head in my hands, I tried to gather my thoughts. *How did I end up here?* I wondered. Then it came flooding back to me.

'Des!'

I cursed under my breath, glancing at him, sleeping comfortable on someone else's grave. How had I let him talk me into his latest scam? Here we were only two days in Spain and already we were in trouble with the local mafia and the dreaded '*Guardia de Seville.'* I lay down again with a groan and as I closed my eyes, I could hear his voice in my head telling me,

'Don't worry, I've got it covered.'

1

It had all started three weeks before when Des had come up with his latest plan.

Des is the youngest of the family, followed by the second oldest Vin. He is the successful one, something that our mother is always pointing out to us. I am the oldest, and the one who always seems to be involved in Des's schemes.

I had just recently spent a scary time in front of a very angry judge. This was a result of an altercation I had with some fella who, unfortunately for me was endowed with a glass Jaw, which resulted in him been wired shut and drinking through a straw and me spending a night in jail and the judge binding me to the peace for the next six months!

I had a call from Des inviting me to meet for a drink. That is when he informed me, he had just arrived from Spain. He had a tough-looking fella in tow.

'This is *Carlos*. He doesn't speak much English,' he informed me. By the look of *Carlos*, it did not matter what language he spoke. The cold stare in his hard-black eyes said he was used to getting his point across!

'Excuse me for a minute, would you?' I asked him, as I dragged Des out of earshot. 'Who the fuck is that?' I whispered. 'He looks like a hit man or something.'

Des just grinned.

'What are you involved in now and what did you drag me here for?' I snarled, staring at him in horror. 'Forget that I don't want to know. You are not getting me involved in another of your schemes, especially with him,' glancing in the Spaniard's direction. However, he had lost all interest in us and was trying to chat up a girl at the bar in whatever language he spoke.

'Calm down will you, he is all right. He is one of the chaps,' he quipped, as if being 'one of the chaps' an expression he had picked up from some of his dubious friends from across the water explained everything.

'What the fuck has he got to do with the 'chaps', he's a foreigner!' I sputtered.

Des put his arm around me and patted me on the shoulder, as if I was a confused little boy.

'Chaz, listen to me, this is what we have been waiting for,' he said, excitedly. '*Carlos* represents some business owners who are living down in Spain and they need some outsiders to manage some of their interest. They are involved with a lot of characters from here and over the water, nodding his head in some direction, which I suppose was to indicate anywhere which was not here! I convinced them we were the men for the job, they will even fly us down business class!' now grinning at me as if we had just won the lottery.

'Businessmen, interests, are you mad or have you just lost your mind? From the look at that guy the only business he is interested in is bad business.'

'Wild horses would not get me down to Spain or anywhere else that guy is going, and nothing you can say or do would get me on that plane!'

2

We filed out of the plane into the muggy heat of a Spanish summer day. I felt like one of those prisoners who were been extradited back for some major crime.

Carlos was in front looking every bit the terrorist, while Des took up the rear in his best *Miami Vice* disguise.

He had done it again!

I don't know how, but Des had convinced me that the idea was worth a look.

'What have you got to lose?' he had said. 'If you don't like the idea, we still can have a free holiday. You won't believe the place, the streets are lined with girls and the drink is dirt cheap, I bet you won't want to come home,' he had laughed, thumping me on the shoulder as he ordered another round.

I don't know if it was the drink or looking at Des standing there brimming with confidence, his blond-curly hair cascading down around his suntanned face that convinced me to give it a try. The truth was that things were not exactly great for me in Ireland at that moment, due in no small part to my recent run in with the law. Also, the word on the street was that glass Jaw's friends were supposed to be looking for me to settle the score.

This did not worry me that much, as I was well able to look after myself at 6'3", 15 stone and a boxing background. But the courts had me on probation, and I had no wish to get 'banged up' again! The sound of sunshine and girls began to sound okay, as I tried to convince myself that maybe this time his scheme would work out. Boy was I wrong!

We walked out to the front of the airport, where the rest of the tourists were trying to trample each other to death in their rush for coaches to ferry them to their two weeks of debauchery in the sun and escape the drudgery of their boring lives, if the expression on their faces was anything to judge by!

An elderly woman was stabbing me in the back with her sun brolly, trying to ask me in broken English if I was her tour guide and which was her coach. She would not take no for an answer, so in order to save myself from further injury I directed her to the furthest bus I could see.

Des tapped me on the shoulder. 'This way, there is a car waiting,' he said pointing to where *Carlos* was getting into a black Mercedes. I followed them; glad to get away in case the old woman came back seeking revenge.

I sat in the back with Des, while his 'friend' rode up front with some other dubious looking character. The person who was driving just glanced in our direction, gave a nod then lost all interest and began speaking to his buddy in Spanish.

I relaxed and began to check out my new surroundings. This was my first time overseas other than England. Des had filled me in before we left as to our destination. He had said we were going to *Mallorca*, an island off the coast of Spain. According to Des this was the 'in' place, whatever he meant by that!

The airport lay to the east of *Palma*. 'This is the main city,' Des pointed out, as we made our way through the crowds of rental cars and taxis all heading to their respective destinations.

'We are heading to a place called *Palma Nova,*' Des informed me gleefully He was giving me the conducted tour as if he was a native.

'Spain was where many of the criminals from Ireland, and all over Europe ran their operations when things got a bit too hot for them at home,' as he proceeded to give me a history lesson about Spain.

'Now back in the day when Spain was a Dictatorship under a guy called *Franco*, he apparently ran the country with an Iron fist. He realised the Spanish were not the best at understanding the needs of the tourists and the greed of the foreigners trying to get in on the action, which was becoming the main source of income for the devastated country at the time.

So, they decided that he needed some foreign know-how and investment.

However, he had a problem. Now that he was in control, he was not about to sell his country off to anyone, therefore he came up with a plan to allow '*extraneous*' (non-Spanish) to invest in businesses over here.

They passed a law that prohibited any non-national to own more that 49% of any business. Of course, that was all changing as the country was becoming a democracy and joined the fledgling common market, which was still trying to get its act together. Add to that the Balearic Islands had always been a law on to itself, even having their own separate language!'

Puffing his chest out, at his newfound knowledge. 'What has that got to do with anything?' I muttered, 'I did not come here for a history lesson, I have no interest in this *'Franco'* fella, or for that matter Spain.' Little did I know how wrong I would be about that!

'This is where we come in,' Des explained. 'I got to know some of the foreigners that own a lot of the bars and night clubs down here.'

I interrupted him. 'But I thought you just told me that they could only invest in the places do not own them,' he looked at me as if I was a two-year-old to whom he was trying to explain the theory of relativity. 'Don't be a gobshite. Do you think these people are going to trust their cash with some Spanish dropkick? Let me explain how it works.

In the past, they get some Spanish waiter or some other nobody and put him in as a front man, even though the laws had changed in many cases the system remained, as a lot of the politicians and police were in one pocket or another.

As I said this is where we come in. Our job is to make sure that they follow the unwritten rules.' 'What kind of rules?' I asked, a little afraid of his answer.

'I don't know. I think we are to make sure that they don't have their hand in the till or something like that I guess,' he replied.

'That doesn't make sense. Why do they need us, surely they have their own people down there to do that kind of thing?'

'Well, it's like this,' he continued, 'we won't be officially working for them, they told me that it would look bad if they appeared to be controlling the clubs.'

'To whom ?' I asked.

He threw his hands in the air. 'The police of course or I should say, the *Guardia de Seville* they were like *Franco's* secret police back in the day, and not much had changed. They keep an eye on all the foreigners to make sure that they follow the rules, which by the way is impossible under Spanish law. That way if they step out of line, he has them over a barrel.' Grinning at me as if that explained all I needed to know.

'But,' I started to say.

'No buts, I have got it covered, relax, we are going to have a great time,' he grinned.

It all sounded fishy to me; Des did not run in the same circles as I did back home. He was best described as a lover not a fighter, as he had an amazing ability to talk himself out of trouble and when that failed, he would turn to me to sort things out. Also, by the look of *Carlos* and his buddy he was well out of his depth, I hoped I was wrong this time. As far as I could see, Des true to form, had no idea what was going on and was doing his usual and winging it.

As I looked at the beautiful place we were in, I hoped that for once maybe he this time had 'got it covered.'

3

After we passed through the city, we followed the coast for about half an hour. I began to wonder where the nightclubs were.

All we had passed were some small bars, blaring out Spanish music to the passing traffic. I guess in the vain hope we would stop. Eventually we came over a rise and a wonderful scene appeared before me.

I could see a large bay bursting with all kinds of sea craft. Along the beachfront were colourful bars and restaurants surrounded by beautiful hotels and apartments. The place was a hive of activity, bustling with holiday-makers enjoying this lush paradise. I could see what attracted Des and I had to agree with him, this seemed to be the 'in place'.

The car slowed and we pulled into a sandy track that ran between two hotels. Stopping just before the beach *Carlos* and the driver got out and started to make their way towards one of the restaurants.

'What should we do?' I asked.as Des jumped out.

'We are here. Come on,' he roared, as he took off after them. I followed him, while at the same time taking in the sights. This place was something else! I had never seen sand so white. It was like something off a postcard. Now this was a beach!

We have lovely beaches back in Ireland, sadly not the climate! We had at best, a couple of days per year when you could venture out to the sea and when that happened it was packed with the sun starved heading out so you could not move on the roads or the beach, usually resulting in road and 'beach rage'!

The place was packed with scantily clad women and wealthy looking guys lounging in the sun. The bay in front was filled with every conceivable type of watercraft; from small peddle boats to the largest yachts. I now understood what Des meant by the 'In place.'

We had to be here!

I looked around to see where he had got to, he was standing in front of this flashy restaurant and if the 'in place' had a headquarters, this had to be it!

In front was a sundeck. The tables were filled with beautiful people all relaxing in plush chairs. They were being attended to hand and foot by an army of waiters. While their boats bobbed gently at anchor in the water in front, awaiting their return.

'Chaz,' Des roared, much to the displeasure of the crowd as they looked in my direction.

I hurried over before he embarrassed me any more than I already was. Compared to the clientele of this elite restaurant I could have been from some other planet. With my dark complexion and thick black hair coupled with the scar that ran in a white line through my right-side eyebrow down to my chin, courtesy of another of my misdeeds, that was compounded by me being dressed in a worn suit, collar, and tie!

At that moment, that is what I felt like, from another planet!

4

Moving inside I could see that the decor was as opulent as anything you would see in *Vogue* magazine. The only reason I knew this was from leafing through them on the few occasions I went to the dentist!

We followed *Carlo*s over to what appeared to be a private section of the restaurant and were seated at a table was a smooth-looking character. Draped on both side of him were two of the most beautiful women I had ever seen. They were wearing the skimpiest of bikinis. It was all I could do to keep my eyes focused on a spot about a foot over their heads!

'Sit down guys, pull up a seat,' he invited in a strange accent. 'Ah! This must be the famous Chaz that I have heard so much about.' Grasping my hand in his and shaking it firmly.

I looked at Des in confusion but before I could utter a word, he kicked me on the shin so hard it brought tears to my eyes.

'Chaz is very discreet about his talents as you can understand,' he interjected, glancing at me with a smile that told me to shut up and follow his lead.

'Of course, I understand and please call me *Antonio* all my friends do,' he instructed, as he indicated for us to take a seat.

I nodded in agreement, convinced that being his friend was definitely not a good thing! Des could see I was starting to get angry and took over the conversation.

'This is Chaz, you will have to excuse him; he is a man of few words,' he said, reaching over to give me a playful slap in the back. 'Chaz this is *Señor Antonio De Sota* that I have told you so much about,' trying to put on his best Spanish accent.

All I could do was nod as I pulled my ankle out of reach of another of Des's well-aimed kicks. Fortunately, *Mr De Sota* took over the conversation at that moment.

'*Antonio*, I insist,' he laughed, 'Drinks!' he said, raising his hand a fraction of an inch. To my amazement not one, but two waiters appeared.

'What would you care for? I can recommend the *Sol e Sombre*,' he offered with a flourish. I glanced at Des in confusion, not having a clue what he was talking about.

'We would love a beer, nothing like a beer on a hot day, that's right isn't it, Chaz?' he asked, nodding in my direction.

I nodded back, wondering when the last time was we had a beer because of the heat; considering hot days in Ireland were few and far between. Within seconds the drinks were in front of us. I could not help thinking that Irish waiters could learn something from these people!

The conversation turned to small talk, with *Antonio* asking Des many details about Ireland. Des did all the talking for us, mainly because I had no idea what he had got us into, but I had a bad feeling I was about to find out.

As the next round of drinks arrived, *De Sota* settled back into his chair and with a dismissive wave of his hand signalling to the girls that it was time for them to go.

'All right, let's get down to business. I am sure Des has filled you in on our little problem,' he inquired, looking in my direction.

'Well, I …' I was about to answer just as the pain in my leg from one more kick caused me to yelp.

'Are you in pain?' *Antonio* inquired. Des jumped in.

'No, he has got an ulcer that gives him a bit of bother, he is not used to this heat. And yes, I have filled him in on the problem you would like us to help with,' he replied.

Smiling at me as he punched me on the arm, in case I tried to say anything. He did not need to worry as I did not intend to open my mouth except to perhaps bite his head off!

'I see,' he said, nodding his elegant head. 'I am afraid the problem has escalated. It seems our friend has a companion in the *Guardia de Seville,* and he now believes he is untouchable. So, it now appears it will require

Charles's special talents to resolve the problem,' he replied, his coal-black eyes burning a hole in my skull.

I glanced at Des and, to my surprise, I could see that he was in shock. There was silence and I could see the expression on *Antonio's* face suddenly harden. Now it was my turn to say something. 'Before we go into that, perhaps it would be better for us to check things out for ourselves,' I replied. as I lashed out, connecting with Des's ankle and as if I had flicked a switch, he immediately started to talk.

'I agree, what exactly is the problem? Can we inquire what has happened? I thought all that was required was to keep an eye on this guy,' he asked.

Antonio shook his head. 'Let me explain. The little faggot has forgotten his place. He now believes he really owns the club and is filling the place with all his '*maricon'* friends, which, I would not mind if they had any money! All they do is drink water and play the music so loud that it has driven away all the paying cliental. But more importantly, it is causing problems for me and my associate's other interests. I paid him a visit to remind him what his role was, but to no avail, he has continued as if he is untouchable. He had a cop there that it turns out is his boyfriend. He believes he is protected, which in fact does present a problem hence this is why we had to look outside of our island.'

He said this as if this answered all out our questions. 'However, enough for now, I can see that both of you are tired from your journey, I have an apartment arranged for you.'

I'd had enough, 'Hold on,' I interrupted. 'None of this makes any sense to me, what are these other 'interests'?'

There was silence from all around the table and *Carlo*s stood, glaring at me. He was wasting his time; I had been glared at by the best of them and I had just about enough of this dickhead. He had been trying to intimidate me ever since we met back in Ireland.

I stood up ready to sort him out when *Antonio* jumped in. 'Let's all take a breath and relax. Chaz is correct, but as they say a picture paints a thousand words. Finish your drinks and my driver will take you by boat to see the place from the water so you can check it out. So, everybody, drink up!'

'*Salud!'* raising his glass. Draining it and slamming it down, 'I will see you tomorrow. Then we can discuss the matter more, ' he said, then with a nod to his 'boys', he stood and shook our hands.

Des stood, pulling me up by the sleeve. 'See you then,' he replied.

I just nodded as he headed for the door.

5

One of his cronies stood and indicated for us to follow him. As we passed *Carlos* who stood there with rage in his eyes, I imagine he did not get fronted very often.

'See you later,' I said as we passed. Somehow, I knew things between us were not over by a long shot. Des was about to say something to me but shut up when he saw the look in my eyes.

Outside we accompanied our supposed driver, he took us on a short walk to a jetty where numerous boats were moored.

'*Aqui,*' he said in Spanish, indicating a flashy powerboat.

We hopped in and again I was aware of been overdressed, Des , as decked out in all the right gear, shorts, and t-shirt so I discarded my jacket, shoes, and tie, not that it helped much. Now I looked like a tourist from Blackpool!

We proceeded to make our way around the point from *Palma Nova* towards *Magaluf,*

'We are heading for *Cap Falco* it is just around the other point.' I have been there once before with some chaps, Des informed me. I looked at him and indicated to stay silent.

'We will talk later, I don't know what you have got us mixed up in, but that story is full of crap, there is something else going on here and it is not just over some ownership dispute.'

Des went to say something but one look from me shut him up! As we came around the second headland, I could see that the coast was much less developed. Instead of gaudy hotels, bars, and restaurants, it was instead, apparently reserved for exclusive private villas with the exception of a small marina in front of this amazing grotto. The entrance was at least one hundred feet high, cut out by nature over centuries. The cliffs towered above, sparkling in all their stark beauty.

In front was what appeared to be an external restaurant and judging by the way it was decked with beautiful couches in the form of giant conch shells. Only for the 'in crowd' as Des would say. There were few boats moored and I could see that there was not a lot of activity.

'This is the place,' Des pointed out. 'The club is inside and is only open in the night you have to be one of the 'chaps' to get in,'

I glared at him, enough about the fucking 'chaps' let's just figure out what the fuck is going on so we can get out of this place. He looked at me in shock as if I was trying to spoil his great plan.

I tapped the driver and indicated for us to be dropped off, at first he did not seem so happy about the idea, eventually he agreed, shaking his head, and pointed to a small beach a little further along. I guess that he did not want to be seen checking the place out.

I nodded, indicating that would be fine, he maneuverer the boat's nose into the beach and allowed for us to climb out over the front. As we jumped out, he pointed to the spot as if to say he would remain there for our return.

We set off in the direction of the club, we must have seemed like the 'odd couple', Des perfectly decked out for the occasion, while I looked like I had just got out of jail (Not too far from the truth). 'You will have to get some summer gear,' Des pointed out.

'What for? I don't expect to be here that long,' I pointed out.

He laughed, 'If you want to stand out you are doing a great job!' I begrudgingly had to agree; seeing as I had been stared at since we had arrived.

We walked into the bar at the front of the club and were immediately accosted by a waiter, 'á table for lunch?' he inquired, holding out a menu.

'Not at the moment,' Des replied, 'we will have a drink first,' he turned losing interest as he walked off. Poofter, Des growled. I nodded in agreement.'

We got our beers and took a wander to check out the place. The entrance to the grotto was cordoned off; before we could even attempt to enter, the waiter appeared again. 'The night Club is only open in the evening' he declared, haughtily.

'Just checking it out,' I informed him, as he strutted off again.

Standing in front of the grand entrance, we could see the cave extended into the depths even though the sunlight penetrated deep into the interior. The ceiling appeared to vanish into the mountain top, there was no doubt it was an amazing creation of nature.

'Shit, this is really something,' I whispered. 'Have you seen it at night?' I asked Des.

'Not yet,' he replied. 'I have only been here like this, for lunch.'

To my surprise, I could see that there was a cutting, which allowed boats to enter into the interior; there was a natural lagoon where patrons could disembark onto a luxurious landing area. No doubt to allow the beautiful people to alight in style. At the futurist point of the lagoon, it narrowed down and was sealed off with solid-steel gates, I could see a notice in Spanish '*Pelegrosa, no entrada*'. I could guess what this indicated: 'Keep out!' This was looking fishier by the second!

We sat down and ordered a couple more drinks. 'This makes no sense,' I said. 'Why the fuck does this guy need a couple of Irish guys to deal with some wayward partner, there has to be more to this, it does not feel right!'

Des nodded. 'Okay, so what, we just string him along for a couple of days, pretend we are checking things out and when we have had a good holiday, we piss off home.'

I shook my head, somehow, I do not think this guy likes to take no for an answer. 'What have we got to lose?' he asked.

That's what had me worried. 'Okay, let's give it a couple of days,' I said. 'Let's go shopping for something for me to wear.'

6

When we arrived back, *Carlos* was waiting on the dock for us. Without a word, he indicated for us to follow him to a car that was waiting.

It was only a short drive to the apartment which was directly on the seafront. We sat in silence until we pulled up in front of the modern apartment block. Getting out I looked up at the name '*Los Delfines*.' *Carlos* must have seen me looking.

'The Dolphins,' he said. This was the first English words I had heard him speak.

'What?' I queried him.

'The name of the apartments, it means the dolphins,' he replied, in excellent English, seeing the shock on both of our faces. He sneered. 'Because I did not speak English before does not mean that I can't. Your apartment is 401, here is the key. I will pick you up at 10 in the morning, don't be late,' he warned without saying a word.

He got into the car and drove away, leaving us standing. 'That guy is pissing me off,' I snarled, starting to lose my temper.

'Well, what do you know, he speaks English,' snorted Des. As if that was all that mattered.

'It seems that is not all that you didn't know,' I roared. Grabbing him by the shirt in rage. 'What have you got us into now and what does he mean by my 'Special talents?'' I snarled in his face.

'Well, if you stop choking me and calm down for a minute I can explain.'

'Go ahead, I would love to hear this,' I roared even louder.

'Well, keep your voice down before you get us into even more trouble.' Indicating over my shoulder at the stares of people who were passing by. 'Let's go up to the apartment so we can talk,' he said, making his way through the door.

7

We found 401; it was a large two-bedroom apartment, clean and comfortable with a large balcony overlooking the bay.

'Nice place.' Commented Des, as if nothing had happened.

'Fuck the place, you don't have any idea what you got us mixed up in, have you?' I demanded.

'Shut up and calm down,' he snapped. 'I know things have not worked out quite as we planned, but we will work it out, don't worry. Come on, let's see if there is anything to drink, and let's relax,' he said, making his way to the fridge. To his surprise, it was stocked with plenty of food and beer. We took a drink and headed out to the balcony.

'Okay, tell me how in hell all this came about?' I asked, downing the beer in one gulp. He sat down, indicating that I should do the same.

'Well as I told you, our job was to watch this guy and to keep an eye on proceedings. I had no idea that it would get to this,' he replied.

I glared at him. 'So why did you need me and what does he mean about my 'Special talents?'' I asked again, as I paced up and down trying to calm down. He got that sheepish look when he knew he had put his foot in it.

'Look, the only way I could get this job was by telling him I had a brother who had been involved with some tough problems back in the past and resolved them in his 'Unique way.'

'What!' I gasped. I could not believe my ears.

'Calm down will you. I had no choice I had to tell him something. I had no idea we would ever have to do anything,' he replied, trying to ease my fears, without much success.' Before I could reply, he continued. 'I told him that you handled problems for them. For example, if somebody was giving them trouble you would convince them to back off or else, they would have an accident.'

'You told them I was a hit man!' I gasped. This was getting worse by the minute.

'No, of course not, if that's what he wanted he could use one of his own men. He needed somebody with no connection to him that could convince this guy to behave, make him think there was a possibility for him to have an accident,' as if that explained everything.

'What's the difference? That is just a fancy way of saying fix him up!' As I looked over the balcony to see if throwing him off was an option.

Des stood up and started to pace. This was something he did when he was trying to talk himself out of trouble.

'That is just the point!' he exclaimed, 'I could see that what he wanted was someone that if it came to that, it would have to be a real accident, nothing that anyone would suspect. That is when I came up with the idea to say it was your 'Specialty.' I never thought for a second it would come to this!' he moaned. As the predicament he had created started to sink in.

'My God, so that is my specialty, making accidents happen. We are screwed, you have really done it this time Des.' I snarled, not believing the shit he had got us mixed up in!

We spent the next few hours drinking the free booze and trying to figure how to extricate ourselves from this nightmare. Finally, we decided the only thing to do was to play along for a few days until we could bail out of this place before we were turned into an accident!

Finally, I decided to confront Des, I knew he wasn't telling me anything like the real story. 'This time you have bitten off more than you can chew, brother! If we are to get out of this, you would be advised to have me on the same page,' I snapped.

I knew my brother, he found it very hard to face facts, or the truth for that matter. So, I was not surprised when he just stared at me, then dropped his head and mumbled something. At that point I knew I was not going to get anything out of him at this time, considering the shape we were in, so I decided the best thing to do was to play along until tomorrow and then I would try to get us out of this place before we were turned into an accident!

8

Finally, we decided that we should go shopping to try to get me looking a bit less like the 'fixer' that Des had labelled me!

Heading out, within a couple of hundred yards we were confronted by a row of shops selling more or less the same things. Stuff for dumb tourists (like me) that did not bring the right gear. In less than half an hour I was decked out with shorts, t-shirt, sandals, and cheap sunglasses. I bought a couple of changes and some 'smart casual' in case we had to go the club. Looking at myself in the mirror, I reckoned that I was starting to blend in a little better.

We dropped my old clothes back to the apartment and then decided to check our surroundings.

'We should head in the direction of this club and get a feel for what's going on,' I suggested. Des nodded, 'good idea, I know a few good places in *Magaluf.*' It was a beautiful evening, so we decided to walk. 'What is the score in this place?' I asked Des, if there was one thing, he was sure to have done was to try to figure out what was the best way to make some money, and by that, I mean the local scam.

'Much the same stuff as back home, fleecing the tourists is number one, but the real money seems to be counterfeit alcohol, and the usual drugs (something we had always shied away from) this place is ripe for the pickings, although this island is geared towards package tourists, it also attracts the rich and famous, there is some fabulous marinas, besides *Palma Harbour* . They recently completed a marina near to *Palma Nova*, called *Portals Nous*, it is almost exclusively the home for the biggest luxury launches and yachts, and some are so big they have to moor on the outside wall,' he informed me.

'How does this have anything to do with fake booze, and while we are on the subject, what are you talking about, do you mean Potheen?' I asked.

He laughed, 'Everything, they copy everything, even down to the identical bottles, as well as selling it here. I believe a lot of the crew from back home are smuggling it back and are making a packet.'

I looked at him, 'I assume that this is not legal, so how do the cops not come down on them?' I asked. He looked at me as if I was brain dead

'How do you think? Backhanders, this place is still to a great an extent operating under its own rules and as far as the mainland is concerned, as long as it is kept low key and there is no blowback, they look the other way. Remember this place is a major cash cow for Spain due to the tourist money and I am sure the black economy due to the 'chaps' is a great incentive as well.'

He could see that he had my attention, so while he was on a roll he continued. 'Well because it is an island, most goods arrive by boat and as well as the shipping traffic it also includes all the rich folk that come and go, are allowed to do so, with very little interference from customs, as a large percentage are Spanish craft and anything from foreign waters only get an occasional search and that again is usually dealt with by a greasing of the palm. Especially as this place seems to operate by its own rules, remember before *Franco* all of Spain was made up of independent provinces, all trying to operate independently I nodded, 'How does that help?'

He shrugged, 'I guess due to the fact that not only do they come from all over Europe I also found out that a lot of the rich crowd, came in their boats from South America, and were pretty dodgy.' Then the light came on.

'So now, I get it! It would be easy to land them anything here and then distribute whatever all around Europe, 'Exactly'!' he replied.

I was beginning to understand why this place was attracting the likes of *Antonio.*

I also remembered a lot of the old crew from back home had moved their operations down to this part of the world. Armed with this new information I decided we should checkout this ultra-rich marina to see if I could get a handle on what was going on, and figure out what exactly, my beloved, but sometimes naive brother had got us involved in!

9

I could not believe my eyes!

This place was like somewhere Gordon Gecko would hang out! It was crammed full of all types of the best luxury cars, and that went for the boats as well, if you could call them that.

The smallest was at least 100 feet long and all had a full crew, dancing in attendance on the people lounging on the decks. They were all dressed in what could be considered the highest of fashion, which was to say: the smallest scrapes of material of the most expensive kind!

It was like a candy shop, but well above my pay grade. Restaurants and bars surrounded the extensive marina including all the top-brand boutiques, as well as real estate brokers and yacht chandlers. They certainly had all the needs of the rich and powerful covered.

We were wandering along checking out what was going on when a voice called out, 'Charles!' I turned to see someone I had not seen for a long time signalling from a table in what looked like a cocktail bar.

He indicated for us to join him. Des looked at him in confusion 'It is someone I knew back in the day,' I explained. The name I knew him by was Bruno Reilly; his family had immigrated to Ireland from some part of Italy and after that had intermarried with an Irish family the Reilly's, a tough bunch from the north side of Dublin. They opened an Italian restaurant which I later found out was a front for their drug operation. We had a few clashes when we were young but soon found out we were a match for each other, but in reality, he discovered I had been getting the better of him and that was before I had filled out with a larger size and muscle. So, a truce was unofficially declared. He was cut from a different cloth, and soon had become a full-blown gangster. As long as he kept his drugs and other illegal activities away from anyone connected to our family, he did not bother me, but as far as I was concerned, he was bad news.

'What are you guys doing down on my part of the world,' he roared, as he gave we a big hug as I introduced him to my brother. He gestured for us to take a seat.

'Only for a minute,' I replied, 'We have to be somewhere.' Not wanting to give Des a chance to speak out of turn. 'Come on, a quick drink with a couple of Irish lads.' Pointing to his friend. '

This is Mick Ryan; you will have to forgive him he is from Carlow, so he speaks a little funny. The guy gave me an ugly look. I could not remember where, but I had a run with his guy before.

'This is Chaz and Des, they are from Dublin, we used to butt heads back in the day, but everything is grand now, right?' he grinned.

'Sure,' I replied, 'what are you doing down here?' I asked.

'Well, you know the story, things got a bit hot for us, so we followed a lot of the crew down here. With internet and mobiles, we can run things from here and enjoy the high life at the same time.

'What about you guys?' he asked.

Before I could stop him, Des blurted out, 'We are helping a fella called *Antonio* with a little problem.' I could have killed him, right now he was the problem, and he could not keep his mouth shut!

Before he could say any more, I interrupted, 'Don't mind him, we are only down for a bit of a break, this guy that he is talking about is someone Des met the last time he was here, he asked could we look at something, but I said we weren't interested.'

Bruno suddenly got a cold look in his eyes, 'What the fucks are you doing with that Colombian shithead?' he asked.

'He is not Colombian; he is Spanish,' piped up Des. I wished the floor would open up and swallow us.

Bruno shook his head, 'Be fucked, he is not Spanish, he had to bail out of *Bogotá* as the police and CIA were after him, again what are you doing with him?'

I stood up, 'look, I do not know what this guy is about or where he is from, but we are not involved in any way with him, okay!' Bruno tried to stare me down, but he knew he had no chance. He started to relax a little,

'If you say so Chaz that is good enough for me, but a word of advice, that fuck is far out of your league all he can bring you is trouble you can't handle, now sit down and have that drink.'

I stood for a minute then decided to calm things down. 'Sure, why not,' as I sat again. 'So tell us what is happening with you?' I asked, he looked at Mick then replied, 'Not here, Chaz, maybe later.' I could tell something had changed dramatically since Des had mentioned *Antonio*.

'Sure. I understand,' I replied as the drinks arrived. We chatted for a while; I nodded to Des, 'Well, thanks for the drink, maybe we will see you around.'

He gave us a nod. 'Sure, I am usually around here, drop down anytime,' he said, with not a lot of sincerity.

We shook hands and we made a beeline for the exit.'We need to get somewhere that we can talk, this is getting too weird for my liking,' he said.

Des went to say something, but the look on my face must have told him to keep his mouth shut.

10

We found a cab with a driver that had a fair grasp of English. I asked him to take us in the direction of the infamous club we were supposed to be sorting out.

He looked at our attire. 'Not open till much later *Señor*, it is a place for *los ricos,'* he said, as if to say, we would not fit in.

'I know , we just want to check it out before we buy it,' he looked at us as if we were crazy, then burst out laughing, 'You Irish, the same as the guys there, always joking!' he smirked.

What the hell was he talking about, Irish in the club? I decided to shut up, I could see that there was a lot more we had to find out about this mystery club!

We travelled about two kilometres past *Magaluf* when we arrived at a crossing, indicating a sign that pointed to a small road leading to the coast. 'Just at the bottom of that road, sure you want to go there now? It won't be open,' he informed us.

I spotted a tavern on the opposite road alongside what seemed to be an abandon church. 'This will be fine, just drop us there,' indicating the pub. I paid the taxi driver, as he roared off in a cloud of dust, leaving us standing outside 'Billy's Place.'

'Look' said Des, pointing at a something written on the window, 'A place for the chaps! Looks like we have found the right place.'

I looked at him in bewilderment, even though we were in all this trouble, he still seemed to believe that as he would say, 'He had it covered.' I just glared at him and marched towards the door to get some relief from the oppressive evening heat.

Just before we entered, I stopped Des. 'Not a word inside to anybody about what's going on, got it?'

'Of course, what do you take me for?' he asked, as if that would never happen! 'Come on then, let's get a drink and try to figure how to get out of this mess.'

Inside I was pleasantly surprised to find the decor was a mix of comfortable alcoves and traditional Spanish bar, restaurant. We took a cubical that had a view of the outside, which had tables to sit outside, if you could stand the mosquitos! We had only just sat down when a beautiful Spanish server came over, 'What can I get you?' she asked.

Neither of us said a word, which is saying a lot for an Irishman! She laughed, 'I get it, the accent, my dad is from London, and I learned my English from him and his mates.'

I finally broke the silence, 'You are right there, I could not believe my ears, you sound just like an English girl, what do you think Des?'

'You are a lot better looking than any English woman I have ever seen,' he declared, raising an imaginary glass, 'Slainte'. Laughing She raised her hand '*Salud*' that is how we say it in Spain, now what can I get you Irish fellas?'

'There you go again, shocking us, I guess it was the accent, so what would you recommend?' Des asked, taking control of the situation, I could see he had not taken a blind bit notice of what I had said, as soon as the girl arrived, I could see where his focus was, not that I blamed him, but now was certainly not the time! Fortunately, I could see this young woman was well used to advances

She just laughed. 'Okay, I will just surprise you,' walking off, with a provocative flick of her well-rounded hips.

'Shit,' Des blurted out. I put my hand up, 'Forget it, now is not the time, we have enough problems without having her father after us.' A couple of minutes later she arrived back with the drinks, 'These are on the house, from my dad,' she said, pointing to a fella waving from behind the bar.

We nodded and raised our glasses to him, 'Tell him thanks,' Des replied.

'You can tell him yourself, he said he will be over in a minute,' she said, again giving a sexy smile as she walked away, confident we were watching her every move.

'Remember, if this guy comes over, not a word about your 'chaps.' I warned Des. 'Don't ...' he started.

Before he could finish, I interrupted him. 'I know, 'you have it covered',' I snapped

He shrugged and proceeded to drink his pint. 'Well, what's the plan?' he asked.

I paused for a minute, and then replied, 'Look, as far as I can see this is far bigger than anything you or I have ever been involved in. As far as I am concerned, we string him along tomorrow, and then head for home as quick as we can.' Des got a worried look on his face, but before I could question him, I spotted the girl's father on his way over with a tray of drinks.

'Welcome chaps, what brings you to my fine establishment?' he asked, putting another round of drinks on the table. He portrayed an air of confidence and approachability. He was just less than six feet, with the look of a bodybuilder or boxer; although he looked like he was heading for fifty, he had a barrel chest and arms that looked like they could crush you to death if he was so inclined.

'We were just checking things out, only arrived yesterday,' Des informed him.

'Well, you are welcome here,' laughing in a relaxed manner, sliding onto the seat in front of us. 'Bill Heart is the name, and you have already met my daughter *Maria,*' pointing in the direction of the bar, where the Spanish-looking girl was chatting to a couple of clients. Before we could say anything, he said, 'Her mother is Spanish, as you can see she got her looks,' he laughed. He went on to say he had left Britain back in the seventies, to, as he alluded, 'Relax, and get away from it all.' Whatever he meant by that!

He met his wife down here, she is *Mallorquina*, and the head of the 'Manor', which I was to understand was to mean she was in charge. 'Anyway, as usual I am talking too much, what's your story, usually only locals come this far down the coast?' he asked.

'We were going to check out the club,' replied Des. I should have cut out his tongue! As usual he had forgotten to keep his mouth shut. I noticed a complete change in the demeanour of the affable English man.

'Are you talking about *Cap Falco?'* I jumped in,

'Somebody we met told us that it was worth a look, said it was built in an underground cave.'

He paused, taking a sip of his drink, 'You seem like nice lads, so I am going to give you some advice about this Island. although on the surface it may seem like it is all sun, sand and fun, there is a lot going on here that you would do well to avoid, that club is one of them,' he warned.

I decided to see what I could find out. 'We had heard from some of the guys me met in a bar last night that it was a one of the, in places around here,' I replied.

He leaned forward, looking us straight in the eyes. 'For a couple of guys that just arrived yesterday, you are well informed.' He pointed at me, 'You look like have been around the block, take it from someone from the same background, the crowd that are involved with that place, even though they may come from your part of the world, are out of your league, there are things going on there that quite frankly don't make a lot of sense, my advice is to be careful.'

Before I could say anything more, an attractive woman came out of the back of the restaurant, I would guess from the kitchen, making her way in our direction.

'I hope you are not frightening anymore of our customers with your stories,' she announced, putting her arm around Bill with obvious affection.

He laughed. 'Say hello to a couple of Irish chaps that have come to join us, this is? He stopped. 'You have not told us your names?'

'Chaz and Des,' I replied. 'This the boss, I call her '*Guapa*' but for you chaps she is *Maris*.'

She sat down to join us, nodding to a young waiter that had just arrived, she spoke to him in Spanish, issuing him with instructions, then sent him on his way. We chatted for a while and to our surprise, he quickly arrived back with a tray laden with a selection of dishes. 'Eat up, you are our guests tonight,' she instructed, pointing at the delicious spread. We did not need to be told twice, and got stuck in.

The drinks and food kept on arriving. I had no idea how hungry I was and judging by the way Des was attacking everything he was the same!

That is how the evening went, Bill regaling us with stories from his time as a barrow boy in the east end of London, and from the sound of it we had a lot in common. Finally, I realised our problem was still alive and well and we had an appointment with Des's mate in the morning.

'Got to go, before I collapse,' I announced, 'how can we get a taxi?'

'Don't be silly, you are our guests, *Roberto* will drive you home,' as he signalled to the young waiter that had served us.

'No don't do that, I am sure he is too busy,' I replied. They both laughed, '*Rob* is our son, and he is always driving Bill's 'chaps' home.'

They introduced us to him, He spoke better English than most of the people I knew back home. 'See you outside,' he said, making his way to the door. Neither Bill nor his wife would take a penny from us. As we said our goodbyes, Bill pulled me to one side and whispered, 'I can tell you are playing your cards close to your chest, remember what I said, watch you back, you know where I am.'

I nodded in thanks, believing that was the end to that. How could I have been so wrong!

11

We made our way outside to find *Rob* waiting in a latest-model Range Rover. 'Nice car,' Des commented, as we climbed in. 'The bar business must be better than I thought!'

He laughed. 'Dad loves his cars he is sort of a Godfather to all the Brits down here and drives anybody home that has had a bit too much.'

Somehow, I did not think he was talking about the average grey-haired retiree. We chatted about life in general, living in such a beautiful place.

He laughed 'It is like a pretty woman, who lulls you into a false sense of security then, *BOOM*! Crushes your balls.'

We roared in laughter; he was just what I needed to take my mind off the predicament we were in. I found him relaxed and very confident and we agreed to catch up again, although with us deciding to head home tomorrow I could not see much of a chance of that. He dropped us off at the apartment, waving as he roared off.

'Great guy, will enjoy catching up with him again,' Des said, as he waved to the departing cloud of dust.

'Well not too much chance of that, have you forgotten we are out of here tomorrow,' I snapped, annoyed that Des could put any trouble out of his mind without a second thought.

He got a sheepish look on his face, 'That could be a bit of a problem.'

I looked at him. 'What does that mean?' I asked.

'Not here, wait till we get upstairs,' he mumbled, making a beeline for the door. We had no sooner got into the apartment than he turned to me, 'Okay, I think you had better get a drink.'

'What the hell are you talking about, get a drink?' I snapped. Ignoring me, he poured a couple of large shots of Spanish brandy, handing me one of them he turned and squared his shoulders,

'Well, here is the thing, I don't have my passport,' he blurted out. I froze, feeling a chill creeping through my body,

'What are you talking about?' I snapped. 'He sat down heavily in one of the chairs, head slumped. Finally, he raised his head, looked me square in the face,

'I am in a lot of trouble Chaz, they have me over a barrel over a bit of business I got into while ago.' The expression was enough to tell me this was going to be bad.

I sat down, took a strong slug of my brandy, then, looking at him said, 'You better start from the beginning.'

12

DES
BARCELONA, 10 MONTHS EARLIER

Des felt a cold shiver in the base of his neck, which worried him as he was sitting on the balcony of his apartment, on that warm start to another beautiful day, overlooking the busy *Las Ramblas.* As the locals and tourists packed the busy walking street, looking for their early morning coffee or breakfast, he leaned back and shrugged off the feeling, putting it down to the old saying, 'Someone walking over your grave.'

Everything had been going smoothly for him lately, as his latest 'venture' seemed to be going on without a hitch. When he had arrived in Spain a couple of months ago after having to beat a hasty retreat from Portugal, where his sunroof business had suffered a major setback.

He had come up with the idea of supplying DIY sunroof kits that he had sourced for somewhere in Eastern Europe. It had gone fine until he discovered that the sale of such aftermarket items were, illegal, so when the local police came looking for him, he had beat a hasty retreat across the border into Spain, leaving a trail of angry costumers behind.

He relocated to the beautiful city of Barcelona, where he met up with one of his 'chaps' from England, called *Diego,* where they had worked together as barmen. So, when *Diego*, whose mother came from Spain, and had decided to move back home.

He was the first-person Des looked up as soon as he arrived. It was when they were sitting at a bar one evening, having a *cana* and trying to figure out how they were going to make their fortune that the idea came to Des. What had happened was, that he noticed the tourists seemed to always be asking directions from the staff in the bar and that's when the light came on. 'I've got it,' he cried.

Diego nearly spilled his beer in shock. 'What?' he spluttered.

'Tourists, we will make tourist maps, you used to work in printers, and you speak the lingo, we will make one in English, we will clean up.'

One thing you could be assured of was his enthusiasm, perhaps that was why he seemed be able to convince his brothers and friends to go along with his many schemes. In any case *Diego*, who was not endowed with the sharpest mind, was prepared to give his idea a go.

So, they proceeded to the planning stage. The first thing they discovered was you needed a licence to engage in any venture that involved tourists, a very guarded species in this country that relied on their much-needed cash. This did not deterred Des. He discovered an old map of Limerick, a city back in Ireland, with the unfortunate nickname of 'Stab City' due the frequent occurrences of this nature. With the help of *Diego*'s skills, they were able to insert the names and details of the tourist attractions in *Barcelona*, using the similar outline of the two cities.

It was an instant hit! *Diego* came up with the idea of putting them in a simple case with the maps inside and attached a box where you could help yourself and deposit the cash in an honour system.

Next, they deposited them in any hotel reception or tourist money exchange. To encourage the owners, they allowed them to take 30% and leave the balance, which they would collect and restock at their leisure. It was working like a dream, so when he felt that foreboding feeling, he dismissed it and headed off to catch up with his partner. That was a mistake!

They met each morning to have breakfast and plan their day, so Des was surprised to discover *Diego* already there, not renown for being an early riser—Des usually was on his second coffee (a habit he had picked up since leaving home) before he arrived. He had a grim look on his face, and it matched the white tablecloth perfectly!

'What's up?' Des asked.

He signalled him to sit down, then shifted in close and whispered, 'Have you seen the news?' Which was a stupid question to ask, as Des did not speak a word of Spanish. 'What?' he asked. 'We are fucked,' he exclaimed, pushing a copy of a local newspaper in front of him, pointing at a story on the front page.

'What's the point of showing me that?' Des said. 'What does it say?'

He shifted even closer, and proceeded to give Des the bad news. As the story was reported in the paper, the son of an important diplomat from the USA recently arrived with his new bride on their honeymoon had been attacked and mugged in a part of town where even the police were not inclined to go.

'So, what has that to do with anything? If they were foolish enough to go to that place, what would you expect, looking for drugs?' he asked.

Diego looked at him in frustration. 'I'm not finished,' he snarled. 'They were discovered walking in the street with nothing on but their underwear, they were taken to the nearest hospital, where a sharp-eared reporter who was there interviewing someone, recognised who they were and managed to get their report of the incident.'

Des shrugged, losing interest in the story. 'So?'

He stuck his finger up to silence him, then continued. 'She reported that early in the day they had purchased a map of the area, and were trying to find *Barcelona*'s famous football stadium, but it directed them to where they got robbed instead,' he paused and looked at Des.

At last the penny dropped. 'Shit, do you think it was one of ours?'

He looked at him in amazement, then read on. 'The police are trying to locate the culprits with a city-wide search, according to the reporter, who could see her Pulitzer Prize looming. She had done her research and was able to report they were looking for a light-skinned fella with thick-blond hair down to his shoulder who spoke with a foreign accent, his accomplice appeared to be a local, they reported. When the lead detective was questioned, he said that they believed that blond chap was from one of the European countries and the other was Spanish. He said that they would be in custody very soon, the American embassy were reported to have lodged a major complaint with the government and were assured the people responsible for this terrible crime would be brought to justice.'

Putting down the paper, he again turned to Des, 'Now do you see we are screwed?'

They decided to head back to Des's, as out of the pair of them, *Diego* was pretty well known, thus going back to his place was not an option. As soon as they arrived, Des could see that his pal was at the point of total panic. He began to pace up and down in the apartment.

'Will you sit down so we can figure out our next move?' Des pleaded.

'Move' he screamed, 'I don't know about you, but I am out of here, as soon as I can figure out where.'

Des tried to calm him down, while at the same time beginning to realise that perhaps this was a lot bigger than any of his previous skirmishes he had with the law. The more he tried to reason with his panicked friend, the worse he got.

'You just don't understand, this place is not like anything you are used to, one thing you do over here is not mess with the government, I should have never let you talk me into this!' Des decided not to remind him that he was the one that was the most enthusiastic when he had suggested it, figuring that it would only make him more out of control.

'Let's calm down, it's not like we have robbed the crown jewels,' he looked at Des in horror.

'We might as well as have. A crime against the State, which includes defrauding the tourism industry. Plus on top of that, we have succeeded in getting an American official's son and wife mugged on their honeymoon, causing a diplomatic incident. I would not be surprised if they reintroduced the death penalty just for us,' he groaned. Shaking his head, as his eyes rolled in his head, I could see that there was no point in trying to reason with him.

He suddenly stopped. 'I am out of here, and I have just remembered that my cousin has a fishing boat here, he will drop me off in France.' As he bolted for the door, he stopped and turned, then asked, 'Do you want to come, he will take you I am sure.' Judging by the state *Diego* was in he was not sure that his cousin would be as obliging as he imagined.

'No, thanks but I will wait and see what happens in the next few days,' he nodded, then without another word, was out the door and gone.

13

ISLAND OF MALLORCA, THREE DAYS LATER.

Stepping off the ferry, he stopped to take in his new surroundings. He had decided on this location, mainly because it put a body of water between himself and the authorities back on the mainland, plus the fact that a good buddy of his had been on to him to come over and help him out with a new venture he had started. It was in a place called *Magaluf*, which as it happened was the place where most of the English-speaking tourists resided.

So, he had called Giovani to let him know that he was on his way.

'Great news' his pal cried, 'I can sure use the help, come over and you can crash with me, until you get a place.'

Des agreed, not wanting to tell him the reason for the hurried departure from *Barcelona*. 'Sounds great,' Des lied, as all he wanted was somewhere to keep his head down until the trouble blew over, 'I will see you in a couple of days' as he hung up.

'Des,' he heard his name being called out, it was Giovani, they had met back in Ireland where his family had a fish and chip shop. Not surprising as they were originally from Italy, the Scarpa family had emigrated just after the war. Des and 'The Shoe', a nickname he had acquired as he had foolishly told his mates that his surname, Scarpa, was Italian for shoe!

They went to school together and had become good friends, even though he had nearly got him thrown out of his family because of an incident involving some stolen fireplaces!

'Jump in,' he yelled, as he waved from his open-top jeep. 'The Shoe' was an avid sportsman, helped by his natural ability to excel at almost any type of sporting activity, be it football, tennis, swimming, or for that matter anything that challenged him in the sporting arena. So, the jeep fitted his personality perfectly.

'Great to have you here, Des, business is booming, and you are just the man I need.'

Des looked at him with suspicion, 'It's not hooky, is it?' he asked, as at this moment the last thing he wanted was to attract any unwanted attention. He roared laughing, 'It is water-sports activities, sailing, scuba diving, water skiing, and all other types of activities, and before you start I don't expect you to do any of that stuff. What I need is someone with your personality to deal with the hotels and clubs that send a lot of the clients, we are on the beach, it is the perfect life, sun, sand, and girls' slapping him on the back.

Well true to his word, in no time Des slotted right into the operation, within a few weeks had even got proficient enough to start giving windsurfing lessons. Des started to relax a bit and the situation he had left behind was receding in his memory. He had given Giovani a brief outline of the problem, downplaying it. He only told him about it was because he was always in contact with his family at home and he did not want anybody to know where he was.

'It was no big deal, but you know what the brothers are like, so as far as anybody is concerned, I have been here all the time, okay?'

He agreed, seeing as Des had become a big help to him. This was to come to an end!

They were sitting outside at the restaurant bar, which served as an office-come-reception for their activities, as well as a gathering place for the young lively crowd that gathered there every evening to continue their holiday festivities. They were enjoying a couple of drinks when a couple of guys arrived, they could not have been more out of place. One was smooth-looking Latin type, who could have easily passed as a film actor or a drug dealer, dressed in a stark-white silk shirt and matching linen pants with slipper-type shoes. He was flanked by a tough-looking character who looked like he had been carved out of stone. The smooth one headed straight to our table, sitting down across from us, the other one stood to one side with a stony look on his face. Des looked at Giovani, a question on his face. He had a concerned look.

'This is *Señor Antonio De Sota,* a business associate of mine,' he said.

Stretching out his hand, he spoke with a strong accent. 'Ah, you must be the famous Des that Giovani has told us so much about. I believe you are from Ireland, one of the true Irish, of Viking origin if he is to be believed.'

Des could not believe his ears, for once he was lost for words. The guy could see the effect he was having, he smiled. 'Don't be concerned, we are all friends here, for instance, this whole operation here' indication the surrounding area, 'would not be possible without the support of some of our very important officials who are also some of our friends and this works because 'friends' help 'friends', correct Giovani?' fixing him with a look that defied any disagreement.

Giovani glanced at Des sheepishly, 'It's true and that without *Señor De Sota's* help with getting the proper permissions the business would not have been possible,' he looked from him to this dubious pair and began to get a very bad feeling.

'I believe you can be of assistance to us with a very special problem we have, I have to discuss somethings with Giovani, allow me to introduce my associate, *Carlos*. He looks after all my security arrangements and will explain everything to you,' indicating for his sidekick to join us, while standing and indicating for a worried looking Giovani to join him. He stood slowly, then as he turned to leave said, 'sorry Des' with a frightened look, then walked off.

The other guy took the seat across from Des, 'You must be wondering what this is all about, allow me to inform you,' he said, raising his hand to silence the response that was on Des's lips.

'We require an Irishman with special talents, which we have been reliably informed your brother has got,' glancing in the direction of the departing Giovani. 'Now before you start to mount your objections to helping us, let me inform you what is at stake. Your friend has explained the dilemma you have left behind you on the mainland, I have many contacts in the *Guardia de Seville.* In another life I have been of some assistance to them. So, when I made enquiries as to their search for a pair of unknown criminals that had caused an international incident, I put two and two together, and before you begin to deny it, the photo of you which we provided has positively identified you, so down to business. Then he proceeded to tell Des what was needed of him.

'He will never agree to it! Anyway, he is in Ireland and would never agree to come over here,' Des tried to explain.

'Perhaps you don't understand, if by any chance you can't convince him to help, I am afraid you can expect to spend a very long time as a guest of the Spanish government, and I can tell you they are not four-star accommodations ,'

Des dropped his head. 'The only chance I would have to convince him is face to face at home.'

'Then it is settled we are off to Ireland.'

Des looked in shock. 'We?'

'Of course, you did not think I would let you make that journey alone, especially with the problems you have, no I will be accompanying you, taking care of all the arrangements' then paused and added, 'Oh, and taking care of your passport!'

14

MALLORCA
APARTMENT 501, PRESENT DAY

I sat in stunned silence, of all the jams he had got himself into, this one was at a whole other level. We sat for a while, just staring at each other, finally Des broke the silence. 'Okay, you might as well give it to me, and get it off your chest, I know I screwed up this time, I really did not want to get you involved, but *Carlos* has me convinced that if I didn't, I was really going away for a long time, I did not know what else to do.'

At first my reaction was to tear into him, but based on his incredible story, and the obvious pain he was in I could not bring myself to pour salt on his wounds. 'Time for that later, first of all we have to find a way out of this mess.' Whatever trouble we had got into in our rocky journey in life, one thing stood true with 'The brothers Savage', we would screw with each other, but if anybody made the mistake of trying to get one over on any one of us, would soon incur the wrath of all of us!

Des lifted his head in surprise, expecting me to blow my top, a look of relief crossed his face. 'I knew you would figure a way out of this, so what is our next move?' he asked, as if all I had to do was wave a magic wand.

'Des, listen carefully to me, we have never had to deal with this class of people before, you have to understand we are just guys that bend the rules from time to time, and these guys are at a whole other level! They are full-on gangsters who in my opinion are capable of doing real harm, remember, we are in a foreign country with no backup, so from this moment on, do not do or say anything without clearing it with me first, got it?'

He nodded his head sheepishly, 'Got it,' as he refilled his glass from the bottle he had brought from the cabinet, so kindly provided by our captors. 'So, what are we going to do?' he asked.

'We are going to do nothing until I can figure out just what they want from us, and before you start with the bullshit story they have handed you, there is no way that they have gone to all this trouble just to sort out some wayward shithead front man.'

'But *Antonio …* ' he started to say.

'Stop!' I snapped, 'Let me ask you, who has your passport?'

'The Boss, I suppose.'

'Well, that's where we put our focus for now, remember all we want to do is get it back and then get the hell out of here, so this is what we will do.'

15

Exactly on the dot of 10 am, there was a knock on the door. It was *Carlos* arriving to bring us to the main man.

'Are you ready?' he inquired. He had suddenly got very polite. This made me even more uncomfortable!

'Sure, we will be right down,' I replied. We had got up early and decided that until I could get a handle on what was going on we would see what unfolded, convincing ourselves that we could sort this out, looking at this guy's demeanour I started to have my doubts. As soon as we got into the car, they took off without a word.

'Alone today?' Des asked, trying to make conversation.

'*Marco* had something else to do,' he replied, without turning around.

I prayed to God that Des would not ask him what that was. I was sure it could not be anything good! Thankfully, Des glanced at me; my expression must have given him the message because he left it at that.

As we sat in silence, I went over in my mind what we had decided to do. My plan, if you could call it that, was to carry on as if we were on board with his request until I could figure out how to get the passport back. This time we did not head to the beach club, instead we headed towards some place called *Calvia*, at least that what the signs said.

'Where are we going?' I asked.

Without turning his head *Carlo*s replied, 'Don't worry, we are going to *Señor Antonio's* estate'

'And why would you think we would be worried?' I asked, wanting to judge his reaction. He shrugged, without replying, as we continued in silence. The journey took about a half hour into the hills behind the coast. We arrived at the gates of what appeared to be some sort of country estate, proceeding up the driveway, on both sides were carefully maintained pastures; on one side, I could see some beautiful horses following the car like some sort of escort. Arriving to a Spanish-style hacienda where there were a couple of fierce German shepherds standing guard.

'Stay in the car until the dogs are put away, unless you want to be torn apart,' growled *Carlos*.

I glanced at Des, who was grinning. He nodded to me, with that, I jumped out, stood by the door of the car, and waited as the dogs charged towards me. I dropped on to one knee and put my hand up as if to say stop. They slowed in confusion not expecting this response, one of them trotted up to me, I remained in the same position as I spoke to them in a singsong voice that I had cultivated a long time ago. One came forward cautiously and proceeded to sniff my hand as the other one began to circle me and check me out from all sides, then the first one started to nuzzle my hand as the other pushed in for some attention. In a couple of moments, we had become best friends.

You see, since a young age I discovered I had a special connection with animals, especially dogs, and had been able to control them with ease. Inside the car, *Carlos* was in complete shock. Des grinned at him as he stepped out to stand beside me. 'There is a lot you still have to find out about us Savage boys,' he snipped back at the shocked tough *Carlos*.

'You are full of surprises,' we heard from the door where *Antonio* was standing. Beside him was presumably the dog handler, who was staring in disbelief. *Carlos* exited the car and with obvious fear of the animals, approached us. The dogs turned and immediately proceeded to snarl at him.

'Your dogs are a good judge of character,' I quipped to the shocked *Señor Antonio*.

With an angry look on his face, he nodded to the trainer, who called to the animals to come to him, they turned their heads and proceeded to ignore him, while continuing to enjoy been stroked. Seeing the anger on his face, I indicated to my new friends to follow me. They trotted alongside with their tails wagging. 'Nice little pups,' I said, as we made our way to the door, followed closely by *Carlos*, who kept glancing in the direction of the dogs in fear.

Antonio stood to one side and invited us inside, 'Welcome to my home,' indicating to the spacious open plan of his magnificent home. He ushered us out on the patio, which was alongside an Olympic-size swimming pool. 'Take a seat, drinks?' he asked, without waiting for a reply he signalled to a servant that was standing nearby. 'Well, you have seen the club yesterday, sorry I could not accompany you, but I could not be seen in your company, you understand, so was that helpful for you?' he inquired, as he relaxed on one of the poolside chairs.

I decided I had enough of this game, 'Before we get into that I have a couple of questions. First, why have you taken Des's passport?'

A surprised look crossed his face, but he quickly recovered. 'When you rent a property here in Spain your passports must be lodged with the Municipality here in *Calvia*, it will be returned shortly,' looking in *Carlos's* direction, who nodded in assurance. This was getting really weird. *Who is running this show?* I thought.

He continued, 'In the meantime shall we get on with our meeting?'

Des was just about to jump in when I stopped him. 'Here is what will happen, I am not sure what you have arranged with my brother, but I make my own arrangements. So why is some low-life front man so important that you must bring in some unknown, when you have seemed to have enough 'help' around here,' looking pointedly at his henchmen surrounding him? 'Also, what is the Irish connection with that place?'

Antonio froze. 'Who has been talking to you?' he asked.

'You are not the only one that has connections,' I replied. He stood up and at the same time, *Carlos* reached inside his jacket. 'If you keep reaching for whatever is inside your coat, I could think you were looking for trouble,' I snapped, as I also stood, for a moment I was sure that all hell was going to break out when I heard *Antonio* burst out laughing.

'Relax everyone, we are all friends here,' as he nodded to his sidekick. 'So, Señor Chaz, what is your suggestion?'

Remaining standing, I replied, 'Tomorrow is Friday, I presume that this guy will be there, by the way does he have a name?'

'*Juan*,' he replied.

'Fine, so can you arrange for us to get in without a fuss, also have someone to contact inside?'

'No problem,' he replied, as if nothing had just occurred. All that you require will be delivered to you tomorrow, I bid you goodnight,' as he turned and walked off.

*Carlo*s indicated for us to follow him, we headed out where he turned to the guy who was supposed to be in control of the dogs, jabbering to him in Spanish. I suppose he was to get him to call his dogs who were happily trotting alongside myself and Des. Finally in frustration, giving the poor fella a clout on the side of the head, to send him on his way, as he walked off, I could hear the guy mumble, '*Puta Gringo.'*

I glanced at Des, to see if he understood. 'Foreign prick,' he whispered.

This was another twist in the tale, so *Carlos* was not Spanish, I didn't know what his game was, but I had the feeling he had a different agenda going on.

I stopped and turned to him, 'You and I will have to have a chat soon, seeing as we are to be working together,' I said, as I told the dogs to follow their 'former' handler. As they trotted back, passing *Carlo*s, at the same time giving him a savage look. He backed away, glaring at me.

'The car is waiting to take you back to your apartment,' then turned, going back inside. I called out to him, 'Don't forget our chat, and I will expect you to have that passport with you then,' as he vanished inside.

16

Antonio was striding up and down on the patio, obviously very unhappy. 'You assured me this would not be a problem, the older brother is not as gullible as the young one, he concerns me,' pointing an accusing figure at *Carlos*.

'I assure you all is under control; I agree that this Charles is cleverer than anticipated, that is not your concern, remember the primary reason we came up with this idea, is to remove that *'maracon'* and his cop friend, which I hope I don't have to remind you is why we came up with this plan?'

SIX MONTHS PREVIOUSLY

'Those Irish are going to wreck everything,' *De Sota* ranted, letting his Latin temper break through his usual calm, suave demeanour.

Carlos nodded in agreement, 'Correct, but as we discussed, if we make the move we have planned, it will give that *Bruja* a reason to remove her son and more importantly his 'companion.''

The deal in question was one that *Antonio* had hashed out with the 'governor.' At this time the Island, due to its autonomous statue, allowed it to govern itself under the guise of the 'Insular council of Mallorca', a body of thirteen closed appointments, usually made up of titled family members and influential businesspeople, one who was reported to have given a 3.5 million yacht to the King of Spain for a gift! The present leader or as she was known '*La Gobernadora*' a graceful woman, in her late thirties, who, due her marriage to a wealthy shipping magnet and the fact that she was closely related to the Royal Family had placed her in a powerful position, something she embraced with fierce pride.

Christina de la Vega was not a woman to be trifled with, as those who were foolish enough to do so, soon found themselves stripped of any 'benefits' from their association with her and more importantly the council, which had on its board people with connections to the feared *Guardia de Saville.* The deal that *Antonio* had presented to her was, as he announced was a 'win-win'.

C*arlos* was the one who had made the meeting possible, due to his family connection. He had been born in Argentina to a German mother and a *Mallorquina* father, who had dubious connections to the Germans that had fled to there after the war, helped by his family connections back in *Palma*, who aided them in return for a boat load of cash. Many of the family were old aristocracy of *Mallorca*, dating back to the time of the Moors, this family tie was the only reason which enabled him to arrange a sit down with .the boss lady.

What *Antonio* had presented to her was an idea that he and C*arlos* had for an old club '*Cap Falco*', the brainchild of an eccentric Englishman with too much money and not enough sense. The Club was constructed inside a natural grotto, something which this volcanic Island was famous for. The result was a beautiful creation, embracing the natural splendour of the cathedral-like caves with modern music and lighting. Sadly, the story, although glamorous was also tragic, due to massive cost overruns, topped by problems with acoustics making the rocks inside unstable. The result was it was closed down, the poor man went broke and was found floating in the spectacular mini harbour he had created inside, where it had remained closed until that day.

Antonio's main business was cocaine, or rather the distribution of the same, due to his connections in Latin America and *Carlo's* scheme for the club, which due to its location on the Island and more importantly, its direct access the sea due to its natural harbour, made it a perfect cover for the movement of their product.

'And how exactly does this benefit our community exactly?' she inquired, arching her eyebrows, while directing her gaze in the direction of *Carlo*s, as if to indicate that *Antonio* was only being given this opportunity due to this unique connection.

Unfazed he continued, 'As far as the community is concerned, a guarantee that none of the product would remain on the Island, simply a distribution point, and of course the financial benefits to the people who facilitate this venture,' and then outlined how his operation could be used to incorporate cash from other 'sources', allowing them be 'returned unblemished.' This was *Carlos*'s contribution; he knew that the main problem facing the people involved in running the Island was how to clean their earnings from the numerous bribes and kickbacks they received.

So, an agreement was reached, *Antonio* could reopen the club, all permits would be provided, and a 'licence fee' was agreed upon. Then came the sticking point, *Christina de la Vega* had a son, the result of an unfortunate error, when she was very young.

Juan de la Vega was what you could call the black sheep of the family, by the age of eighteen, he had already developed a reputation as a 'wild child'. His mother tolerated a certain amount of his bad behaviour, so long as it did not distract her from her other ventures. The main problem the mother faced was that he was gay. At that time Spain, being a staunch Catholic country, took a poor view to the practice. So, she saw this as an opportunity to resolve that problem and put him to work.

'My son will be my representative at the club, as you know in order for any foreigner to have a business here, requires Spanish participation.'

All of *Antonio's* objections fell on deaf ears, so after the final details were ironed out, the club got the green light to reopen.

17

For a time, all proceeded smoothly, with the help of *La Gobernadora* arranging all necessary permits, plus *Carlo's* ability to motivate the workers to whip The Club back to its previous splendour. His efforts resulted in not only the club operating successfully, but he also seemed to be able to control any interference from *Juan* and his friend. This was to come to a swift halt!

'We have a problem,' *Carlos* announced, as he marched into *Antonio's* office, slamming down a package on the desk.

'What's this?' *Antonio* glanced up from the line of coke he was snorting.

'This is what's wrong, I have just found out that the little shit has got a side deal going on with that Irish crew.' The crew in question was headed up by Bruno Reilly and his Hench man Mick Ryan, they had relocated to the Island a while back when things got a bit hot for them back home.

'What!' screamed *Antonio,* spilling a couple of hundred euros of coke all over himself and the floor.

*Carl*os ignored his display of petulance, continuing, 'From what I can find out, Mick Ryan had got on the right side of his 'friend' and convinced him that the club could be used by his crew as well, and before you ask, I have spoken to the son, but in his eyes, his pal can do no wrong, he then pointed out that he has, and I quote, 'The full support of his mother'.'

Antonio slumped in his chair, 'If the cartel get word of this, I am dead.'

'You are correct, so we will have to resolve this quietly, but we can't be seen to be involved for a couple of reasons, if we upset the *Gobernadora* or the police it will bring everything down.

'So, what do we do?' he asked, diving into his drug supply again.

'Relax I have a plan,' he replied. *Antonio* lifted his head, wiping the powder from his nose. *Carlos* laughed, clapping him on the shoulder. 'We let the Irish sort it out!'

18

PRESENT DAY

'How are we going to make your plan work now?' asked *Antonio.*

Carlos nodded, 'Simple, remember as I outlined in the beginning. The idea of bringing this couple of Irish guys on board, giving them the idea that their task was to bring a wayward associate back into line, we would infiltrate them into the club, giving them time to make some waves, while I arrange for problems to escalate to the point that the 'son' had lost control. We can then move in to remove the 'Irish gang problem', blaming it on our patsies'

'Yes, but what about when they say we employed them in the first place?'

Carlos, shrugged his shoulders, 'Who do you think the Queen Bee will believe, the guys that solved the problem, or the ones that caused it? Remember, I have the brothers over a barrel. If they're any trouble, I'll just remind them of the problem Des had with the *Guardia de Saville*.'

This seemed to relieve *Antonio*. 'You are right, and if they become a problem they can always disappear and again blame it on the Irish crew cleaning up their mess.' So, it was agreed that things would proceed as planned, they would give them a visit to the club and make sure that they would be noticed, so when things started to flare up, they would be remembered. 'You sure that you have it arranged for them to be noticed?'

Carlos nodded, 'It is all in hand, they will be the centre of attraction, leave it to me.'

Antonio clapped his hands, 'So time to get to work, I am heading back to the beach, I will leave everything to you, to make sure things goes according to plan' as he marched out to his car.

Carlos watched him drive off in a cloud of dust, lighting a cigarette with a sly grin on his face. 'The question is, whose plan?'

19

Carlos arrived promptly at 9 am to drive us to The Club. As soon as he was in the car, he passed a slip of paper back to me. 'This is your contact inside; he will assist you with whatever you need.' On it was a single name: '*Franco*'.'

'How will I know him?' I asked.

'He will find you' was the curt reply. We continued in silence, travelling the same route, taking us past the area where Bill's Bar was located. We turned into a driveway that led in the direction of the coast. It was a gravel track, lined with Olive trees on both sides, which only served to add a more sinister feel to the journey. We carried on for a kilometre or two until we came to a small building right on the edge of a cliff that overlooked the sea. It had a sign '*Cap Falco*' in lights above.

Getting out of the car, I notice *Carlos* was staying put. 'You are to get a cab home when you are finished, it would not be wise for us to be seen together,' he informed us. 'You will be contacted tomorrow.' Then without another word, he drove off in a cloud of dust.

'Fuck you,' we both muttered, as we watched him vanish.

We were met at the entrance by a stunningly beautiful woman who directed us to a lift, which was located in the back of the small but plush interior. We entered, accompanied by our host, she pressed the button and it instantly descended at amazing speed.

The doors opened and a kaleidoscope of lights and sound assaulted us. It was so loud I could feel it thumping in my chest. We stepped out to the most amazing sight!

We were standing on a ledge with stairs on both sides. They descended into a vast grotto that had three levels and at the bottom was a huge dance floor surrounded by plush seating. 'Is this not the most amazing place you have ever seen?' Des shouted in my ear, over the incredible sound.

I reluctantly nodded. 'Some English millionaire squandered his fortune building this place. It was an underground cave and he cut this place out of the solid rock, just before it was to open government engineers banned the place. They said it was too unstable. It drove him bankrupt, and he committed suicide,' he informed me

'How is it open now?' I roared back in his ear.

He shrugged. 'Money talks I suppose.'

We made our way down to the next level; I could see that in the front of the vast cave was the large opening out to the sea that went all the way down to the cavern floor. They had constructed a marina so people could arrive by boat. It was obvious judging by how many boats were moored that the place was attracting the 'in crowd.'

When we got down to the dance-floor level, we made our way over to one of the lounge areas. Making ourselves comfortable on one of the luxurious couches, I cast my gaze around at this incredible place.

The ceiling was at least 30 metres high and in the walls above were alcoves for dancers to perform. I felt a presence beside me. '*Señor Antonio* sends his regards. My name is *Franco*, and I am here to assist you.'

I looked up to see a young fella, dressed as a waiter beside me. I tapped Des. 'Your pal's assistant is here.'

He glanced across. 'Great, bring us some whiskey,' he asked.

'And some beer,' I added, not quite ready for the hard stuff yet! Before he took off, I grabbed him. 'Where is the owner sitting?' I asked. He pointed across to the other side of the floor to a raised section. I could see there was a table protected by a red velvet rope. Seated there was a handsome fella of about 20 years of age. Sitting beside him was a tough-looking fella in uniform. I did not need to be a rocket scientist to figure this was the front man and his cop boyfriend. As soon as the waiter departed, I leaned over to Des. 'That story about the gay problem is a load of crap, just look around,' I said, indicating how the place was pulsing.

He nodded in agreement, 'What's the plan?' he asked, a troubled look on his face.

'As I told you, we do nothing! Remember, we are only putting on an act, until I figure how to get your passport back, so let us have a few drinks until I figure out our next move, I think I'll have to try to talk to this guy.'

Before he could say anything, the drinks arrived. As our assistant placed them on the table, I indicated that I wanted to speak to him. 'Is there somewhere we could talk?'

He glanced around, and then indicated for me to follow him. I signalled to Des to remain and keep an eye on our target. Following *Franco* we made our way to a small alcove, where we were somewhat insulated from the sound. 'What is the problem here?' he looked confused. I tried another tack. '*Antonio* told me you were his inside man here, so what have you seen out of place?'

He glanced around. 'Señor, all that I know is that there is some problem with the shipments,' he replied, nervously.

I froze, then quickly gathered myself, 'Who told you that?' I snapped. I could see him visibly shake, 'Please, Señor, don't say anything, I am only telling you what I have heard.'

I fixed him with a cold stare. 'Don't worry, just tell me what you know.'

'All I know is that I heard *Señor Juan* yelling at his business partner that some shipments had been mixed up and the big bosses were not happy, that's all,' he stammered.

'Are you talking about *Antonio*?' I asked.

'No Señor, the BIG bosses,' pointing towards the sky. 'Please Señor, do not tell them I was talking to you, I have a wife,' he begged in panic.

I could not believe my ears, not wanting him to freak out, I tried to reassure him, 'Relax, I am on your side,' indicating I was ready to head back. He seemed relieved as we returned to Des.

The music was so loud that you could feel it pulsing through the seats. The one responsible was a wild-looking DJ who was perched on a huge ledge, hewn out of the rock face. It extended out like a massive-male appendage, below it an artificial waterfall cascaded down the cave wall directly behind where *Juan* was sitting with his partner.

I did not know if it was the drink or the noise, but it seemed as if the whole place was shaking. Everything was swaying, as if in time to the music.

'This place does not feel right; I have never felt like this.' Fed-up sitting around and getting my head smashed by the sound and vibrations, I decided to do something ... looking around I spotted our waiter, lifting my hand to signal he instantly headed in our direction.

'What are you doing?' Des asked.

'Shut up and keep your eyes open,' I replied, as our waiter friend arrived.

'Si senior?' he inquired.

'I want you to do me a favour,' I shouted over the din. 'I would like to meet *Señor Juan*, could you arrange that?'

He glanced around nervously, then nodded, 'Follow me.'

Together we made our way across the dance floor to the platform where he and his pal were seated, as if surveying his domain. 'Just wait here a moment while I speak to him,' heurged me, fear in his voice. As we reached the roped-off area where they were seated, he quickly went over to *Juan* and whispered in his ear, who then looked in my direction and I could see that the cop had spotted this and immediately sat up, glaring at me.

This was not starting out well! He whispered something back, then turned to his friend and gave him a reassuring pat on the leg. The waiter signalled for me to approach. 'This is '*Señor Juan,'* he said, and then with a nod, departed. He greeted me in Spanish, '*Ola, como esta*?'

I looked at him blankly, 'I am sorry I don't speak Spanish,' I replied.

He laughed, as a smile crossed his handsome face. 'No problem, we speak English,' nodding in the direction of his friend. 'Is this your first time in *Mallorca*?' he asked.

'Yes,' I replied. 'I am here with my brother. We arrived today.'

'*Bueno*,' he said, with a laugh. 'And already you have found a club that caters to your tastes. *Verdad*.' He chuckled as he gave me a wink.

I realised he thought I was gay! How dumb was I? Of course, what else could he think? I was in a gay club, and I had asked for a private audience with him!

'I just wanted to compliment you on your fantastic club,' I blustered. 'I have heard so much about it and its wonderful history.'

He got a strange look on his face. 'Yes, some would say a dark history, it is said these caves are haunted with the souls of all who perished here.'

I looked at him in confusion.

'In the past these caves were used by pirates to smuggle in all types of contraband. Later when this ill-fated construction was underway, many died under mysterious circumstances, either by accident or simply disappeared,' he obviously could see the shocked expression on my face, laughing, he continued, 'But not to worry my friend, the ghosts have all gone, perhaps it is the music?'

'Wow,' I replied in feinted wonder. 'Great story, I was wondering if I could look around up there,' pointing to where the disc jockey was perched.

'Normally, it is off limits, but seeing as you are so interested in the history, you can check it out, just don't go where it is signed not to go. I would love to accompany you, but as you can see, I am occupied now,' he replied with a sly grin, as he placed his hand on his pal's leg!

'No problem, I will be fine,' I replied, trying not to look where his hand was.

'Stairs,' he said.

'What?' I said, confused. 'The entrance to the upper floor,' he replied, pointing to roped-off stairs by the side of the music booth. I thanked him and beat a hasty retreat.

20

Making my way up to the upper floor, I could see that it was where all the machinery needed to operate The Club was housed. I had not a clue what I was looking for, anything that would give me an idea as to what was the real reason for our involvement in this mystery! I poked around in a few of the rooms, if you could call them that, most were converted natural alcoves with doors attached. I was just about to give up, when I heard someone shuffling around behind a door with a big sign, 'No admittance.'

I quickly ducked into a storage room, holding my breath, I had been around enough dodgy situations to get the feeling that something was up!

I heard the door of the other room being opened, and the sound of someone leaving. I waited a few seconds as the footsteps receded to look outside, to the sight of somebody disappearing down the way I had come in. I only got a look at his frame for a second, he was shorter than I was, but at least as solid, most remarkable was his head and shoulders, it was almost as if they were cut from the same stone as this cave. He was solid with his blocky head planted directly on to his shoulders, I could see he had a buzz cut of almost white-blond hair, no way was he from this part of the world. He glanced around just before he vanished out of view, to display a tattoo of a cross on his face!

I checked that I was still alone, and then headed over to where he had been.

I ducked inside and pulled the door closed behind me. I was in a massive room, which housed from what I could see was a monstrous machine. I went to examine it, to discover that it was a huge water pump.

I knew enough about engineering to know it was far too big to be just for the club's plumbing needs. Then as I examined it further, I suddenly realised what it was for.

As this whole cave system was interconnected with the sea and had to be drained continually to prevent it flooding. By following the pipes, some were feeding the water features like the waterfall below the disc jockey. At intervals there were glass inspection points where I could see that water was been pumped at great pressure out through vents and back to the sea. I wondered what that person had been doing. I was just about to give up when I noticed paint flakes on the ground. On inspection I could see that valves had been rotated, instead of pumping out they were diverting the water pressure into, from what I could see was a giant holding reservoir, and from the groans coming from it was not happy!

Discovering this I realised that it was about to blow and started back to warn Des. In my urgency I became disorientated, because I suddenly found myself overlooking the dance floor. I had entered the DJ's platform by mistake.

I stood there in shock for a moment. Then I spotted Des across the floor waving at me with *Franco* standing beside him, in shock at the sight of me in full view!

I started to wave frantically at Des to indicate to get out, but before I had a chance to react, I felt a massive pressure shock, and my world dissolved into blackness!

21

Down on the floor of the club *Franco* was frantically tapping Des on his shoulder to get his attention over the din of the music. He was pointing in the direction of the disc jockey's perch. Des looked where he was indicating and to his amazement saw his brother gesturing frantically. At the same time, he felt a massive vibration beneath his feet.

Suddenly there was a huge sonic boom, which drowned out the sound of the music. He could not believe his eyes; Chaz disappeared in a cloud of dust and rubble. At the same time the DJ and his platform was starting to lean at a crazy angle. Then as if the giant penis had decided to lose its erection, it tilted downward!

It seemed to hang for seconds before, with a terrible rumble, it started to plunge to the ground followed by a huge volume of water, transforming the decorative waterfall into an inundation!

'Chaz!' he roared, as he saw his brother's limp body plummeting down in the deluge of water and rubble. The whole place froze for a moment, everybody stood in amazement. Then all hell broke loose!

As people scrambled for their lives, he sprang into action. 'Come on,' Des yelled grabbing F*ranco*. He followed him as they pushed their way through the crowd over to the pile of rubble that was the platform.

Des stopped in horror at the sight in front of him! All that was left of *Juan* and his pal were their feet sticking out from under a few tons of granite. Nothing was going to separate them now!

In panic he grabbed *Franco*. 'Help me, we have to find Chaz,'

He resisted, 'No time, you have to get out of here at once, nobody must find you here, follow me.'

Des grabbed him by the neck, 'We are going nowhere without my brother' shaking him.

He nodded in terror. Des pushed him in the direction of rubble that was the remains of the sound stage. Just as they started to move the whole place started to shudder, looking up at the gaping hole where the stage had crashed down from, a deluge of water, rock and slush increased in intensity. He jumped on top of the remains, ignoring the former partners squashed below, dragging poor *Franco*, who could see his future being flushed away with the remains of the club.

As he urged him to search for Chaz, at the back of the scene of destruction, he spotted somebody lying motionless. Scrambling over, he recognised his brother at once. 'Give me a hand,' he ordered the hapless waiter. Rolling him over, he started to shake him. However, before he could say anything, Chaz's eyes started to flutter. 'He is alive, give me a hand.' Responding at once, they took him by each arm placing them over their shoulders, 'Okay, get us out of here before the whole place comes down.'

He did not need any urging. 'This way, there is a back entrance.'

Des could see they would need it; the main stairs were jammed with panicking patrons, scrambling over each other, trampling anybody who fell in the rush. He led us through the pandemonium to a staircase in a back corner, cut into the rock face.

'Follow the stairs to the top, we will find a door to your right, it will take us outside,' he yelled over the screams. Needing no urging they lifted Chaz, dragging him between them.

They charged up the stairs, knocking an unfortunate couple over the edge in the process. 'Never mind them, they are okay!' *Franco* cried.

Des looked back, 'Hurry up unless you want us end up like *Juan* and his pal?' he urged. He realised he had a point, pushing forward to help him to clear a path!

22

They pushed their way outside, still supporting Chaz. By this time, he was starting to recover his senses. In front of the main entrance, it was jammed by the escaping crowd.

Des yelled, 'This way,' as he pointed to a taxi that was parked in a corner of the parking lot. They made a dash while still steering Chaz between them, they were not the only one with this idea. Another couple had made a dash for the cab just before us. Des grabbed one of them by the arm. 'We have a choice. Fight over it or share it, make up your mind!' he snarled. They took one look at the expression on our faces.

'Share,' they agreed in unison. They all crammed in just as the rest of the panicked mob arrived.

'Go!' *Franco* screamed. The driver looked at us and said something in Spanish. 'He wants to know where we want to go to,' he asked, his voice cracking in terror.

'Anywhere but here,' Des snarled, 'Just get moving while we still can!'

The driver must have got the message because he floored the accelerator scattering people in all directions. They careered down the driveway slewing left and right until we got to the main road. He jammed on the brakes sliding to a stop, and then looked to us for directions. Chaz had started to recover and pointed to the other side of the road where he recognised the bar where they had spent time with Bill Heart.

'Drop us here,' he struggled to blurt out, as he pointed in the direction of the assortment of bars and restaurants.

'Where do we go?' Des asked.

'Anywhere but back to that apartment, we need time to think,' Chaz replied. The other couple just clutched each other in terror, probably wondering if they would have been better walking!

'There,' he said, pointing in the direction of the precinct that housed Bill's Bar, they were all closed with the exception of one, '*Carlos's Cantina*' as the sign above the door announced.

'This will do fine, drop us here, what do I owe you?' he asked the driver.

'*De nada,*' he stammered.

Des shrugged his shoulders, 'Fine, seems that nobody wants our money tonight,' he said as we got out.

The taxi took off in a cloud of dust with the two in the back peering out the rear window, with a look of relief on their faces. 'I think they were glad to see the back of us,' Des commented.

Franco had got out with them; it was obvious that he was in a state of panic. 'I am leaving now, please do not tell them I helped you, they will kill me,' he begged. Before they could say anything, he took off running down the road.

Chaz grabbed Des by the arm. 'Let's get a drink. We need to talk!' Chaz spluttered, his throat clogged with the dirt and dust from his lucky escape.

'There,' said Des, pointing to the dingy late-night joint at the end of the strip.

They entered the bar, which, except for a couple of locals, was practically empty. Taking a couple of seats at the back of the bar, they ordered drinks and instructed the waiter to keep them coming.

'What happened back there?' Des asked.

Chaz took a deep breath and began to explain about his investigation upstairs before all hell had broken loose, shrugging his shoulders in complete confusion.

'Í spotted this guy coming out of what turned out to be a pump room to control the water level in the caves. After he vanished out of sight, I snuck in to see what he was up to and discovered that he had jammed the return valve to the sea outlet, causing all the pump pressure be diverted to the water reservoir tank. From the sounds, I could tell it was going to blow, so I made a dash for it and, well you know the rest!'

'Why would they want to destroy the place that seems a bit extreme just to get rid of a few queers?'

Chaz punched him on the shoulder, 'Get a grip Des, this has nothing to do with a few gays, I have no idea what the plan was or who is behind it, and worse than that, what our role is in all of this fiasco!'

They sat in silence for a while trying to make sense of what had happened, finally Des spoke, 'We have to get out of here.'

Chaz looked up. 'Easier said than done, seeing as you have no passport and the *Guardia de Seville* is probably looking for us, not to mention your pal *Antonio!'*

Des dropped his head into his hands. 'I have really screwed thing's up this time,' he moaned, signalling the waiter to keep bringing the drinks!

23

I kicked Des in the ribs to wake him up. The movement only increased the pain in my head. He sat up rubbing the sleep out of his eyes.

'Where are we?' he asked.

'In a graveyard and considering the trouble we are in maybe we should make reservations,' I snarled.

'Take it easy and keep your voice down will you, my head is pounding,' he mumbled, as he proceeded to relieve himself on the grave where he had slept last night.

'For the love of God have a little respect, you just slept on the poor bugger, you don't have to piss on him as well,' I groaned, as I dragged him away.

'Her,' he said.

'What?'

'It's not a man, it's a woman,' he replied, pointing to the headstone.

I shook my head in despair, nearly causing myself to lose the contents of my stomach. 'I need coffee,' I groaned.

'Good idea, where?' he asked. I pointed in the direction of Bill's Bar which appeared to be open. We stumbled out of the graveyard Des glanced up at *Carlos's Cantina*. 'Looked better with lights,' he remarked.

'Shut up, please, I need coffee,' I moaned, making our way to Bill' place in search of a friendly face.

The harsh Spanish morning sun was blinding as we entered the shady bar, which to all appearances did not look open for business, as my eyes adjusted to the gloom, which offered some relief to my pounding head I spotted Bill's son Rob behind the bar.

Making our way over to him, I asked, 'Do you have coffee?'

He nodded his head, with a sly grin at our obvious discomfort. 'Two strong black please, and a beer,' mumbled Des from behind.

'Really?' I mumbled to myself, then muttered, 'Better make that two.' With a nod, he indicated for us to sit down turning to the coffee machine.

We made our way to a corner booth, heads down in silence until the coffee and beer arrived. I took a sip of the coffee and with a groan quickly realised that it was not the answer, switching to the beer looked up at Des, raising the glass. 'Here's to really screwing us up this time,' and looked at me for a second, then continued, 'Could always be worse, we could be under that pile of rock with *De la Sota's* pals.' and shrugged.

'Unless we figure out what the hell is going on, we might as well head back to that graveyard and save whoever is behind all this some time!' I snarled, gulping down a mouthful of drink to try to stop the pain in my head hoping that I would wake up and this would be a bad dream.

'You lads look the worse for wear, I hope you were not mixed up in that fiasco in *Cap Falco* last night.' It was Bill, standing there with a coffee in his hand. We looked up at him and I guess the expressions on our faces gave us away. 'You have got to be kidding!' he gasped, he slid in beside us, 'What the fuck happened up there?'

I glanced at Des, and he nodded in agreement, turning to Bill we proceeded to fill him in all that had happened from the moment we arrived, to awaking in a graveyard this morning. The only think I omitted was the mysterious fella I had spotted, I decided that was something I would keep to myself until I could figure what the hell was going on.

He sat there shaking his head in disbelief, 'I have to say lads for blokes that only got here a few days ago you sure have got yourselves into some deep water, these are some nasty people, not to mention very powerful. I would suggest that until you get to get to the bottom of what is going on you should lie low, for sure don't go back to that apartment.'

We looked at him in despair. 'I guess we could go to a hotel.'

He shook his head. 'Out of the question that is the first place they would check; besides that, you would need your passports for that. Here is what you will do, *Rob* will take you to a farm I have near here, and you can lie low there until I try to get to the bottom of what is going on.'

We looked at him with a mix of surprise and suspicion, seeing as we had trust issues with everybody we had met since we got here!

I looked at Bill, 'I have to ask, why you would stick your neck out for a couple of guys you only met a couple of days ago.'

He sat for a moment with a grin on his face. 'Fair question. First, I like you guys, but in truth in the last few months there have been rumblings of a power struggle between the islands power base and the different 'enterprises'. 'Where you guys fit into this, I have no idea, but I intend to find out. Now let me get you something to eat before you head off, you look like you need some soakage!' he laughed, signalling for a waiter, telling him to bring breakfast for us. 'I will be back before you go. In the meantime relax, and Chaz try to remember as much as possible about last night.'

24

As soon as we finished filling our hungry stomachs, *Roberto* came and fetched us to head off to our new hideout.

'Dad said he will follow us out a bit later, better to make yourselves scarce until he checks things out.'

Nodding in agreement, we headed outside where the car was waiting, we were just about to jump in when we heard a cry from behind, *Maria* was running out of the bar waiving something in her hand.

'Des, this is for you,' waving a hat in the air. 'The sun is too hot for you with your blond hair!'

Rob and I glanced at each other in surprise, but it had nothing in comparison to the look on my brother's face. He was bright red, and it was not from the sun.

'Thank you very much,' he spluttered. *'Denada*, it is nothing, you have to take care of your lovely hair.'

Smiling and blushing as she turned to go inside. 'What about Chaz?' cried *Rob*, teasing his sister. The look she gave him could have killed!

'Looks like your brother is in trouble.'

I looked confused. 'I know my sister and when she sets her mind to something, nothing can stop her.'

I groaned. That was all we needed, more complications, and by the look on Des's face he seemed perfectly happy with the situation.

As we made our way to the farm, not a word was spoken until Des turned, 'Not a fucking word!'

I just put my hands in the air as *Rob* burst out laughing. 'Nice hat,' he said, with that for the first time in what seemed forever I burst out laughing as well.

When we arrived at Bill's 'farm', it would have been better described as a county estate. The main house was a single-storey *hacienda* that seemed to stretch forever. Olive tree and lush lawns surrounded it.

Rob could see our reaction. 'In Spain they call this a *Finca*, just a fancy name for a property,' he said dismissively.

'In Ireland we call this over the top,' I replied. Inside it was every bit as grand, and yet very much with a welcoming-home feel.

'Hi there,' we heard someone call out, 'you must be the mad Irishmen Dad was talking about.'

We stopped in our tracks; standing in front of us was a carbon copy of *Rob*! Des and I did a double take in shock, they both burst out laughing, 'Have you never seen twins before? This is my 'younger' brother *Victor*,' he punched *Rob*. 'By about a couple of minutes!' he laughed.

'Well, you better get name tags, you are spitting images,' spluttered Des.

'Come on let's get you settled in and show you around.' Afterwards they gave us a tour of the property and introduced us to Dawi, their housekeeper. 'Just ask her for anything you need, she runs the place actually, come on let's show you to your rooms, the swimming pool is out back and if you need a change of clothes, you can use some of ours until it is okay to pick up your stuff.'

After they showed us to a couple of rooms down a long corridor we thanked them. As they left, I turned to Des. 'Let's do as he says, I don't know about you, but I need to have a shower and try to get my head around what we are going to do, when you are ready we will try to figure our next move.'

'Okay, see you in a while,' replied Des. 'I am going to check this place out,' as if he was inspecting the place as his own. Typical Des, could shake his problem off as if water off a duck's back!

25

It was approaching dusk when I finally surfaced; I did not have much sleep. Every time I closed my eyes, the events of the last couple of days kept playing in my mind like a nightmare.

I found some shorts and a t-shirt and made my way towards the sound of voices and laughter. Des and the lads were beside the pool, with drinks in their hands.

'Here is sleepyhead, I have just been telling the boys how our trip has been going so far, come on get a drink and join us,' pointing to a bar in the corner.

Vic jumped up. Come on I will fix you up, let me get you a beer, your brother is quite the storyteller,' he said, as he handed me a tall glass of red liquid. *Sangria* it is, *Dawi's* special recipe.'

I took the glass and joined them, taking a big slug of the powerful liquid. 'Look, before we go any further, you guys are being terrific, but my brother has no sense of when things have got serious, and I can tell you this is no joking matter, these people he has got us mixed up with are bad news. I would not want to bring any trouble down on your family,' glaring at Des.

He avoided my stare.'I will just get a top up,' heading to the bar.

'Don't worry about us, Dad is not without influence here on this Island, he knows where all the bodies are buried, you are in good hands, relax until he gets home, he has been on the phone and says he has some news,' as *Rob* indicated for me to sit down.

Bill arrived home a couple of hours later. 'Well, how are the Irish bombers settling in?' he asked his sons, as he got himself a drink.

'Des is fine, regaling us with his version of what happened, he even told us he has another brother who is also named Vincent, Chaz on the other hand is another story, where are Mum and *Maria*?' he asked.

'They are happy to be at the bar tonight in case they pick up any more news, or I should say *Meris* was, but *Maria* was anxious to get home for some reason,' looking a Des with a serious face.

I jumped in quickly before Des could get us into more trouble than we already had. 'I cannot thank you enough, this is too much trouble for you.'

He shrugged, as if to indicate it was nothing, as he signalled for me to sit. 'Let's get something to eat, then we will talk, I have news for you, there is a lot more going on than you could imagine.'

We all sat around the pool and *Dawi* served plates of different dishes of her own versions of traditional Spanish food. '*Dawi* is part of the family, she is originally from Bali, but that is another story.' I looked at him in confusion. 'I will explain later, enjoy the food for now,' giving me a look that now was not the time.

Later, we all adjourned to the veranda area and at once Bill became serious. 'I will tell you what I have found out so far. First, they are trying to say that the incident in the Club was all an accident, which nobody believes! The good news is the police are not looking for you guys, all the focus is on the death of the Governor's son and his 'friend'. She is sure to discover very soon that this was no accident and knowing her, will do whatever it takes to get to the bottom of it. She is a powerful woman and will take the death of her son as a personal affront, she had no love for him but will want answers,' and for once Des did not make one of his jokes.

'The club, or to be more accurate, the caves, have been used for a long time to smuggle in all types of contraband especially during the time of the *Franco* regime. After his demise and Spain adopted Democracy, the Island continued as before and created their own type of fiefdom. As far as Spain was concerned the Islands were a main source of income from its growing tourism and a source of foreign currency. For this reason, they were allowed to govern itself and the position of Governor became a position of great power and corruption,' he could see the confusion on our faces. This is why I believe you became involved. Your friend *Antonio* and his Colombian cartel are in bed with the Governor. *Christina de la Vega*, through her son and the club, has been distributing their contraband.

Because of its easy access to boats through its private sea entrance and its many secret entrances, plus its activity as a club made it a perfect cover.'

'But then why would they want us to disrupt things, gays or otherwise?' Des blurted out.

'Good question, recently there is word that the Eastern Europeans, have developed a liquid form of Cocaine that is more concentrated, therefore easier to transport. I am told that a litre would supply all of Spain for a month! And before you ask, we, indicating his family, are not involved in that type of business. We stick to ourselves,' as he waved a dismissive hand. 'Let's take a break and refill our glasses.'

I nodded, as I could see Des was in the same state of shock as I was. After we topped up, Bill resumed, as if this was his usual evening topic. 'From what I can gather about a year ago *Antonio De Sota*, through his connection with some character from South America, has a connection to one of the leading families. This is the only way that *De Sota* got to negotiate with '*La Bruja*'. This is a nickname, it means 'Witch',' he explained. 'Anyway, he worked a deal to reopen the club, but part of the deal, was that her son had to be a 'partner'. Nonetheless, things seemed to be rolling along nicely until the son did a side deal with the Irish mob, which really pissed off *Antonio*.'

'So, did he get someone to screw with the water reservoir?' I asked, remembering the blond guy I had spotted, which to me looked more European than Latin.

'That's where it gets interesting; it would seem there is another player involved.'

'Who?' I asked.

Bill grinned, 'That is something I am sure *Antonio* would like to know!'

'So, who then?' Des asked.

He shrugged his shoulders, 'That's a good question I do not know, but one possibility is this bloke. There is word of a particularly nasty piece of work, a Russian named Rostov Janko, they call him '*El Diablo*'. He showed up here about six months ago making a big impression with the most luxurious yacht, reputed to have cost six-hundred-million dollars. It is so big they have to moor on the outside of the harbour at *Portals Nous*.'

I shrugged. 'So how is he involved? I take it he did not make his money by winning the lottery.'

Bill grinned. 'So right, they say he is into everything back in Eastern Europe. However, he dirtied his bib with the Russian mafia and more importantly their country's beloved leader, Boris Melnikov. So, he supposedly has moved his operations to Israel,' he could see the confused look on our faces. These people are involved in the worst kind of things imaginable; Human Trafficking and the epicentre is in Israel. It is run by their version of the Mafia. Moreover, word is that Rostov is in bed with them up to his neck. They use his extensive connections throughout Europe and the Middle East to move the 'merchandise', usually young girls looking for a more glamorous life. *Dawi* is an example,' pointing to their housekeeper. 'She was one of the lucky ones; I will keep her story for another time.'

Des asked, 'So how is the club involved in all of this?'

Bill shrugged, 'I am not sure, but why they would want to disrupt the operation of the club I have no idea. Anyway, that's all I have for now, as far as you guys are concerned, I would just focus on getting your passports back so we can see about getting you out of here.'

Des nodded, 'We are onto it first thing tomorrow.'

He had no idea how wrong he was!

26

'What happened?' *Antonio De Soto* screamed at *Franco.*

'I did just what you told me to. I looked after the Irishmen and introduced them to *Señor Juan.* The big one went to speak to him, and then went up to the platform floor. The next thing the water came, and everything collapsed. The younger one grabbed me to help, as he saw his brother, he had falling down with the rocks and water. When we got to him, I thought, he was dead. I remembered that you told me not to let anybody discover he was there. His brother and I carried him out the back way'

'So, how did the bastard sabotage the water containers?' he ranted again.

Carlos stood by impassively, his cold eyes fixed into space, something *Antonio* perhaps should have noticed. 'But he couldn't, he was only up there for a short while, he did not have time to be responsible,' pleaded the waiter. 'We grabbed a taxi that was outside and got out of there, on the way he started to mumble, I could not make out what he was saying, only one word he kept repeating, 'Blondie', that's all I know *Señor!'*

'*Rubia*' using the Spanish word for blondie. 'What the hell does that mean?' he roared, turning to *Carlos.* He just stared impassively and shrugged, then turned to stare outside so as to avoid his boss seeing the concerned expression that crossed his face.

Antonio started to lose it. 'Where are those Irish bastards?'

Franco shook his head. 'I don't know? They got the cab driver to stop, jumped out and took off.'

'Get out of my sight,' he roared at the hapless waiter, who scurried out as fast as he could, glad to escape his wrath. He turned to *Carlos.* 'Find them before the *Bruja* does, if she thinks we had anything to do with her son's death, it will be war.'

Carlos looked at him. 'Don't you think you should inform our friends in *Bogotá* about this development?'

He threw his hands in the air. 'Let me do the thinking, you just find those Irish. We have to find out who is behind this!'

Carlos nodded then turned and walked out, without a sound. *Antonio* poured himself a big glass of Scotch. Downing it, he muttered, 'Who the hell is this 'Blondie'?'

27

CARLOS

As *Carlo*s left, the fury on his face was hard to disguise. 'How had things got so screwed up?' he fumed to himself. He was sure he had those mad Irish men under control, perhaps he had misjudged the older one, it was obvious that he was suspicious, which was only to be expected, considering what they were being asked to do.

The young one was easy, seeing as he had a hold over him, and he could see that his older brother would protect him whatever, all he had needed them to do was let them be seen at the club engaging with the 'problem child'. He would then take care of him personally, so that *La Bruja* would believe that they were involved with the Irish crew and the Russians and hold them responsible. Now, due to this fiasco, the club was closed, and more importantly sealed from entry, putting his personal plans at risk and it was all the fault of those fanatics back home and their interference!

Immediately his thoughts shifted back to his youth back in *Argentina*, he could hear his grandfather scolding him for this error. Carl Von Ginsberg was a powerful figure, even though by that time he was starting to show the signs of stress hiding out after his escape in the final days of the War. As he was one of the most prominent members of the dreaded SS, his capture would have meant the firing squad. *Carlos* (he had been named after his grandfather) was the apple of his eye. He would spend hours regaling him with his war stories and his special relationship he had with his beloved leader, Hitler, and it was one of these stories that was to lead him to where he was now.

Snapping his thoughts back to the present, he realised what his *Abuelo* would say at this moment, 'Just deal with it, trust no-one, remember, your future and our family depend on it. No time for looking back, move forward, crush anybody that stands in your way!'

Yes, he agreed to himself, only his concerns were not for his family, they had done enough damage. No, now it was his turn. The first thing he realised he needed to do was take care of the fool who had wrecked his plans by destroying the club. Now that he knew the big Irishman had seen him, the last thing he wanted was for the police to question him first. No, he had to speak to them, but first he had to locate them, and with that in mind he made a quick call.

Juan Forteza answered at once. *'Si,'* he responded, he knew who it was, as he and *Carlos* had a working relationship. In his position as a mid-ranking official for the *Guardia de Seville*, he took care of any 'problems' in return for a healthy consideration.

'I would like you to keep an eye out for a couple of friends of mine, I would like to speak to them.'

'Friends?' he asked, with suspicion.

'Yes, I only want to speak to them, they are not to be touched, understood?' He got his agreement, then gave their details and description, 'Let me know when you have something,' then hung up. He then realised he would have to contact *Bogotá* to let them know that their operation was in ruins. A cold shiver ran down his back, realising the balancing act he had in play, so many acts involved, the Irish crew, the Russians, the Colombian cartel, not to mention the *La Gobernadora*, and the police.

He felt like one of those performers, with spinning plates on sticks, all in motion at the same time and if one falls ...

He put that thought out of his mind. 'Failure is not an option,' he could hear his grandfather say. 'Keep your eye on the prize,' he muttered to himself.

He entered his apartment, poured himself a stiff drink then stepped out on to the balcony. Looking out over this tropical paradise, he took a big slug of his drink, looking out into the brilliant sunshine, asking himself

'Where are you two idiots?'

28

Des plunged headlong into the sparkling water of the pool followed by *Maria,* landing on his back, as they came up spluttering in glee. Bill and I were sitting at the side, discussing the ongoing saga.

Bill glanced at them, 'I have not seen *Maria* this happy in a long time, they are getting on like a house on fire.'

I glanced at them, preoccupied with what to do next, as I sipped a cup of Dawi's perfect coffee. 'Sure, typical Des, nothing bothers him for long,' I grumbled.

Bill laughed, 'Don't you think he has the right idea? Worrying never fixed anything, I have found in my long career, all that matters is the outcome, when all is said and done, then you can look back and figure how you could have done it better.'

I sighed. 'I suppose so, as long as it is not from a jail cell,' I grumbled.

'Okay, let's see can we figure out how to avoid that,' he replied, continuing with what he had been able to discover so far, 'Well the good news is that 'officially' they are not looking for your guys yet, although my contact in the police tells me *Antonio's* 'inside man', a low-level police chief, is ...'

'What?' I yelped 'Police chief!'

'Relax,' he replied, 'he is small potatoes, all he is doing is asking his men to keep an eye out for a couple of guys, with a brief description, nothing else, I would guess that *Antonio* is just trying to cover his tracks.'

I looked at him. 'It's a bit late for that don't you think, with the head boss woman's son and his pal turned into hamburger meat! They are going to find out sooner than later that this was not an accident, then all hell is going to break loose!'

He looked at me strangely, 'How can you be sure that is was not something going wrong with the pumping system?'

I quickly realised that the blond stranger was still my secret, I was not sure why, but I still wanted to keep that bit of information to myself until I could figure what the hell was going on. 'What, I can't work out is what makes this club so important? Surely that is not the only place that all the crews are operating from?'

Bill nodded in agreement. 'I was of the same mind, sure it has the benefit of the sea entrance, but there are many similar places dotted around the island. They may not be night clubs, but that should not be a deterrent to the likes of these guys.

'There is another thing I have been thinking,' I replied. 'Why did it have to be Irish guys, to sort things out? More importantly, why go to all the trouble of getting something to hold over Des's head, as well as having go all the way to Ireland with *Carlos* in tow, when there are plenty of homegrown 'Irish' here on the Island?'

He nodded. 'More questions than answers,' he replied, shrugging his shoulders.

With that Des and *Marie* arrive, shaking water droplets all over us. 'You guys should come in, the water is beautiful'

'Sorry,' I snapped. 'But I am a bit occupied trying to figure how to keep us out of jail, and in case you haven't realised it, this is Bill's place. Without him allowing us to stay here we would probably be in jail by now, or something worse!'

'Papa,' *Maria* cried, 'Des and Chaz can stay here can't they?' as she hugged Des, giving me a sideways glance, as if to say, I was only welcome because of my handsome brother.

Bill laughed, 'They are welcome as long as they like, providing you behave yourself,' he warned.

'Don't worry Bill, I will make sure Des behaves.'

He fixed them with a stare, 'It isn't Des I am concerned about!'

Maria suddenly decided that there was something important to do in the kitchen, avoiding her father's glare.

'That girl will be the death of me,' he moaned.

Great, I thought to myself, as if I hadn't enough to worry about, now this romantic entanglement could cause even more trouble.

'Okay, listen up, I am heading into town to see if I can get some answers.'

Des piped up, 'Okay, I will get changed.'

I stopped him. 'No, I have something else for you to do. I have been speaking to Bill and there is something strange about all the interest in that club, so I would like you and *Maria*,' glancing at Bill for approval, who nodded, 'I want you guys to do some digging, somebody around these parts must know more about its history, see what you can find out.'

That was right up his alley. 'On it, leave it to me!'

I groaned. 'Remember, keep our involvement out of the conversation,' I warned.

'Of course,' he snapped, as he rushed off in the direction of his scantily clad lady friend.

Bill turned to me. 'There is a 4+4 van out the back you can use, you don't have to worry, it is registered to one of my companies, nobody will bother you in it. What's your plan?' he asked.

I stood, 'I am going to do what they brought me down here to do, shake things up!'

29

The 4+4 was a late-model Nissan Patrol, grey in colour, so it blended in perfectly, as this seemed to be the go-to vehicle at the moment.

I headed in the direction of *Portals Nous*, while I figured out my next move. The first thing I wanted to find out was why *Antonio* wanted the Irish crew out of the way so badly to have gone to all the trouble of recruiting us. The best way I knew of finding anything out was to go directly to the source, so I was going in search of my old nemesis Bruno Reilly. This was why I was heading to where we had run into each other only a few nights ago, although it seemed like a lifetime to me after all that had happened since.

I parked and made my way to the bar where we had met, it was approaching lunchtime and the place was buzzing. Full of all the beautiful people from the adjourning yachts, as tourists wander past all the luxurious shops, gazing at the amazing range of goods on offer, with longing in their eyes, knowing that they were only on display for the select few that could afford them.

There was no sign of Bruno or his sidekick, Mick Ryan, so I sat down at the bar and ordered a drink. When the waiter returned, I thanked him then struck up a conversation. Luckily he spoke perfect English, something that more or less everybody that worked in this tourist area did.

'I was here the other night, and I ran into an old friend of mine,' I lied. 'His name is Bruno. I was wondering if you would know where I could find him, I lost his phone number.'

I then went on to describe him, but before I could finish, he stopped me. 'Sure *Amigo*, but you won't find him here this early, he is a late starter.' Glancing at his watch, 'You might find him at the *café* at the end of the pier, he sometimes stops in there if he spends the night on his friend's yacht,' pointing to this monstrous boat, that was so big it had to moor outside the harbour wall, I quickly realised this was the yacht of the mysterious Russian.

I thanked the waiter, finished my drink, and headed towards the café when I spotted *Carlos*. He was climbing down into a speedboat moored at the side of the pier, and his back was to me. So, I moved quietly forward to see what he was doing, as he dropped in the driver turned to the person sitting in the back and said something. Indicating to the approaching *Carlos*, who jumped in and began to gesture furiously with the guy, who whipped off his cap and started to gesture back, I stopped cold. It was the guy from the nightclub! Before I could react, the boat took off and headed out of the harbour, heading in the direction of *Palma.* I could not believe my eyes. What was *Carlos* doing with the guy that had destroyed the club?

One thing was for sure, now I was determined to get to the bottom of this mystery, and what was the mysterious *Carlos's* up to. I continued to the end of the pier in search of Bruno, the place was packed, there was seating inside and out, glancing around I could not see him. I was just about to leave when I spotted his pal, Mick.

Now my history with both of them was not the best and the other night when we met, I pretended to not remember him. I had an occasion to have a run in with this guy before, I knew I would get nothing out of him, he hated me because I had stopped him striking some poor girl that had the misfortune of crossing his path, since then he had vowed vengeance on me. I was not concerned about him, but the last thing I needed at the moment was to attract attention.

I was turning to leave when, unfortunately, he spotted me. 'You!' he roared, 'You big prick!'

The whole place turned to see what was going on, I had no option but to respond, so I wandered over to him. 'Your wife tells you everything,' I replied, smirking. He looked at me confused. So, I continued, 'What you just called me. That's what she says, whenever she sees me,'

He started to gasp with anger, and I knew there was only one way this was going to end, so before he could rise, I sat down in front of him and asked, 'Can you swim?'

'What?' He growled as he began to rise again.

Now before I put myself in a precarious situation, I always look for a way out, rather than fight. Because of this I had noticed his chair was placed against a low ridge at the edge of the pier. Before he could move, I placed my size 13 boot against it and gave it a push. Because he was in the motion of standing, he immediately toppled backward, and he and the chair disappeared over the edge.

There was a scream followed by a mighty splash.

I looked over the edge, followed by most of the cliental. He was bobbing in the water a good six metres below, spluttering and screaming for help, somebody threw him a lifebuoy, which he grabbed frantically.

'Sorry, thought you said you would like a swim, maybe you should stick to water wings for a little longer,' I shouted.

The place erupted in laughter, as he swallowed more water in his efforts to say how he would end my life.

Then I heard, 'Nice one, Chaz.'

30

I turned to see who was calling. It was coming from the direction of the outside wall. Looking up I could see it was from the giant yacht and there standing on the top deck was Bruno.

'Well done, Chaz!' he roared in laughter. 'Come on board before he gets out and makes a bigger idiot of himself,' indicating the gangplank leading up to this magnificent vessel.

As I made my way on board, I realised that this was the first time I had been on a yacht, especially one of this calibre. A stunning girl in a micro-bikini greeted me, 'This way, sir,' indicating that I should follow her.

Not sure where to look, trying to avoid ogling the sway of her hips, I decided to inspect my surroundings. Everything was painted a sparkling white, all the wooden rails and fittings seemed to be more suited to fine furniture than a boat, but then who was I to say?

Bruno was waiting to greet me as we arrived at the palatal top deck, it was the size of a small football field with a full-size swimming pool in the centre, surround by sunbeds, most of which were occupied by more beautiful creatures, who in turn were accompanied by some hard-looking guys.

'Chaz, come over here,' he said, indicating a bar, which, like everything I had observed so far, was way over the top. Bruno signalled to an attentive waiter, 'What will you have?' he asked, indicating a vast selection behind the bar.

'Just a beer,' I said. 'In fact I was down here looking for you,' I added, which did not seem to surprise him.

'Funny you should say that. We were just talking about you and your newfound friends,' as he handed me my drink, offering his as a salute, 'Slainte!' raising his glass in the Irish greeting for health. 'Come on, there is someone I want you to meet,' pointing to some stairs that led up to an upper level.

I followed him, not sure who we were meeting, but as far as I was concerned, this was exactly what I had hoped for. A chance to stir the pot!

'Chaz, I would like you to meet a business associate of mine and the proud owner of this fine vessel, say hello the Mr Rostov Janko.'

Sitting on a large lounge was a heavy, large man somewhere in his forties, I figured, though it was impossible to tell by his chiselled features. His thinning hair was carefully arranged to compensate for the lack of coverage, and from the look of it there was not a lot of fat on his large frame.

I made my way over, and extended my hand, which he took and proceeded to attempt to crush it. That was a lost cause, as I returned the favour, he quickly realised that I was more than a match for him, so a silent truce was declared, but the expression on his face told me I had just been ticked off his Christmas-card list.

'Bruno has been telling me all about you and your brother and how you are involved with *Señor Antonio,'* he growled with a voice like broken glass.

Just the opening I was looking for. 'That's exactly what I wanted to discuss with him,' indicating Bruno, 'it would appear that you may have similar interests. Perhaps we should talk, I believe it will be to our mutual benefit?'

He indicated for us to sit, then dismissed the couple of tough-looking guys that were sitting behind him. We sat, and they waited for me to start the proceedings,

'As you are no doubt aware I only arrived here a few days ago,' nodding in the direction of Bruno. 'Yes, he mentioned that you were involved in all the problems at *Cap Falco.*

'Let's stop right there,' I interrupted. 'As I told him,' pointing at Bruno, 'my brother has a habit of jumping into things without giving them a lot of thought. As soon as I spoke to *Antonio* and his sidekick, *Carlos*, I knew something was fishy. Why bring us all the way from Ireland just so we could, as he described, deal with some issues he had with his 'partner'? So I just fobbed him off until I could figure out what he was up to.'

The Russian grunted. 'Then what was the disaster at the club about?'

'That's just the point, we were never there,' I lied. 'But when we heard about what happened at the club and considering he had asked us to cause 'disruption' and I since discovered that Bruno was involved, I put two and two together. I figured the reason he wanted us was because of the Irish connection and the disaster could perhaps be blamed on Bruno and his crew. Anyway, that's my theory, now it is up to you guys to figure it out from here, just wanted to let you know we have no interest in all of this. I just want to make sure that we don't get mixed up in a couple of deaths, one I believe is the son of a very important person.'

There was silence for a moment, then Bruno spoke, 'So where is *Antonio* now?'

I shrugged my shoulders, 'No idea, I have only met him twice, once at a posh restaurant on the beach in *Palma Nova.'*

Rostov glanced at Bruno, '*La Baraka,'* he informed him. On a roll I continued, 'The only other place I met him was at his villa in a place called *Calvia.*'

Again, there was silence for a moment, then the Russian burst into laughter. 'You Irish, always straight to the point, I like that, we have a lot in common,' as he jumped to his feet and gave me a bear hug, something I guess was a Russian thing. As far as I was concerned we had nothing in common, but decided to keep that to myself.

I stepped back and looked the pair of them in the eye, 'So we are good then?'

Rostov fixed me with a stare, 'All good, Irishman, we will take care of this *Antonio*,' he replied.

I nodded, then turned without another word, as my back was to them a smile crept on my face. *That should stir things up!* I thought, as I made my way down the quay side.

Just then who should arrive but poor Mick, looking like a drowned rat. He was shaking with rage, but before he could say anything I stepped in, 'Before you get started, I suggest you have a word with your boss,' pointing to the bridge above.

He looked up to see Bruno, indicating that he should come aboard.

Moving over to the gangplank, shaking with cold and rage, he placed his hand on the rail, spinning to hurl some abuse at me, which caused him to lose his balance. Then he reached out in panic. As I gripped his wrist, he glared at me.'I will, get you,' he threatened.

Smiling, I said, 'Never bite the hand that feeds you, or is holding you from falling,' as I released his arm.

With an ear-splitting scream, he disappeared off the side of the quay, down between the boat and the wall, as I walked away, I could see the deck hands rushing to rescue him before he drowned or was crushed.

I turned and shouted, 'You really should consider getting swimming lessons if you are going to continue diving into the sea!'

Continuing on my way, I could hear laughter coming from the top deck of the ship.

31

Arriving back at the car, which I had parked just out of sight of the only entrance to the marina, I sat and tucked into a sandwich and a drink I had bought earlier, waiting to see if my plan would hatch.

I didn't have to wait that long, about forty minutes later, four *Escalades* with heavily tinted windows roared out of the entrance of the marina. I grinned to myself. I guessed the cars belonged to the Russian as Bruno did not have the class, or the money for that level of transport.

I started my 4+4 and followed them at a discrete distance, which was made easy as I could see quickly where they were heading. One peeled off in the direction of *Antonio's* beach hangout, while the other three made straight for the only road that led to *Calvia*.

It took about twenty minutes to arrive at the villa. They slowed as they approached, and then one of cars drove up the driveway, while the other two proceeded to block the entrance. The occupants stepped out, it was a mix from what I could see from my vantage spot of Bruno's crew, and the tough-looking guys I had seen on board the yacht.

I smiled to myself when I saw Mick Ryan take the lead. I could see he had changed his wet clothes and looked ready to kill anybody that stood in his way. As he charged up the driveway followed by the rest of the gang, I expected all hell to break loose, but instead, after a few minutes the staff started to stream out the front, clambering over the car in their efforts to escape whatever was happening inside the house. Then there was silence, at least from what I could hear from where I was parked. I was just about to sneak up to investigate when ear-splitting screams of terror started to come from inside!

I stopped in my tracks as the mob came scrambling out of the house, throwing themselves over the cars blocking their escape, followed closely by the straggler. I could see no sign of *Mr De Sota*, and so I guess he was not at home to welcome them.

Then, closely following them, tumbling through the door came Mick and a few of his cronies, accompanied by my two friends, the guard dogs!

One of them had a firm hold of Mick's leg and was trying to drag him back inside, the other one was quite content to chase the others towards the blocked entrance. One of the men made the error of trying to get into the safety of the car, while the others bailed out over the roof. Mick had succeeded dragging himself and the dog outside, while one of his mates tried to distract his attacker. I could see that a few of them had their clothes ripped and there was plenty of blood covering them. By this time one had got the doors open as they tried to bail inside, followed by the other dog.

Finally, Mick succeeded in getting himself free and with the help of the others managed to get into the cars, while the dogs continued to bite any stray limbs that were exposed.

As they roared off, the dogs settled down, so I wandered up to them. Immediately they recognised me and started to look for affection. 'Good boys,' I said, scratching their ears, much to their delight. They followed me inside as I decided to check that what had happened, as I surmised the place was deserted. The house was wrecked. I guess when they found out *Antonio* was not in residence, they decided to make their presence felt.

As I wandered through, the trail of destruction led out to the enclosure where, unknown to them the dogs lived, some smart guy had made the error of opening it, presumably to check if anybody was there. Big Mistake!

I could hear the sound of police sirens in the distance, so decided to make myself scarce. Hurrying back to the car, I opened the door to get in and was bundled out of the way by the dogs clambering in! They jumped into the rear and sat there patiently waiting for me.

'No way, I have enough problems going on without you two adding to it,' I said, directing them to exit. They just sat and looked at me as if to say, 'Yes, anyway we have had enough of this place.' The sirens were very close, so I had no option but to depart, dogs and all. 'This just gets better and better, as if my brother and his pals are not enough to contend with now it would seem I have you two!'

By this time, they had made themselves comfortable, as if this was their new home. I passed the police cars on their way to *Antonio's* place, so I decided I had stirred the pot enough for today and headed back to Bill's place to see what he had found out. At the same time I wondered if Des had any success with his *Cap Falco* investigation?

32

DES

As soon as Chaz had left, Des threw himself into the task he had been given, glad of the chance to help get them out of the fiasco he had created. He grabbed Bill and *Maria* to see if they could help.

Bill responded at once, 'The person you need to ask is your mother,' he suggested to *Maria*. 'She, or more important, her family, have lived in this area forever. If anybody can help, she is your best bet.'

Maria jumped up, 'Of course, I am right on it!' glad of the opportunity to get involved in, which to her was a great adventure, and rushed off in search of her mother.

Des just stood there until Bill pointed in the direction she had gone, 'If I were you, I would follow her, or you might be left behind.' Des dashed off in her direction, to the sound of him laughing.

At first Maria's mother refused. 'There is only trouble in those caves, misfortune befalls anybody that disrespects them.' Finally after persistence from her daughter, she reluctantly agreed to help. 'The person I think you should talk to is old *Ricardo*, he has been in and out of every cave and grotto, around this island, and he was involved with the original construction of the first club all those years ago.'

Maria clapped her hands with delight, 'Where does he live?' she asked.

'That's a great question, but impossible to answer,' she replied.

'Why?' she cried.

'Because for as long as he been around, the only place he has been known to live in is those caves.

'So how do we find him?'

Her mother smiled, 'Luckily in recent years, most mornings he can be found having a *Carajillo* in the restaurant on the beach in *Portals Ves.* But a warning, he has a reputation for not trusting strangers, so if you find him, mention that your mother, '*Meris*', and he have a connection to *Diego*.'

'Who is that?' she asked.

'His son,' she replied.

'And how do you know him?' *Maria* asked, curious.

'None of your business,' she snapped, a blush coming her face. 'Now on your way, I am busy,' as she shooed them out.

'I reckon there is something going on there,' Des said as they headed out.

'Oh, I am sure of it, remember she is Spanish!' giving Des a mysterious look. If his brothers had been there, they would have told him to watch out, 'woman trouble', something he'd had plenty of experience.

'How far is this place?' he asked.

'Not far, but the access by road is not the best, almost all the clientele that go there, go by sea.'

An hour later after a scary drive over a steep and winding hill, they arrived at this enchanting, enclosed bay. Cut off from all the usual tourists, it was only frequented by locals or wealthy boat owners. The whole restaurant was more or less outdoors, a completely rustic setting.

There were only a few people there, as it was mid-morning. They made over to the bar and *Mari*a ordered some drinks. When they arrived, she introduced herself, and it was obvious from the waiter that her family was well known. They chatted for a while, then the waiter wandered off to serve some other customers.

'Well, what did he say?'

She put her finger to her lips and indicated to take their drinks over to a table in the shade. They sat and she leaned in, 'Yes, he still comes here, but according to the waiter, he always sticks to himself, especially in the last few days since the trouble in the club. A lot of strange people have been looking to speak to him, but he is avoiding them like the plague.'

Des shrugged his shoulders. 'Can't say I blame him, I hate answering questions myself.' *Maria* just shook her head, as if beginning to understand that her boyfriend 'marched to the sound of a different drum'.

'Not the point, the waiter told me that he should be here shortly, as today was when he picked up some meals they gifted him from time to time, he will arrive in a small boat from that direction,' pointing to a small inlet which seemed to vanish into the mountainside.

They settled to wait and shortly as predicted, a boat appeared in the inlet, heading towards the beach. The old man that stepped out of the boat was of an indeterminable age, he could have been 60 or 90, it was impossible to tell. He was tall for a Spaniard, with thick-gray hair flowing out from under a sailor's cap, as he made his way the to the bar his stride showed no sign of decay.

'Wait here,' *Maria* said as she got up. 'If I succeed in bringing him over, whatever you do please stay quiet,' she implored.

Des shrugged his shoulders. 'No problem, I won't say a peep.'

She glanced at him with not a lot of conviction. *Maria* stood beside the old guy and started to speak to him. At first, he shrugged her off angrily, but as she made herself known to him, he calmed down considerably, either the family name or his mysterious son's name had the desired effect. After he collected his food, they made their way over to the table. *Maria* introduced Des, and he looked him up and down, then disregarded him and turned back, jabbering away in Spanish to her.

Not a good move, if there was one thing that was sure to get the Savage brothers upset was to ignore them. 'Lovely to meet you too,' Des shouted, grabbing the guy's hand, shaking it firmly.

Maria looked in horror, so much for keeping quiet! She started to apologise but the man raised his other hand to quiet her, then turned to Des, staring at him with his startling blue eyes, then he spoke, 'My name is *Ricardo*, many people call me *El Cavernicola*, it is an '*apodo*' a nickname, you call it,' in English that was very passable.

Before things got any worse, *Maria* jumped in, 'I did not know you spoke English, I am so sorry, can we sit down please?'

They sat down, there was an awkward silence, then *Maria* spoke first, in Spanish. She spoke quickly to him for a few minutes, the said in English, 'I will translate for Des; he does not understand anything,' then quickly added, 'In Spanish.'

The old guy gave Des a sly look of satisfaction. She continued, 'His nickname translates to 'Caveman'. He is called that, he believes, because his father was involved with the construction of the submarine pens for the Nazis in the last war.'

Des looked at Maria in confusion, then back to this guy, 'Can you ask him if he can help us with some information about what goes on at the club?'

She translated, but Des could see this old man could understand him fine. They chatted for a while, then she turned back to him, 'He says that when they were built, they had asked for his help, but when they explained what they intended to do and he told them of the dangers, they brushed him off and brought in engineers from outside.'

Maria continued to ask him questions, but he cut them short, picked up his rations then took off to his boat.

As he vanished out of sight, they looked at each other, then in unison and laughed, 'Weird!'

33

When they got back to the house, Chaz was at the pool with Mari's dad, deep in conversation.

'We found somebody that lives in the caves,' *Maria* yelled, unable to contain herself, as she rushed over to give her dad a hug.

'Calm down, what is all this about?' Sitting her down and indicating for Des to follow. They related their encounter with this strange guy, and explained his history and nickname, 'Caveman.' Bill asked for more info, then Des told them about the guy's father and how he was involved with the submarine pens.

'Submarine pens?' Bill questioned, 'Don't be surprised what you hear from *Ricardo*, his family have been involved with all sorts of skulduggery, which included smuggling, because of their knowledge of the grottos and caves, remember this island is volcanic, the underground is like Swiss cheese'.

'Some people say they were used as back as far as the slave trade,' came this voice from the direction of the kitchen. It was her mother, as she came out with a plate of sandwiches.

'Now I know how this pair found out who to talk too,' Bill laughed, 'You don't know the half of it, we Spanish women always keep a little mystery in our past,' she replied with a delightful Spanish tilt to her accent. A troubled look crossed Bill's face, the first time we had seen him look uncomfortable!

Before another word could be spoken, *Maria* let out an ear-splitting shriek, 'Look out!' as she jumped up, pointing at the two monstrous dogs that we're trotting behind her.

Meris glanced back and laughed, 'Meet the new members of the family that Chaz brought us,' scratching their ears.

After she joined her mother and quickly started fondling the dogs, much to their pleasure, Chaz proceeded to fill them in on all that had happened, when he concluded with the dogs joining the group, they all started to babble at the same time.

'They attacked his house?' Bill asked, in disbelief.

'Correct, I was surprised at their blatant disregard for the police. It was lucky I suppose that nobody was there, I didn't want to start a gang war, only create a little mischief,' said Chaz. 'I hope that they didn't do the same to that club.'

They all turned in unison. 'What club?

34

La Baraka was in an uproar as they drove past.

Deciding to have a look for themselves, we had all piled into one of Bill's wagons to see what was going on. The sight of one of the Russian's Escalades engulfed in flames shocked them.

'Drive on,' commanded Bill, his son *Victor* driving. As we passed, a crowd were pointlessly throwing their drinks on the flames, while waving their arms in anguish. We pulled over and Bill turned to his other son *Roberto*. 'Go back and see what you can find out, but remember keep a low profile,' he grinned, nodding his head as he stepped out. 'We will see you up at the Blue Bar.' *Rob* winked, then shot off.

The 'Blue Bar' was located on the peninsula that divided *Palma Nova* from *Magaluf*, called *Torre nova*, explained Bill. 'It has become the accepted meeting place for the 'Chaps' (Des had used this expression so much, I had come to understand it be a 'trusted one'). It is owned by the grandson of one of the original families that founded this Island in modern times, they used to own most of this coastline, even, and I believe the grottos,' he added.

I glanced at Des, who nodded in understanding at a possible other source. We arrived at the bar and were greeted as if a long-lost family had arrived. I was beginning to understand there was lots more to Bill than met the eye.

After we were seated and drinks were ordered, he proceeded to fill us in on the history of this beautiful place, perched on the cliffs overlooking a beautiful bay. 'Back in the day, *Miguel*,' indicating to the young guy who had greeted us, as he carried over a tray of beers and wine, 'became good friends with my boys. They grew up together, our families are intertwined, he is married to *Meris's* sister, she is younger,' he hastily added, as *Miguel* placed the drinks down.

'Telling stories out of school again?' he asked, in a strong English accent. By the look on our faces, he guessed, 'So these are the two Irish '*Tios*' you have been telling me about, they would not by any chance be the two, *Guardia* are looking for 'unofficially?'

'This is *Miguel*, he is like a son to me, his grandfather was my saviour back when I first arrived here, bringing some trouble with me. Enough to say that I would trust this young man with my life,' looking straight at the two of us.

Des immediately piped up, 'Great to meet you. I thought *Maria* had an English accent, but you sound like you were born in London,' grasping his hand, giving it a good shake. At once everyone was talking at the same time, I guess, on our account they were all using English.

Bill had brought *Miguel* up to date, which didn't take long as besides what he had heard from Bill, the news and gossip had echoed around the Island. We were all chatting away, while at the same time I observed Des deep in conversation with *Miguel*. A smile crossed my face, as he had not missed the possibility of finding out some more about the mysterious caves. Just at that point *Rob* returned, excited to share the news.

'Shit! You were not joking when you said you were going to stir thing up a bit! All hell is breaking out back at the restaurant,' at the same time giving me a hefty slap on the back,

I started to bluster when Bill cut in, 'Will you sit and calm down a bit, so we can hear what you have to say.'

Rob did as he was told, accepting a drink which was pushed into his hand. 'Well as you can guess after Chaz's visit, the Russian sent a couple of his crew to pick up *Antonio*, but he wasn't there. But from what I could get out of the frantic barman, they had made the mistake of trying to rough up a couple of the French crew, trying to locate *De Sota*. In the ensuing ruckus which ended up outside, a bottle of whiskey was thrown at the one of the Russians, missing him and exploding on the side of their *Escalade*, which had a door open. The driver, who was waiting nervously smoking a cigarette, as soon as he was soaked with the liquor burst into flames!'

'What a waste of good whiskey,' Des decided to comment, not known for his sensitivity.

'So, what happened?' I asked.

'He jumped out in a ball of flames, the crowd tried to help by throwing their drinks on him, but this only added fuel to the fire, literally. Finally somebody from the restaurant threw a carpet over him and managed to dowse the flames. The car was not so lucky, it was still burning merrily when the *bomberos* arrived. By the time the ambulance and police had arrived, the Russians had bundled their toasted friend into a taxi that they commandeered, and were gone.'

He took a deep breath, while Bill began to speak. 'As Des has said, Chaz, you really stirred things up, along with the deaths at the club, this will bring a lot of unwanted attention.' Before I could respond, he put his hand up. 'Before you say anything, we are all on your side, this type of response is out of order. I am just saying I would expect the powers to be, here on the island and by that I mean the *Bruja* to react. The good thing is that it takes the attention away from you guys for now.'

Des looked, first at the group, then to me. 'So what next?' he asked.

'Good question, first thing is to locate *Antonio*'

Bill replied, 'We can probably help with that, but what then?'

I looked first to Des and then to the others, 'We have found that when you stir the pot, it usually exposes the people that work better or worse under pressure, I want to chat to him to see where he falls, so where do we find our friend *Antonio*?'

35

CARLOS

While their meeting was going on, *Carlos* was dealing with his own personal problem. It was in the shape of a blond-haired guy seated in front of him. 'Do you realise the chaos you have created?'

The guy just shrugged his shoulders. 'I did what I was asked to do ... I disabled the pumping station.'

Carlos tried to keep his composure. All he wanted to do was put a bullet in this idiot's head, yet he kept his calm; Klaus Becker came well protected.

When he discovered that what he was looking for had a night club sitting on top of it he, had to come up with a plan to remove prying eyes. It was all going fine, he had the two Irish guys to misdirect all the interested parties, until his family connection had come up with the idea of sending him this fool. He, like himself, was a descendant of a Nazi-party member who had fled with many of his cronies to Argentina in the waning days of the war.

When he had discovered his grandfather's letters and the secrets they contained, what he realised was his opportunity to break free of these fanatics. It would then give him the life he believed with all the heart he deserved. In the beginning he needed their connections with the Colombians to infiltrate their crew on the Island. He had convinced them that they were been short-changed by *Antonio* and his mates in the government, which put him in a position to form his own plans, then this idiot arrived!

'The members felt that things should be moving quicker and sent me to give assistance,' he had reported when he had rocked up at his villa a month ago.

The party he was referring to be the remnants of 'Third Reich' who were using the fanatical youth from Germany and the likes of Klaus, who still believed in the return of their beloved party, for their own ends. He guessed at once that this guy had been sent with the express purpose of keeping an eye on his progress. He had no choice but to except, so as to avoid suspicion, that is when he had made the fatal mistake of using him for the simple job of disabling the pumps, in order to speed up the disarray in the club.

'Do you not know the difference between disable and destroy? Oh, and to add to that, killing the son of the most powerful person on the Island, and let's not forget a high-ranking member of the *Guardia de Seville*,' he snapped.

The blond hulk squared his shoulders. 'A minor setback I am sure that the party will be happy with the results, it will show that we are in control and not to be trifled with,' as he snapped a Hitler salute.

It took all of his constrain not to strangle this moron on the spot, but his grandfather had trained him well, 'Keep your friends close and your enemies closer.' Bearing this in mind, he softened his approach. 'Perhaps you are right I may have overreacted, come let's have a drink, and figure out how we can use this to our advantage, now they tell me you're are good scuba diver?'

36

Carlos continued to ply Klaus with drinks and praise, as he explained what he had in mind.

'There is no doubt that what you did disrupted the arrangement between 'The Witch' and our advisories, the only problem is that the lower chambers of the grotto are flooded, perhaps we can use this to our advantage, with your help we can recover the drugs and cash that are in one of the caves. It would seem that there is some discord between all the parties, who seem to be at each other's throats at the moment, we can use this opportunity to make a private killing for the party.'

Klaus practically exploded with pride at the mention of his beloved clan, he jumped up and with an outstretched arm, and 'To the Fourth Reich!' he roared, seeing himself as one of the future leaders.

*Carlo*s raised his glass, nodding in agreement. 'Here's to our success. Now the details: in two days' time there will be minimum security at the site, as it is a *Fiesta,*' then refilling the glasses.

'How will we enter and what about equipment?' Klaus asked.

'All taken care of. We will enter by boat, a secret entry and I have all the equipment ready, all we need is your expertise,' again boosting his ego.

Two days later, the small but nimble speedboat made its way out of a private harbour just as dawn was breaking. Klaus sat in the prow of the boat, fully clad in a diving suit, as he knew the waters inside the caves would fall to freezing temperatures the deeper he went.

As they navigated along the coast, Carlos started to head in the direction of a sheer, black-faced cliff. As they came closer, Klaus started to panic as they continued straight for the rock face. 'Don't worry, I know what I am doing,' *Carlos* said to calm him, and continued on what seemed a fatal path. Just as it appeared they would crash against the face, an opening appeared, as if by magic.

A strange illusion was created by two vertical walls of rock that angled inward, giving the appearance of a rock face. Unless you were to venture close which, due to the danger of the rocks, nobody in their right mind would do. They navigated their way in through the entrance, and *Carlos* motored slowly deeper into the natural grotto. He headed in the direction of what looked like a natural landing place. As soon as they arrived, Klaus hopped out, looking around he could see the signs of activity around the place.

'So this is where they operate from?' he asked.

Carlos nodded as he secured the boat, 'One of many, we go on foot from here' as he grabbed the gear and headed off, deeper into the cave system.

After going through a series of narrow cuttings they emerged into a larger cave, fed with light from higher than they could make out. 'How deep are we?' a worried Klaus inquired.

Carlos looked up, 'Deeper than you will be buried when you die.'

'Fuck you,' he muttered. 'How much further?'

'Just over here,' he replied, pointing to an opening in the cliff face. They entered and *Carlo*s set up a spotlight on a tripod.

'There,' he pointed towards what appeared to be a well, but flush with the ground.

Klaus moved closed to inspect the opening, he could see that it was flooded up to what appeared to be steps leading down into the black depths. 'It's down there?' he inquired.

'Yes, it's all down there, that's where they stored stuff before shipment,' he could see the doubt on his blond-friend's face. 'I can assure you, I have seen it, and before you destroyed the pumps that room was as dry as a bone, but now we can turn that to our benefit.'

Again, Klaus thrust out his chest, 'For the party!'

Carlos nodded, 'Of course.'

They quickly kitted out Klaus, who carefully checked that his tank was full, not trusting anybody with this task. After he was ready, *Carlos* handed him a torch, then tapped him on the side of his full-face mask to indicate he could talk. 'Can you hear me okay?

He nodded and gave the thumbs up.

'Now remember when you descend the steps, you will see you are in a large chamber, ignore the door at the end, it is flooded also, look to the far right you will see a watertight panel, there is a touch panel there, enter the code I have given you. It will open a panel on the opposite wall, which is where the merchandise will be.'

'How do you know?' he asked.

Carlos smiled, 'Because I put it there.'

As he descended down the steps, Klaus swung the light around to familiarise himself with the surroundings, it was more or less as had been described. 'Can you still hear me?' he could hear *Carlos* ask. 'Yes, I can hear you fine,' surprised at the sound of his voice, which sounded like he was breathing helium. 'I sound funny?' he questioned.

'Don't worry, it is because of the full-face mask, concentrate on what you have to do, now go to the panel.'

Klaus made his way to the panel and located the touch screen, 'Entering it now,' he said, as he imputed the code he had been given: my struggle. He smiled to himself at the translation of the title of Hitler's infamous book, *Mein Kampf.*

It never crossed his mind as to why *Carlos* would be using a German reference password in a Spanish drug hangout. As soon as he entered the code, he could hear something opening behind him. Turning, he could see a portal opening on the other side. 'Its opening,' he said, again surprised at the sound of his voice, it sounded even higher than before.

'Okay, now for the hard part, you have to make you way over there.'

Klaus was confused, it was only a couple of metres across to the opening, but as he tried to move forward, he suddenly felt as if his whole body was made of rubber, it was as if his brain had disconnected itself from all control, he started to panic. 'I can't move, something is wrong, help me,' he cried in his newfound high-pitched voice.

'Relax this is quite normal under the influence of the sedative gas you have been inhaling, shortly you will suffocate. I knew you would check if the bottle was full, but sadly this gas although very good at sedating, carries very little oxygen, I reckon you have about ten minutes if you relax.'

Klaus screamed in terror, 'You are crazy, you will never get away with this my friends will get you' as he started to cough.

'Tut, tut, at this rate you won't last another five minutes.'

'Why are you doing this?' he gasped.

'I am surprised you had to ask; you have been a thorn in my side since you arrived. Your crazy fanatics at home insisted, but after the fiasco in the club you had to go, and before you waste what little air you have left, your buddies will be very saddened to hear of your passing, and it will all be down to your love of cave diving. You took one risk too many and drowned alone. I am sure there will be big memorial for you back home.'

Carlos could now hear Klaus gasping for his final breath. He sat for fifteen minutes or so, then donned a face mask, quickly descended into the room, located the body, which was resting on the bottom just below the touch screen. He re-entered the code and the door behind began to close on the empty room. 'Sorry Klaus, this was only my own storeroom where I used to prepare for my quest, that was until some idiot flooded the place,' thinking to himself as he towed the corpse up to the hatch.

He was just in the process of dragging it on to the cave floor, when to his shock he could hear the sound of voices approaching from deeper in the grotto. How was this possible? As far as he knew nobody ever ventured into this area. All his grandfather's notes and drawings indicated that this secret entrance was the only entry.

'No time to speculate now,' he muttered, as he could hear the voices getting louder. He decided he would have to improvise his story as to Klaus's demise.

He quickly gathered all evidence that could connect to him. Just before he turned to leave, he patted Klaus on his still body. 'Sorry, guess I was wrong. You did die deeper than you would be buried.'

37

Des was deep in conversation with *Miguel*, as Bill gave Chaz directions to *Antonio* 's hideaway. 'It's not hard to find, in fact everybody that knows anything about him knows.'

'Doesn't sound very safe,' Chaz said. 'How will I find it?'

Bill laughed. 'Don't worry you will recognise it, just drive into *Port de Andratx*, and look for the most likely place, you will recognise it. How you will get in is another matter!'

'That's easy,' he said, 'knock on the door. Remember he's looking for me.'

Bill shrugged his head. 'I guess it is true what they say, all Irish are mad.'

'Some more than others,' Chaz replied, 'Anyway I am bringing backup,' as he gave a loud whistle, the two monstrous shepherds appeared as if by magic. Chaz ruffled their ears, 'Want to go visit your old master?'

'Be careful,' Des called out, 'Need me to come?'

Chaz shook his head, 'No I will be fine all I want to do is have a chat, you just find out what all the interest is in that club.' Then nodded and left.

Outside, he jumped into the 4+4 with the dogs sitting to attention on the back seats, and as he drove off, Bill muttered to himself, 'Sure, just chat!'

Des, meanwhile, had continued to pump for information. 'What we are trying to figure out is what is so important about this place that they would go to such trouble, as to destroy the place just to make a point, and more importantly why they needed us Irish guys?'

'I am not so sure that they did, from what I have been able to pick up, all sides are denying having anything to do with the 'Accident'.'

Des went on to tell them about their encounter with the 'Caveman' and the lack of information they had got. Bill then said, 'Not surprising, if not for *Maria's* Mum's connection, I doubt he would have spoken to you. Those cavepeople are a breed on to their own.'

'Cavepeople?' echoed *Maria* and Des.

'Yes there are more than one,' he laughed, 'but they are shrouded in mystery. Rumour is that they have existed for centuries. Those caves have been used for all kinds of weird activations over the years, all manner of smuggling and when *Franco* cuddled up to Hitler in the early days of the war, he allowed the construction of submarines pens. None of this would have been possible without the help of these guys, I am told.'

Des shook his head. 'But what has that to do with the club?' he asked.

'No idea, but for sure if there is anything going on down there, one of them would have to know what is going on.'

Maria shook her head. '*Ricardo* made it quite clear that he did not want to discuss it anymore. He became quite agitated when we mentioned C*arlo*s and his friends.'

That perked *Miguel's* attention, 'Strange, did he mention him by name?'

She thought for a moment. 'Now that I think of it, he called him *'El Extrano Espanol'*—The Strange Spaniard.'

He nodded, 'That's what they call anybody that does not come from the Balearic Islands, but most importantly do you think he was talking about the same guy?'

Des jumped in, 'No question, I described him in detail to *Maria*, he definitely knew who we were talking about.'

Miguel turned to Bill, 'There is no question he has something going on, the cavers, never mix with anybody unless they are up to no good. Perhaps if you have another word with *Meri*s, she is the only one that could make him open up.'

Bill did not look so happy, 'You know she does not like to revisit that time, considering what happened.'

Des was just about to ask what they were talking about, when *Maria* gave him a swift kick, indicating that they would talk later.

She jumped up. 'Well we won't solve anything sitting around here drinking and talking, time for action , let's go and see Mum.

38

Chaz drove into the small village of *Port de Andratx*, he was told that this ancient port was built by the Moors, and their influence was evident in the design of the buildings and narrow pave roads.

He decided to stop at one of the many cafés that dotted the picturesque sea front, he picked one that appeared to be dog friendly, judging by the pets sitting around. He quickly discovered that English was not the spoken language here, but managed to order coffee and water for the *'Perros'*.

He sat wondering how he was going to locate this 'obvious' place. As he was surveying the surroundings, a big smile crossed his face. There alone on the top of a hill was what he guessed was originally one of the many Moorish forts that dotted the landscape. This one had been restored and the outer walls had been rebuilt and fortified, but what convinced him was the fact that the only access was a single road that led directly to the steel gate. This had to be the place.

He finished his coffee and jumped in the car with the dogs. 'Let's see if your old master is home,' he said, scratching their ears.

As he drove up the narrow track to the property, he could tell that raiding the place like the Russians had done at his *Finca* would be out of the question: anybody approaching would be sitting ducks. He stopped at the entrance, and almost at once a tough-looking guy appeared, '*Que*?'

'Tell your boss that the Irish Gringo wants to talk to him.' The guy seemed to understand and put a radio to his mouth and started to speak rapidly in Spanish, then he finished and put it away. He opened the gate and indicated for Chaz to drive on. He could see the house and a couple of guards standing in front. He pulled up and stepped out, followed by the dogs.

'*No Perros*,' growled one of the men. He just nodded to him and proceeded to the large doors in the front of the house, followed by the dogs. The one that had spoken, pointed his rifle in a menacing manner, but before he could react one of the dogs, which he knew *Maris* had named *'Lobo'*, launched himself at the guy, gripping the strap on the rifle and proceeded to drag him along the ground, screaming.

Chaz stopped. 'I have to tell you guys, I grew up with fellas pointing guns at me and they were scary, but you lot wouldn't have lasted an afternoon where I grew up. Let him go *Lobo*,' he commanded.

'Not only do you steal my dogs, but you rename them and then bring them to attack my men.' The boss man himself was standing at the door.

'Antonio, I have been looking for you, I hear you had some trouble at the club and were looking for me.'

He looked confused, 'You must be crazy or have *cojones* of steel. You destroy my club, kill two people, and then have the nerve to come here for a chitchat!'

'Ah, that's where you are wrong, we had nothing to do with that, but I think I can help you find out who did.'

He glared at Chaz and the dogs, which by this time had abandoned the terrified guard. Finally, he dropped his shoulders and indicated to follow him inside.

They made their way down a rather austere passage into the main living area, which was in stark contrast to his former villa. He indicated for Chaz to sit. 'From what I remember, there is very little you don't drink,' handing him a large glass of brandy. 'So, tell me Irishman, why I should not have you taken outside and shot?'

Chaz took a sip and replied, 'I could give you a lot of reasons, but I think the only one you need is that you are not stupid. You know there is no way I, or my crazy brother, who had never been inside that place before that night, could have orchestrated what happened. Your waiter friend can confirm that I was nearly killed myself! No sir, I have come here to clear the air with you, and maybe point you towards the real culprits.'

He looked at him with suspicion, 'Why would you want to help me?'

'That's easy. To begin with, we don't need you or that crazy guy *Carlos* after us, by the way where is he?'

He waved his hand dismissively. 'Good question,' he mumbled, indicating for him to continue.

'If what I have heard is correct your villa and restaurant have been attacked by the Russian mob?'

'The whole situation is out of control,' he fumed. 'We have our problems, but this response is beyond extreme.'

Chaz paused for a moment. 'More extreme than destroying the club?'

Antonio snapped to attention, 'Why, do you know something?'

'Well as I said, all I want is to go home, so if I can help you, that will help me.'

He glared. 'How can you help me?'

Chaz continued. 'Well on that night, I went to say hello to the late *Mr Juan*, I told him I was a visitor and asked if he would mind if I could look around. He agreed and I was on the upper floor where the pumping station is located, as I was poking around I saw this figure sneaking out and vanishing out some back stairs, I didn't think much at the time but when I recovered I guessed he had to be the one that caused the 'accident.'

Antonio looked puzzled. 'So do you know who this man is?'

'No, but I would bet my life he was Russian.'

'Again, how can you be sure?'

'How many Spanish or Irish do you know with white-blond hair?'

He took the glasses and refilled them. As he handed the glass, he asked, 'Would you recognise him if you saw him?'

Taking the drink, he replied, 'Considering he nearly killed me, yes, I would recognise him.'

He then behaved very oddly, grasping Chaz's hand firmly. 'Charles, I wish we had met in other circumstances; you are not what I expected, this whole idea of using you brothers was all *Carlos's* idea. He believed it was the only way to solve the problem with '*La Bruja*.' I would have preferred to negotiate, but he can be very persuasive.'

'So what now?' Chaz asked.

'None of your concern, I will take it from here. That '*Cabron*' better have lifeboats on the piece of shit he calls a boat,' he snarled.

'So, we are good?' Chaz asked.

Antonio nodded. As Chaz turned to leave, he said, 'Stop.'

Chaz turned to see him walking to a desk. Opening a drawer, he took something out and passed it him, 'This won't solve your brother's problems in Barcelona, but at least now you can leave.'

Chaz looked at Des's passport in his hand, he just nodded and left with the dogs at his heels.

As they drove away, he turned to look back. 'Interesting, so *Carlos* is behind the club thing, something to look into,' he thought to himself. In a way he felt a little sorry for the shit load of trouble *De Sota* was about to bring down on himself, but then remembered that he was behind bringing this pair of dumb Irish over to stich them up.

'Well, we will see who the dumb ones are now,' as he scratched the heads of the dogs, satisfied with having stirred things up enough for today.

39

'No, anytime we have anything to do with *Ricardo* tragedy follows,' *Meris* declared.

Bill took her to one side. 'My lovely, please listen to me these guys need our help, but besides that there are a lot of strange things going on that is threatening to disrupt this little paradise of ours. More importantly, if this keeps on going there is a strong possibility of the mainland stepping in, and that is the last thing the chaps or for that matter any *Mallorquina* wants!'

She nodded begrudgingly; it was true the *Balearic Islanders* had a long and turbulent history. Inhabited by the Moors, used by pirates and smugglers who became part of the eclectic history of the place, along with all the seafaring people.

'So, what exactly do you want to know?'

Bill explained that they needed to find out if the club was being used for some reason that was out of the ordinary. 'I have not told the Irish lads yet, but they have discovered that the deaths were not an accident. They have not locked on to them yet, but it is only a matter of time, and more importantly that makes the chaps very anxious.'

Maris was no idiot. She had been involved in Bill's business dealings from the beginning and knew the 'Chaps' referred to the London crew which used *Mallorca* as their place of refuge and relaxation, and they made sure no business was carried out on their own doorstep. She thought for a minute, 'There is one possibility, come with me now, and tell the others to wait here and do nothing, understood?'

He nodded and went to tell the others to hang fire. Of course *Maria* immediately demanded to be included, but when Bill informed her that it was her mother's wish, she backed down at once.

As soon as they were gone Des pounced, 'Can someone tell me what's going on?'

Vic called them over to the table, inviting them to sit. 'I think by now we can open up a little to Des, seeing as you two seem to have become 'friends'.'

Maria blushed, causing her brothers to laugh. 'Okay, enough, carry on then,' she demanded.

Vic quickly explained, ' A long time ago, when *Meris* and her older sister *Monica* were young, *Monica* became infatuated with *Ricardo*'s son, *Diego*.'

'What!' exploded Des.

Miffed at the interruption, he continued, 'So, to cut a long story short,' giving Des a withering look that went over his head. Like a hairnet, as his mother would say. 'This was met by strong objections on both sides of the family, as it was considered an insult for cavers to be with a *'Granjero'* and vice versa. It drove them to run away into the cave together, and sadly they were lost and never found. Since then both sides blamed each other with the exception of Mum, she felt sorry for *Ricardo* losing his only son and tried to comfort him, she is the only one he trusts.'

'How could they be lost?' asked Des.

Roberto cut in, 'This whole island is volcanic and is like a piece of Swiss cheese, most of it is inaccessible and unexplored.'

Vic continued,'Because of this, each caver usually becomes an expert in a warren of his or hers choosing, and that knowledge is carefully guarded.'

Maria broke the silence, 'So what chance have we got if Mum could not get him to open up?'

Roberto replied, 'Perhaps the fact this will be the first time she has spoken to him directly in over twenty years?

They continued to talk for about an hour or so when they heard the sound of the car returning. A few seconds later Bill entered, closely followed by *Maris*, who with her head down went directly to her room in silence. Bill signalled for them to follow him outside to the pool. 'This had been very upsetting for your mother, so please forgive her and give her time, she will be fine,' he assured them. All his kids started to chatter at once, and he put up his hand for silence. 'If you all shut up, I will tell you all that happened,'and he then went on to explain that his wife had spoken to *Ricardo* and had got him to agree to lead you to the last spot he knew the *Gringo* had been. 'So, it is arranged for you to meet him at *Portals Ves* at twelve noon tomorrow and he will guide you to the place he last saw activity. Before you ask, you can cave walk to there, but a word of a caution: don't let him out of your sight, he is not be trusted.'

Des stepped in. 'I will hold his hand if I have to.' Bill laughed, having a good idea what 'holding' meant.

They were just finishing up the arrangements when Chaz returned. They spent the next hour filling each other in on their escapades. Chaz described everything that transpired with *Antonio*, excluding the 'Blond Guy' and the fact he now had the missing passport. It was not that he did not trust everybody, it was something nagging at him that made him stay quiet for the moment. When he heard the news about the caves, the first thing he asked was, 'Is anybody going with Des? I ask because if Bill has some time tomorrow, I would love to catch up to help me plan my next move.'

Bill did not believe a word of it, but immediately agreed, this Irishman was beginning to intrigue him. 'We are,' came the chorus of voices in answer to his question. He could count the two brothers and of course *Maria*, he could guess that they would have tried to dissuade her, but of that, there was no chance.

They headed off to bed, agreeing to meet for breakfast. Chaz indicated to Des to hang back. When they were alone, he said, 'I want you to listen to me brother, this is not one of your scams, these pricks are all crazy, and we have dragged Bill's family into this. Remember, tomorrow there is only one thing for you to take care of. You must make sure nothing happens to his family.'

Des nodded firmly. God help anybody that got in his way tomorrow!

40

CHAZ

Breakfast was over in a flurry, and everybody was getting ready to head out on their tasks. I took the opportunity to grab Bill and ask if I could accompany him.

'Sure, I reckon it is about time we had an honest chat, what do you think?' he asked with a sly smile.

'I figured you would get the message last night, there are a few things I need to tell you, and perhaps you have something to tell me?'

He nodded. After Des and his caving crew were on their way, reminding them again to be careful, and not let their guide out of their sight, they piled into one of their family 4+4' to vanish in a cloud of dust.

'Don't worry, *Ricardo* won't let anything happen to them as long as he knows that he would be held responsible if anything were to befall them.'

Glancing at the expression on Bill's face, I had no doubt that poor guide was very aware that his life depended on their safe return.

As we were driving, I brought Bill up to speed on what I had been with holding back on. I started with the information I had gelled from *Antonio* and how *Carlos* was responsible for the scheme that Des and myself had been brought in for.

'It all makes no sense, why try to disrupt a business that you had an interest in? It would seem to me a better approach would have been a sit down with all the parties and resolve it like sensible people. Add to the fact this is what *De Sota* had suggested apparently. Plus, the destruction and deaths, leaving the please unusable, why anyone of them would resort to that is beyond belief,' replied Bill.

'That's just it, I don't believe it was any of the 'usual suspects.' I then went on to tell him about the mystery guy 'Blondie' I had seen on that night in the club, and how it was all a surprise to *Antonio.* He had no idea who it was, I told him how I used his appearance to link him to Rostov and if he could be found I could identify him, which brought a smile to Bill's face.

'That's going to create some fireworks,' he laughed.

'Should buy me some time to get to the bottom of this crazy trip,' I growled.

He was silent for a moment, then spoke, 'I guess I have not been exactly honest with you also. Me and 'the Chaps' or to be more precise the London crew, have made this place our sort of neutral ground, a bit like 'Ricks Bar' in the movie *Casablanca.*'

I looked at him blankly. 'Never mind. You get the idea, no 'business' is to be conducted on this Island, other than meetings, etc. 'Before you ask, we are not the police, whatever other crews get up to is none of our concern, unless ...' he halted.

I jumped in, 'Like the suspicious deaths of two powerful people and all the publicity that goes with it!'

He nodded, 'Exactly, but all that is our concern, all you need to do is focus on getting the hell out of here.' I reached into my pocket and produced Des's passport. 'Is that what I think it is?' he asked.

I nodded. '*Antonio* gave it to me, and I think he believes we are friends now. I will make it simple, Bill, I can put up with a lot of crap, but when people start threatening anyone of my family, and worse than that, treat me like someone without a clue, well then I am going to see this through until I get to the bottom of whatever this character *Carlos* and his blond friend are up to.' I saw the puzzled expression on Bill's face. 'Oh, I forgot to mention, when I was dealing with Bruno and his crew, I spotted the pair of them leaving *Porto Portals* in a speedboat together, and they didn't seem to be all that happy.'

'Well, I am glad we are on the right side of you brothers, and to think *Antonio* believes you are his friend. A friend like that could become a big problem!'

41

They had arranged to meet *Ricardo* at *Portals Ves*, only this time they went by boat, a choice of craft from the Hearts' family collection.

The thirty-five-foot speedboat roared the four of them to the beach in front of the meeting place in minutes, where they anchored and waded ashore in the warm waters. They were only there a couple of minutes when their guide appeared as if by magic. He seemed a little more relaxed this morning; perhaps talking to *Meris* directly had reassured him, but Des still did not trust this guy one bit. He indicated that they would take as short trip in his dinghy, to where they would enter on foot. The five of them managed to just fit in with the equipment that they had brought, such as torches and some snorkelling equipment in case it was needed.

They didn't have to worry; it was only a short trip into a semi-hidden estuary where they beached the craft a short distance in. 'We go on foot from here,' he instructed. 'I will lead, make sure we stay connected, if you become separated, you might never be found!' he warned.

'Don't worry, I won't be letting you out of my sight,' Des said as he stepped directly behind *Ricardo* and clipped a rope to his knapsack. 'Just to be sure!' he grinned.

They set off down a narrow track which opened out into a clearing, he pointed over to a small opening leading into the hillside. 'We go in through here, this will take us to where the *Gringo* spent some time before the flooding.'

'Is it flooded now?' he asked. *Ricardo* just shrugged his shoulders and headed in with Des firmly connected to him, he was followed closely by *Maria* then *Vic* with *Rob* taking up the rear.

The going was easy at first but the deeper they went into the complex the going got more difficult. 'I can see how someone could get lost in here, every turn looks the same.'

Ricardo picked up on the remark. 'Over the years even the most experienced '*Cavernicola*' vanished, they get disorientated and that's usually the beginning of the end,' he stated ominously.

They all went silent after that, paying close attention to the person in front. 'The blind leading the blind,' Des whispered to *Maria*, which prompted a swift punch in his back.

Their guide would stop from time to time to check something on the walls of the caves, it would seem they he had some personal markings to guide his way. After what seemed like an eternity, they began to see some natural light, he pointed out many fissures that caused light from the outside filter in. 'You can turn off the torches now,' he instructed.

A short time later, he pulled up suddenly, 'What's wrong?' Des asked.

He just stood, listening intently, 'Did you hear that?' he inquired; they all shook their heads. He still looked concerned, but carried on, a few minutes later, the sound of a boat could be heard.

'What's that?' Des asked.

He glanced at him and without a reply, then carried on. They came out into a large cavern, which led down to water which disappeared into darkness.

Maria gave out a sharp cry. 'Look!' pointing to the corner where somebody in diving gear was lying motionless, besides what looked like a small pool. They stood in shock for a moment, then Des went to investigate.

'He's dead,' after checking for a pulse, 'but not long ago, he is still warm and no sign of rigor mortis,' he added.

'Was it him we heard?' *Rob,* asked.

Des shook his head. 'Not from this guy, he might not be dead long, but there is no way he was making any sound, he didn't get out of the water on his own accord, somebody took him out.'

'How do you know?' *Maria* asked. Des pointed to the track marks that the air tanks had made, as he was dragged across the ground.

'Then there was somebody else here, it must have been them leaving when we heard the boat engine sound,' *Rob* replied.

Des turned to *Ricardo*, who had not said a word since they had entered the grotto. 'Do you know who this is?' he asked as he pulled off the head mask to reveal the shock of blond hair and frozen features of Klaus.

Ricardo moved cautiously over to look, obviously fearfully of the dead body. He shook his head vigorously. 'No, never' turning away, while blessing himself.

'So what's the story about this place?'

Glad of the opportunity to move away from the grim scene, they moved down to the water's edge.

It was obvious *Ricardo* was visibly shaken. 'All I can tell you is that some time ago some guy approached me to help in getting access to the submarine pens.'

Des jumped up. 'Again, with the submarines, what has any of that to do with this fecking club?'

'If you would shut up and listen, we might be able to find out,' snapped *Maria.*

Her brothers grinned, with all his hard-man act, they could see that Des was like putty around their sister. *Ricardo* continued to tell them that someone from a connected family had contacted him and 'suggested' it would be in his best interest to help this guy out.

'What did he want?' Des asked.

The guide, looked sheepish. 'This is no time to clam up, there is a dead man here.'

Maria snapped at him in rapid Spanish. He nodded. 'He wanted to find certain areas deep in the caves. I tried to explain to him, that I did not know every inch of the cave system, nobody does, but he would not believe me. He did not know that I had found this place, I tried to look through his stuff, but he must have had it hidden in one of the safes.'

Des could not contain himself, 'Safes!' he cried 'What are safes doing down here?'

Before *Maria* could say anything, *Ricardo* continued. 'That was where the engineers kept their valuables and documents, they were put in during the construction of the club, they are dotted all around the complex.'

Des looked back at the pool. 'Is it down there?' pointing at the well.

He nodded. 'It wasn't flooded before. It must be because of the accident at the club,' *Ricardo* added.

Des stood and went over to the water, avoiding the still form lying beside the edge. 'I am going to have a look,' as he reached into one of the knapsacks, taking out a face mask and snorkel. 'Are you crazy!' his three companions yelled. He grinned, 'Be quiet you will wake the dead,' pointing at the stiff. 'I am okay at this. I have had a few lessons, even some scuba, I will just drop in and check out if there is anything that could help us, here, tie this around my waist,' he said, handing them a rope. 'If I have any trouble, you can drag me out.' They reluctantly agreed, and he proceeded to the steps leading down into the darkness. 'What is the layout of this place?' he asked the petrified guide.

He described a room of about 6x6 metres, with a door at the end which led in the direction of the club, but he had never been through there, he added. Des switched on his torch, illuminating the room and its layout, he could see the control panel in the corner and proceeded over to see if he could discover anything. After a brief inspection he came back up for air. 'Nothing down here, only that control panel, do you have any idea of the password?' he asked *Ricardo*.

'No, it is impossible without the correct '*contrasena*',' he added.

'Password,' translated *Rob*.

'Where I come from locks only keep the honest people out,' Des replied, taking a small hammer and screwdriver out of the pack. 'Be back in a second,' as he dived into the room again.

Quickly going to the panel again, he put the screwdriver at the point of the keypad, then gave it a quick crack of the hammer breaking the seal, allowing the water to seep into the electronics. At once there was a sound behind him as a panel opened behind him, a quick inspection before he came up for air, told him it was a waste of time.

As he stripped off his mask at the side of the pool, they all anxiously waited for him to reveal what he had found. 'Nothing, the place is empty, whatever was there is gone,' he turned to *Ricardo*. 'Have you been into the locker room?' he asked.

Again, he avoided any eye contact. 'I have seen into it, when this guy was not there, all I could see was this kind of stuff,' pointing to the diving equipment, 'and what looked like maps and books, plus a box of explosives, I think.'

'Explosives!' the brothers yelped.

'Well, it is all gone now,' Des added. They looked at him in confusion.

'How did you open the panel without the password?' Maria asked. He pointed to his tools. 'Easy I just added water as soon as the keyboard shorted out the door opened.'

The boys looked at him in wonder. 'How did you figure that out?' they asked.

'Sorry, if I told you I would have to kill you,' he replied with a grim face. They all went into shock, until he burst out in laughter, 'You should see your faces. Come on, time to do something about him,' pointing at the body. 'I am going to check out where this leads, it has to be the way they came in,' pointing in the direction of the outlet at the end of the landing. 'Be back in a flash,' as he slipped his mask on again and plunged into the water!

42

Within a couple of minutes, he could see light. 'The light at the end of the tunnel' he joked to himself, as he came out into the bright sunlight.

Turning, he was amazed to see a sheer-rock face behind him, until he focused and could see the optical illusion they were creating. He returned quickly to the others and explained what he had found. The shock on their guide's face was a surprise, when he questioned him, he told him he had no idea of its existence.

'Okay, here is what we do. *Rob* you come with me outside so you can identify where the entrance is. You and *Vic* can accompany our guide friend back to your boat, then you can come and retrieve us from here.'

'What about him?' pointing at the corpse, 'Should we not call the police?'

Des laughed, 'That is the last thing we want to do, don't you think we have enough trouble already? No, we will take him with us, until we decide what to do.'

After *Roberto* had pinpointed how to locate the entrance, he and his brother, with *Ricardo* in tow, retreated back to recover their transport. Meanwhile, he and *Maria* prepared their package for the journey to the outside. 'We will inflate his lifejacket so we can float him out, give me a hand to get him in the water,' as he grasped the guy under his arms.

'This doesn't seem to bother you at all,' *Maria* said.

He shrugged. 'It is the live ones that bother me, I have found that the dead ones are no trouble at all,' as they paddled outside.

Not long after, the boys arrived and quickly pulled the body aboard, covering him with a canvas. *Ricardo,* who had been silent the whole time, now said, 'Can you drop me back now?'

Des turned to him, 'Buddy, since you were with us when we discovered him,' pointing at the canvas, 'you are not leaving our sight until we figure out what to do with you, so sit tight and enjoy the company!'

43

Bill and Chaz were deep in discussion, trying to decide how to get to bottom of the *Carlos* situation, when Bill's phone rang, He did not speak, as Chaz could see the blood drain from his face.

'We will be right there,' he said as he hung up.

'What's wrong?' he asked.

'I will explain in the car, we have to get home at once,' grabbing his keys as they headed for the door.

As they drove, he explained what had happened. 'They are back from the caves, and according to Vic they ran into some trouble. He would not say what was wrong on the phone, just to get back at once.'

'Is anybody hurt?' Chaz asked.

'He said everybody was okay, but we have a big problem, that's all he would say, just to get back as quick as we can. It must be bad, *Vic* never gets stressed,' he added.

They lapsed into silence until they arrived home. Skidding to a stop outside, they could see the Range Rover that they had used this morning, parked outside the side entrance. As they jumped out, they were met by Des and all the family plus the dogs. Hugs of relief were shared by Bill and the kids, as everyone started to talk at once.

'Stop. Let's wait until we are inside, and everybody has calmed down,' he shouted over the din.

When they moved inside, Chaz and Bill stopped in their tracks at the sight of *Meris* deep in conversation with a strange old geezer. 'Who the hell is that?' snapped Bill.

'That's Mum's friend that led us into the cave,' *Maria* informed him.

'And what the hell is he doing here, can someone tell us what is going on?'

They indicate that they all should sit down, while *Rob* filled them in on what had happened. 'A dead guy in diving gear, are you kidding me?' Chaz gasped. 'Are you sure he is dead?' he asked, incredulously.

'Dead as you can get,' Des chimed in.

There was silence for a moment, then Bill asked, 'So how did you leave him?'

'We didn't,' replied *Maria.* 'He is out in the car.'

Chaz immediately turned to Des. 'That had to be your idea, what the hell did you bring him back here for?'

Des raised his hand for calm. 'We had no choice, it was the only way we could contain the situation. This way we can control the outcome, remember that whoever left in that boat we heard could have come back and covered his tracks. This way, we might be able use this to our advantage.'

Chaz stopped. 'So who is this guy?'

Everybody shook their heads. 'No idea, and before you ask, the crazy guy has no idea either,.I brought him along, until we figure how to proceed and to keep his mouth shut,' Des added.

Bill stood, 'Well let's go and have a look,' as they all trooped out to the car.

'Well that's something you don't see every day' Chaz commented, as they looked at the surreal picture of the fully outfitted diver, stretched out in the back of the 4+4 as if asleep.

Bill reached inside to remove the face mask to have a look at who the cadaver was. As he pulled it off, his face appeared, along with his close cropped white-blond hair. He sprung back, looking at Chaz. 'Is this who I think it is?'

He nodded, which started them all asking questions. 'Cover him up and move back inside, so we can bring you guys up to speed,' Bill said, pulling the canvas cover back over the mystery diver. After they were seated, Chaz told them about his encounter in the club that fateful night.

'And this is the guy?' *Vic* asked.

'Yes, you tend to remember the people that try to kill you no question, but the bigger question is what he was doing at the bottom of some flooded room, in full diving gear; and how is all this connected?'

'More questions than answers,' added Bill.

Des piped up, 'One thing is for sure, whoever was in that cave before us, has got to be involved.'

Chaz nodded his head. 'For once Des is right. You did the right thing to bring the guy back here, I am sure that this guy will be back to check what happened, and I have a good idea who it is.'

'Who?' the boys chorused.

This time Bill spoke. 'One of *De Sota's* crew, a guy called *Carlos*, he is a bit of a mystery. Charles and I have been trying to find out about him, but he keeps a low profile. We know he lives somewhere in *Palma*, but other than that he is a bit of a ghost.'

Maria piped up, 'Speaking of ghosts, if we don't do something about our guest in the car soon he is going to get a bit ripe.'

There was silence for a moment, then Chaz said, 'We will keep him. If it is *Carlos* involved, the fact that the body has disappeared will keep him guessing, we will keep him in reserve until we gauge the reaction.'

'That sounds a good idea, but in a few days from now, he won't be recognisable, and will be on the nose,' Des added.

'So, what do we do?' *Maria* asked.

Chaz broke out into a grin, then turned to Bill. 'Do you have fridge?'

44

After they had the deposited 'the ice man' (which they had started to refer to him as) in a giant freezer that Bill had on his property, they all stood around looking at the strange sight of this guy. He was fully dressed in diving gear, sitting amongst the frozen carcasses of beef hanging all around him.

'He looks peaceful,' *Rob* added, which prompted some gasps and moans from the assembled crew.

'Enough of the jokes,' cautioned Bill.

Vic, who of all of them had the most experience with diving had removed the tanks and face gear, turned to them, 'Check this out,' holding the gauge and face mask out to his brother to inspect. 'There is something wrong here, the tanks are still almost full, so how did this guy die?'

Rob put the face mask to his face and took a breath, he immediately took it away, 'This is not an oxygen mix, it is some type of gas, this guy did not drown, he was poisoned!' he gasped.

'Okay, enough, put it back with him, until we figure out what to do' Bill instructed.

As they moved inside, the atmosphere amongst them had changed, the news that they may be mixed up in a murder, and now had the body hidden in their freezer, changed everything. 'Come on I want to have word with this caver guy,' said Chaz. *Meris* was still sitting with him when they got back to the sitting room. '*Meris*, could you tell this guy that if he wants to get his life back, he would be well-advised to tell us everything he knows about what has happened, and how he knew to go to that spot.'

She broke into a strange language, which *Maria* explained was '*Mallorquina'* a dialect spoken only on the Islands. After she finished speaking with him, he took a deep breath and again explained about his shadowed connection to this family.

When Chaz looked quizzing at *Meris*, she explained how the islands were 'influenced' by this lot of old families with murky pasts.

'Sounds just like back home!' chimed in Des. A look from *Maria* was enough to shut him up.

Chas said, 'Ask him to describe this guy and what specifically did he want.'

Again, *Maris* spoke to him, and they chattered on for a while. When he stopped, she looked at Chaz in confusion.

'What he is saying makes no sense. The guy wanted information about the old submarine pens.' She explained that early in the Spanish conflict, Hitler used the opportunity to test out his war machines before the outbreak of war, then the pens were built. After the war they were abandoned and fell into ruin.'

'So why all the interest in them?' he asked.

'That's just it, there is no secret, their whereabouts are not a secret and they have been explored so many times over the years that they have been picked clean.'

He could see this conversation was causing the old guy some concern. He tapped her and spoke again. After he finished, she continued. 'He now tells me that he explained this to him, but this guy had some maps, or drawings, which he said was to hidden submarine pens, these had been constructed in secret towards the end of the war.'

Rob cut in, 'I have heard those stories about hidden treasure, stashed away in secret by high-ranking members of the Nazi party, but that's all they are, fairytales. Nobody has ever discovered anything of value, in all the years of searching.'

'Tell him to continue,' Chaz directed.

He went on to explain that the fella would not take his word. He was adamant that this place existed, and he needed somebody that could follow the directions to the location. He became angry when he explained that there was nothing in the area that the drawing indicated and also it was very '*Pelegrosa'*—dangerous.

'Ask him what this guy looked like,' he asked.

As soon as *Meris* described him, they knew it was *Carlos*. He asked her to find out what happened after that. 'Nothing, when he discovered that he was of no help, he left and that was the last he saw of him,' she replied.

He nodded and then remembered something. 'Ask him did he ever explore where this guy was interested in?' She spoke to him, and he started to shake vigorously, becoming very agitated.

'What's wrong?' he asked.

She looked at them, her face as pale as ivory. 'He said, never, that is where his son vanished.'

They let him leave then, as he was visibly shaken. 'Tell him, that if he wants to stay out of jail, to keep his mouth shut about all of this, we will be in touch him soon. Until then, it would help him and all of us if he could shed any more light on all of this,' and with that *Vic* agreed to drive him back to his dinghy.

When he left, Bill, Des and Chaz got themselves a drink to calm down and to discuss their next move. 'This has just gone to another level; this is going to explode if we don't get to the bottom of this. One person we have not considered in all of this is the *Gobernadora*, what is her involvement in all of this?' Bill asked.

'Good question, and I know just the person to ask her.'

They both looked at him. 'Who?' asked Des. 'Oh, you know him well, his name is Vincent Savage QC, your brother!'

Des spluttered. 'You are going to ask Vin for help?' he choked.

Bill cut in. 'Are you sure? This *Bruja* can chew the balls off anybody.'

The brothers laughed. 'That won't be any bother to him.'

Bill looked quizzing, 'You see he has years of experience with 'Witches'; he is married to one!'

45

VINCENT

Vincent Savage QC, was sitting in his west-end penthouse flat in London, sipping a glass of expensive French wine, pondering what his life had in store for him now that his soon to be ex-wife had finally pulled the pin and left with a considerable part of his fortune.

He had mixed emotions. He was delighted to see the back of his tyrant-like wife Caroline, but on the other hand hated to part with the money. Not that he was short of a bob or two. He had inherited the Savage's gift of the gab, which he put to good use in his role as a trial lawyer. He defended many of the social elite with their numerous scandals, add to that, politicians, and people from the shady underworld. His success had catapulted him to be the number one go-to guy to if you had a problem. This, as he reflected, had provided him and his ex-wife with a lifestyle that could only be envied. Sadly for him he never seemed to be satisfied. He smiled to himself as he remembered his conversation with his parents, when he let them know that Caroline had taken a hike.

As he expected, he did not receive an iota of sympathy. 'Ha ha, his dad chuckled. 'Told you she was a great housekeeper, she kept them,' he laughed. 'I told you not to call her 'Dear' just call her 'Expensive'.'

The fact that Vincent's success had provided them with a perfect retirement was lost on him. Vin had purchased the old family home and restored it to its former glory, yet they still spent all their time between the kitchen and the bedroom, the only concession was the big-screen TV in both places. The smile slipped from his face as he looked around his palatial flat, and yet he could not raise an interest in any of his success. Perhaps that's why when his phone rang with a totally unexpected call from his older brother, he resisted his first reaction to ignore it.

After they exchanged cautious greetings again, because whenever the Savage brothers reached out to each other, it was seldom for a chat!

After Chaz had spent about an hour bringing his brother up to speed as to what had happened since their arrival in *Mallorca*, he took a breath. 'Well, Des has really excelled himself this time, this is certainly of a far greater magnitude than any of his previous schemes.'

Chaz retorted, 'If you mean by that he has really fucked up, you would be correct. Is there any chance you could lend your expertise to this mess, this is way out of our league? I know it will be difficult to get it by Caroline and will understand if the answer is no,' not expecting a favourable reply.

'That's not going to be a problem. Caroline has taken the advice of her councillor and filed for divorce, it has not been very fair, she keeps the house and a shit load of money, and I get to keep on working.'

Chaz was in shock, he never thought she would release her grip on her cash cow. 'So sorry brother,' he replied.

Vincent laughed. 'Are you kidding, I still can't believe it happened. I have been sitting here with all this freedom, not knowing what to do with it, then out of the blue you call. Count me in!' he roared with delight. 'I have a client in Barcelona that has been on to me to have a look at his problem, I will kill two birds with one stone, see you in a couple of days. Until then gather all the information on the lady in question, and don't get into any more trouble before I see you.'

'No problem, ring me and we will pick you up from the airport,' as he hung up.

'Fine asking me to stay out of trouble, try telling that to Des,' he mumbled to himself as he turned to the group, giving them the thumbs up. 'He is in!'

46

CARLOS

Chaz was completing his call to his brother, when *Carlos* was just hanging up on the second of two very painful phone calls.

The first was to a very angry cartel boss, who was frantically demanding to know what had happened to their operation. All he could do was point the finger at *De Sota*, which did not help. 'I don't care what the crazy idiot wants, he is sampling too much of his own product. This dispute with the Irish and this Russian Rostov Janko, has to stop. The *Gobernadora*, has been in touch with your German friends in Argentina, demanding that this is to be resolved at once. She is furious with the loss of her son and the club, which was raising eyebrows with the powers to be on the mainland. She has sent word that all hostilities are to cease immediately. If this continues the federal government may step in, and that will bring the roof down on everybody. Speaking about roofs falling in, have you discovered who is responsible for the destruction of the club?'

Carlos took a deep breath, 'I am looking into it, don't worry I will get to the bottom of it.'

'Worry!' he roared. 'We have lost this outlet for good it would seem, which is creating havoc with supplies. Get this fixed up; remember the reason you are involved is to keep things running smoothly. If this is your version of 'running smoothly' I am not impressed,' and hung up.

Then he had to deal with the 'party' and about their pal Klaus Becker's disappearance. He had to explain that he had not seen Klaus since he had informed them that he was going diving and had not been seen since.

'Well, find him, people don't just vanish,' they demanded, as he was hung up on again.

'That's just it,' he thought to himself. Klaus *had* vanished, as he had discovered on his return to the cave. Somebody must have moved him, and he guessed that it had to be something to do with the voices he had heard. He cursed himself for not hanging around to see who it was. This was all because of that idiot Klaus, now even in his death he was still causing him trouble!

He slumped down into his chair, putting his head in his hands wondering, how could things have got into such a mess, it had been all in control. He had the Irish brothers to take the heat with this plan to get the Irish mob out of the Club. They had been disrupting his own plans in his search that his grandfather's notebooks had led him on. He recalled the day he had discovered them when he was tidying up after his passing, a couple of years ago. Then the shock as to the involvement that his grandfather had with the Nazi-party upper echelon, right up their beloved Führer. The stories about his beloved party and their crazy leader, fascinated him in his younger years. Although he could not believe how anybody in their right mind could believe in their obscene policies and had little interest in their history. That was until he started to read his grandfather's journals. To his shock and surprise he was to discover that in the early part of 1945 the top brass of the Nazi party knew that the war was lost. Also, that his grandfather was put in charge of the 'relocation' of the party faithful and, more importantly, the wealth that they had stolen in their rape of Europe.

His excitement was tempered when in his investigations he discovered that over the years since then, treasure hunters seemed to have discovered any wealth that was recoverable. That was until he stumbled upon a small notebook which carried a fascinating story. The Führer had commissioned his grandfather in secret to put in place an escape route for himself and Eva Braun, in the final days of the war. In it he tells of utilising their submarine base in Mallorca to construct a secret location for them to escape to by submarine. What he read next had brought him to this point. It was the mention of 'the leader's' legacy and the resources that he would need to revive his dream of a 1000-year Reich. They were to be transported to the secret location in anticipation of losing the war in preparation for their escape to, probably *Argentina*. All that *Carlo*s was interested in, was whatever was stashed in that secret location.

So, with the help of the fanatics, he had convinced them that they needed someone to keep an eye on their 'investments' over here. Because of his unique relationship with his *Mallorca* family and the fact he was half

Argentinian made him perfect to blend in. That was until they had sent him Klaus to 'help him out'.

'I should have killed him the minute I saw him!' he raged to himself. He was snapped back to the present by the phone ringing. It was *De Sota.*

'We need to talk, come down to The Fortress,' which he had dubbed his place in *Port de Andratx.* 'I have news. I believe I have found out who is behind the destruction of the club.'

Carlos froze. 'Who?' Fearing the game was up.

'That Russian prick Rostov, he had one of his men sabotage the pumping system, screwing up everything, it's time for payback.'

Carlos could not believe his ears; how could things get any worse? 'How do you know that?'

Antonio just screamed. 'I will tell you when you get here,' hanging up.

The normally unflappable *Carlos*, proceeded to kick the hell out of the furniture, until he finally regained his composer. He grabbed his keys, muttering to himself as he headed out, 'What is this coke-sniffing maniac planning now ?

47

An hour later, *Carlos* was making his way up *De Sota's* driveway, wondering what he would have to do to contain *Antonio's* rage. He had enough experience with his Latin temper to realise that he could be a loose cannon.

De Sota was pacing up and down in his stark living room when Carlos walked in. 'Where have you been? All hell is breaking loose out here,' *Antonio* roared. Without waiting for a reply, he ranted on. 'I have had *Colombia* on to me. Your 'friends' have demanded answers to the club incident, and fortunately I was able to tell them that I had discovered who is behind it,' he declared triumphantly.

Carlos started to get a bad feeling. 'You said that it was Rostov, how do you know?' he asked.

'I had a visit from one of Irish brother's, he wanted to clear the air as to what happened in the club. As you can imagine, he could have had nothing to do with it.' This coming from a man that a couple of days ago, wanted their heads! 'He told me that on that night he was checking the place out and spotted the person responsible, leaving just before the place flooded.'

Carlos could not believe his ears, 'How did he know that he was sent by the Russians?'

'Because he described him, well built, but most importantly, he had white-blond hair and his description was of an 'Eastern European'. How many Spanish or 'Latinos' have hair like that? It has to be Janko, it is time for pay back!' he roared.

Carlos wished the floor would open up and swallow him, how had it come to this, but he knew the answer: Klaus. 'Boss, the cartel has been on to me also, they are demanding that all hostilities stop. *La Bruja* has sent word that she wants the people responsible for the destruction and the death of her son brought to 'justice': quickly and quietly.'

De Sota flared up, 'Who are they to dictate, this is my operation. I am the one that negotiated for the club.'

'Which is now gone,' interrupted *Carlos*.

He ignored him, 'I will deal with '*La Gobernadora*', meanwhile you see what you can find out about this blond guy. Maybe this Chaz can be of some help, I found him most agreeable,' having a jab at *Carlos*.

'Okay, I will see what I can find out, but until then, please don't do anything drastic,' he pleaded. But he had a feeling that his words fell on deaf ears. Outside in the car, he sat in silence trying to process all that had happened, and what was the common denominator.

'The Savage brothers,' he snarled under his breath.

48

So, it would seem this Chaz fella was a lot cleverer than he thought. He had seen Klaus in the club, but he would have no idea who he was, yet it was clever of him to use the information to stir up that fool, *De Sota*.

He drove, fuming at how his carefully laid plans could have got into such a mess. He knew that his plan to use the brothers to implicate the Irish mob was a good plan. If only that crazy cave guy had been true to his word and been able to help locate the entrance to the secret subbase. But all he had done is strung him along. He had to admit that the part of the cavern system that his grandfather had indicated was only known to a select few *'Cavernicola's'*, of which he wasn't one! Beside his promises that he would find someone who could lead them, he knew that it was a lost cause with this guy; and if not for the fact he also had vanished, he would have joined Klaus in the afterlife.

When the party faithful sent their guy, he had made the mistake of thinking he could use him to speed up the disruption in the club. This had all been brought about because of the increased activity in the cave system disrupting his opportunity to continue with his quest. All caused by the sticky fingers of the *Gobernadora's* son and his equally stupid partner Apparently, they had believed the rumour of this special 'concentrated cocaine' the Russians had boasted about. This happened to be just that, a rumour, but the result was that *Antonio* got word that stuff was going missing and insisted he do something, hence 'The Plan'.

Which would have worked if this fanatic from Argentina had not decided to destroy the place! He took a deep breath, remembering his grandfather's words: 'Keep your eye on the prize, this will not be easy, but the reward will guide you there.'

'Fine,' he thought, but the directions laid out in his notebooks lacked a lot of detail. Fortunately, he was able to locate the entrance to his grandfather's 'bunker' which he used exclusively during the construction of the escape route for his beloved Führer. But he had hit a blank wall as to the location of the hidden cave entrance. He knew that from the notes that his grandfather had, with the help of some cavers, located a deep underwater entrance to a massive grotto. This was where they had, in secret, constructed the hidden sub location. At first *Ricardo* had led him to the war-time submarine bases, believing this was what he was looking for, as he had brought many inquisitive explorers in the past. He knew this was a waste of time as soon as he could see that the place had been picked clean. Besides, what he remembered being told was, that outside of his grandfather, nobody knew of the location at the insistence of Hitler.

Snapping back to the present, he regathered his thoughts. 'So, where the hell are the brothers, and more importantly where had Klaus got to?'

49

While *Carlos* was trying to figure out where his blond friend had disappeared to, at the same time on Rostov's yacht all hell was breaking loose.

Janko was gesturing furiously at a very angry-looking Bruno Reilly. 'You overreacted, I told you to settle this matter, not start a Third World War,' pointing again at Bruno, who was just about to point out that this had been a joint effort, with Janko calling the shots. But before he could say anything the phone rang again for the umpteenth time since the 'incident' at the club. He knew from the tone of the conversations, even though they were in a foreign language, that the callers were not happy. When he hung up from this one, he could tell this was at a whole other level of 'unhappy.' His hands were shaking so much he almost dropped the phone, his face chalky white.

'Everything okay?' he asked the shaken Russian.

He shook his head, then surprisingly began to speak. 'That was word from the very top,' referring to the Russian leader. 'He is so displeased that we have not held up our side of the bargain we have with his friends in the Israeli underground, that he is considering releasing Viktor Vostok.'

He continued, 'He is threatening to release this animal from detention in the Gulag and giving him back his yacht that you are sitting on, and you swopping places with him. Those were his words, now you may wonder why I am sharing this information with you, it is to remind you, in case you were thinking of 'jumping ship', so to say. Remember Melnikov,' referring to the Russian leader, 'Boris? He has a reputation for making sure that the slate is wiped clean using the scorched earth policy of old, do I make my point?'

Bruno and his boys nodded their heads, the history of what happened with people that displeased him, was well known.

'So, what is this plan with the Israelis?' Mick asked.

Rostov looked at Bruno, who nodded for him to continue. 'When the opportunity arose to take over the Vostok operation, the Israelis would only consider it if I brought something different to the table, hence the 'concentrated cocaine'.'

Mick looked at them, confused, 'So, what's the problem?'

'The problem is there is no 'concentrated cocaine'. When Bruno came to me with his connection in the club, this is the story we came up with, and it was working until *De Sota* wrecked everything with his 'Irish Plan' and destroyed the club.'

'But we tested your product, it was off the charts.'

Bruno jumped in, 'It is not hard to produce a high-concentrated product, the problem is it is very expensive and difficult to produce. So, we only had enough to satisfy them.'

Mick, slumped back in his seat, 'So what do we do now?'

Rostov continued, 'We try to calm things down, until I figure a way out of this mess.'

'What do you want us to do?' Bruno asked.

'Just make sure that *De Sota* does not create any more havoc. Is the ship protected?' he asked.

'No problem there, we are covered on the harbour side, and there is no way he can approach from the sea without us seeing him.'

'Good,' he said. 'Bruno, we need to find who destroyed the pumping system, that way we can clear ourselves of the blame.'

He indicated to the waiter to replenish the drinks, who hurriedly cleared the glasses. 'Of course, right away Señor,' replied *Victor Heart*, smiling to himself.

50

'No concentrated cocaine?' chipped in Bill as *Vic* reported his findings back at the *Finca.*

It had been Des's idea to get somebody on the inside. He had volunteered, but of course the fact that he did not look Spanish or speak the language quickly ruled him out.

Vic had stepped up. 'No problem, I know a lot of the guys that work on the ship, I will get it done.'

So, when he returned with this news, it was obvious the news worried Bill. He indicated to Chaz to step outside, while *Vic* filled them in on life aboard this luxury yacht. When they were beside the pool, he told Chaz that the 'Chaps' are very concerned with the situation. 'They want you to know that they appreciate you sticking around. I told them that you had recovered your passport and could leave any time you wanted.'

He shrugged his shoulders, 'Not our style, anyway there is the matter of Des's problem in Barcelona. *Señor Carlos* is going to have to rectify that before we leave.'

Bill did not look convinced, 'Not sure how you are going to do that, we can't even locate where he is staying exactly. We know he has a place in *Palma*, but that place is a rabbit warren, so far no luck. Any ideas?'

'First thing we have to establish is a connection with him and the blond stiff, any luck identifying him?'

'Not a sign, he seems to have appeared out of nowhere. Speaking of that, any idea what we are going to do with him?'

Chaz nodded, 'I am working on that, but in the meantime we need to find out what all the interest in the old submarine pens are. And how they are connected to the club.'

'How do we do that?' he asked.

'I have found, if you want someone to divulge their inner-most secrets, there is only one man for the job.'

'Who?'

'Des of course, his 'secret power' is his uncanny way of making people do what he asks.'

Bill glanced in the direction of the family, who were deep in conversation, and who was holding the floor. Des! 'I see what you mean, so how can he help?'

'Well, until Vincent arrives, and he puts his slant on things, there is a couple of things we can do, I will see if I can find a way to connect *Carlos* and the blond friend. As to the other, watch this,' he said as they made their way over to the group. 'Listen up, Bill and I are trying to figure out our next move. We were wondering about this fella *Ricardo*, from the caves, do you believe that he has told us all he knows?'

Meris spoke first, 'He told us everything,' followed by the boys and *Maria* agreeing, 'He would be afraid of Mum not to.'

Chaz and Bill sat in silence, then Des spoke. 'He might be afraid of *Meris*, but he is afraid much more of someone else. I believe he has a secret, one that is killing him. I will find out what it is if you want.'

Chaz gave him a nod. That was all the incentive he needed. 'On it,' turning back to *Maria* and her mum, to consider his next move.

'We can leave him to that, if that guy knows anything, Des will get it out of him one way or another.'

Bill shook his head, 'If only *Carlos* and his crew had known what he was letting himself in for, he would never have set foot in Ireland!'

He burst out laughing.

51

VINCENT

Vincent Savage QC strode out of the airport after his short flight from Barcelona. He stood in the warm *Mallorca* sunshine, looking every bit the picture of the successful lawyer. He was dressed in a white linen suit that probably cost more than most made in a month. He glanced at his watch, a Rolex® GMT master II. A Pepsi model, a collector's piece of considerable value.

Glancing around he spotted his brother, Charles, as he liked to call him, just to stir him up. He was standing beside a late-model Range Rover, beside him was a large tough-looking guy, which struck a chord in his memory.

He made his way over, trailing his carry on. Chaz greeted him, 'Never thought you would make it, glad to see you,' giving his brother a big hug, which Vince found uncomfortable. 'This is …' but before he could finish Bill cut in, 'I believe we have met before.'

Vince nodded. 'I believe so, I represented one of your colleagues in a delicate matter some time ago, and you were present at one of the meetings.'

Chaz looked at them in surprise as Bill continued, 'Correct, it's a small world for sure, come on let's get out of the heat. I am sure you could do with a cool refreshment, we have some in the car,' as he took his cases, placing them in the back of the vehicle.

As they made the hour-long journey from the airport, which was to the northeast of *Palma* to Bill's ranch, Chaz listened to them swapping names. The 'spots of bother' that Vincent had sorted out for the 'Chaps'.

'I can't believe I did not make the connection when you mentioned you had a brother who was a Brief.' (Chaps' slang for a lawyer).

'Well hardly surprising, considering the circumstances you met Des and me. Not the sort of people you expect to have one of the top Barristers in England, as a relation.'

Bill burst out laughing, 'Now that I realise that it is Vincent, it is not at all surprising, and his reputation for doing things 'differently' precedes him. Not unlike what I have seen you two do in the last few days, you are definitely cut from the same cloth.'

From the expression on Vince's face, something he would have rather Bill had kept to himself. The conversation continued, as they brought him up to speed on what was happening. When it was mentioned about what Des was endeavouring to do, his response surprised both.

'Well, if anybody is going to extract the truth from this cave guy, it will be Desmond.'

They continued to chat until they arrived at *Finca.* 'Now before you start, Chaz has told me that you will insist on staying at a hotel, as you can see rooms here are not a problem. For obvious reasons it will be more secure if we all stay together.' Before Vince could respond, he jumped out calling for one of the staff to fetch the suitcases.

Chaz turned to his brother, 'No point in arguing, remember he took us in after we slept in a graveyard.' He looked at Chaz in confusion. 'Don't worry, I will explain later,' as they went inside.

After all introductions had been made, and drinks had been replenished, Bill indicated for them to proceed outside to the pool where food was being served. Des and *Maria* had left earlier to see what they could find out about the *cavernicola's.*

Des had decided to chat with the guys from the 'Blue Bar' before confronting *Ricardo* again. At that point two thing happened to make Vincent react, one in a way that Chaz had not seen him do since he was a teenager, and the other which he had seen many times. When Dawi entered with a tray piled with food, his reaction was something to behold. He sat bolt upright, his eyes out like organ stops, as she glided in and out of the kitchen, he could not get his eyes off her. Bill looked a Chaz, with a grin on his face, Chaz shook his head, knowing Vince would be mortified if he thought anybody noticed. The last thing he wanted was for him to make a bolt for the airport! Then the second thing happened, she reappeared, only this time she was followed by the two massive hounds. His focus on Dawi was broken immediately, leaping on to the couch in terror.

You see when they were young, he had a mortal fear of dogs, something the other brothers exploited to the max, so his reaction was to be expected. It was Dawi who took care of the situation. As soon as she saw his behaviour she called the dogs over to her side, then brought them over to the highly embarrassed visitor.

'They are quite safe; they only attack when they are told,' she explained to him. 'Lobo, Bear, come here,' she commanded as they trotted over to her, tails wagging.

Vincent tried his best to regain his composure and salvage his pride. 'Nice dogs, sadly I am allergic to their fur, otherwise I would be glad to meet them.'

Dawi smiled, 'No problem, I will put them outside,' as she shooed them away.

'Thinks quick on his feet, no wonder he is a whiz on the court room floor,' Bill whispered to Chaz.

'Pretend you didn't notice for shit sake, he's is very conscious of the fact he is afraid of dogs, considering how they are with me,' he nodded, grinning.

'The truth is I am every bit as afraid as he is, how do you think I feel seeing how they jump to obey that little girl?' referring to Dawi.

'No problem, I am sure we are all afraid of something,' Chaz agreed.

At that point *Meri*s came to let them know Vincent's room was ready. Vince thanked her. 'Just want to have a word with the boys, before I settle into your beautiful home.' She smiled and left them to continue their chat.

'Time to get down to business,' Vince announced.

52

After they had a replenished drink in their hand, they took a seat around the pool. Vince opened the conversation,

'Whilst I was dealing with my client in Barcelona, I checked up on *Christina de la Vaga,* the one you call *La Bruja.* She is extremely well connected; her family is one of premier families in *the Balearic Islands. She* rules *Mallorca* and with a firm hand from all accounts. The death of her son in the club accident, which according to reports is being judged 'suspicious'. Coupled with the violence that has erupted, is putting incredible pressure on her from the federal authorities. Normally, they would leave island problems to the local authorities, namely her ladyship and her 'select panel' made up from the other families.'

Bill jumped in, 'You are very well informed. It is well known that nobody that is not connected to the 'families' cannot get an audience with her.'

He shrugged his shoulders, 'That won't be a problem, but I don't want to chat to her until I am better informed.'

'Chat!' Bill laughed. 'I am told reliably that chatting is not her thing, rather issuing orders.'

'Don't let that concern you, my friend, my client in Barcelona is a personal friend and can arrange a chat anytime.'

'That must be some powerful friend,' he retorted.

'A member of the Royal Family would surely qualify,' he replied, in his best barrister's voice. 'And before you ask, no names 'client privilege' you understand.'

Chaz could not contain himself. 'Was it a sex scandal?'

Vince, putting on a superior look, replied, 'Watch the tabloids, be grateful for the distractions at the moment, it deflects attention away for all the drama here. Our best course of action, until we get to the bottom of this, is to let the dust settle and hope that there are no other 'incidents' to pour more petrol on the flames.'

Bill glanced at Chaz. 'I reckon that ship has sailed,' he mumbled under his breath, as Vincent headed off to his new accommodation.

53

ANTONIO

The atmosphere at *De Sota's* hideout was very tense. His lieutenants stood around sheepishly as he raged at them for not coming up with a plan to exact revenge on Rostov and the Irish. This was not helped by *Carlos* dropping out of sight. He was under immense pressure from the cartel to resolve things and to get operations moving again, something that was proving impossible due to the increased presence of the police and the *Guardia de Seville*. He cursed his bad luck again for listening to *Carlos*'s plan. Now he had everybody on his back. The *Bruja* cops and to top it all, the head honchos back in *Colombia*!

He had to sort things out, but until he could solve the Russian and Irish problems he could not move forward. The frustration of waiting for his so-called 'number one' to sort things was getting to him, so he decided to take matters into his own hands.

'Is there no way we can get to them?' directing his question to the leader of his henchmen.

He shook his head, 'They have all gone to ground in the Russian's yacht. There is no way to approach without creating a major war in the middle of the marina, they are protected on all sides. They have the security of being moored at the end of the pier, so any approach can be seen from a mile away; and on the water side, any craft approaching would be spotted at once. The only boats are the pleasure craft and the *Pedelos* which keep their distance. They use the drop-down swim platform on the water's edge of the ship to allow his entourage to enjoy the sun and sea, and before your suggest it, they have armed guards posted on it with them. So, any approach would be doomed to failure.'

There was silence as they waited for his next explosion, but before he could, one of the youngest guys put up his hand. 'What!' he roared.

The frightened guy stammered, 'I was just going to suggest something, I am sorry,' as he sat down.

'Don't' stop now, it's not like any of the rest are coming up with anything but excuses, what's your name?' The kid replied, *'Pedro,* Señor, I was just going to say, that it is not correct that boats can't get near to the yacht. There is one type that is always getting close.' The silence made him stop in terror, wondering if he was going to get shot.

'Continue, what are you talking about?' Antonio snapped.

The poor, frightened guy stammered on, 'Well I have seen the beautiful girls getting sprayed on the swim platform almost every day, including the guards, but all they do is duck for cover to avoid the water. I guess because they must enjoy the sight of those beauties with their skimpy swimsuits becoming transparent, something that the girls, although screaming in protest, seem to love the attention.'

'And how do you know his?'

The kid smiled, 'Because all of the guys love it. The most beautiful women in the world almost naked, what's not to like!' That broke the tension, the bunch started to laugh, until *De Sota* put up his hand.

'Okay, so how does that help our situation?'

The fella's confidence was growing, as he replied, 'Well if we can get that close, we can mount an attack.'

Antonio was getting impatient. 'So what are these boats?'

He stood up to address his newfound audience. 'They are not boats; they are jet skies!' he declared, with triumph.

There was silence, then they burst out in laughter again. 'What do you want us do, splash them to death' one of them shouted.

'Enough!' *Antonio* roared. 'Let him speak.'

So, the young man started to outline his idea, and as he described his plan, all the laughter subsided as they listened to his outlandish idea.

54

Two days had passed, and a sort of deadly calm had settled over the Island.

The excitement of all the action had quickly dissipated under the influence of the sunshine and other activities. Also, the normal passage of tourists returned to the bars and restaurants, including of course, the luxurious *Porto Portal*. Business was booming, it was the height of the season, so all the berths were occupied, with the biggest luxury craft displayed by where it was anchored. Moored outside the wharf, it dwarfed all the other ships in the place.

Rostov Janko stood on the top deck, deep in thought. The silence was killing him. They had located *De Sota* at his hideout but had been unable to discover what he was planning. The worst part was the waiting. It was time he did not have, the silence from his president, was a sure sign that something was in the works, none of which would bode well for him.

Just them Bruno appeared, he nodded, 'Any news?'

He shook his head, 'It's like everything is forgiven, perhaps the pressure he is sure to be receiving has persuaded him of pull his head in.'

'If it, was you, wouldn't you 'pull your head in?" he asked. He shuffled his feet, then nodded in the negative. 'Exactly, so we have to be prepared for anything?' he replied.

That perked him up 'We have covered everything possible, with the exception of an air attack, and before you react, this is not your home country. Any attempt to do something would endanger the tourism business, their most important asset. It would result in putting the Spanish army on the ground, something nobody wants. So stop worrying about the security, leave that to me, you just figure out how to get us out of this fix we are in!' then beating a hasty retreat to avoid any more questions.

Janko was so lost in thought he did not even notice Bruno's departure, as concern over his predicament monopolised his concentration. He stood at the ship's rail, looking down at all his entourage frolicking below on the swim deck, enjoying their jet-set lifestyle aboard his playboy yacht. An image he had carefully cultivated, a cover, but more importantly because he enjoyed it. He enjoyed looking at the bikini-clad beauties, screaming in mock horror as some young guys on jet skis were spinning out, spraying them with their water. They were being encouraged by the ladies' companions, made up of playboy sons of wealthy parents and a smattering of would-be film stars.

He shook his head in anger to see Bruno's guards joining in the fun, encouraging the jet skiers to continue, enjoying the impromptu 'wet t-shirt' competition. The sea surrounding the boat was alive with pleasure craft, which he idly observed. Then something caught his eye, one of the jet skis that had been coming closer and closer, suddenly seemed to lose control, and headed directly for the platform. Before he could react it hit the edge, launching itself into the bowels of the recreation area. At the same time the young guy who was on board the offending craft did a back roll off, just before the collision. At the same time, the rest of panicked ensemble scampered into the water, followed by the so-called guards, in their effort to avoid the runaway ski.

Then everything went black. The next thing he remembered was finding himself, flat on his back, looking up at the sky. He tried to sit up, but the deck beneath him heaved suddenly. As he fell back into unconsciousness, he could hear the sound of alarms shrieking, drowned out by the screams of people fleeing in terror!

55

FORTY MINUTES EARLIER.

Antonio surveyed the scene from an innocuous fishing boat, anchored just offshore. He had a front-seat view of Janko's yacht and the water activities going on in front.

'Ready Señor,' *Pedro* informed him, referring to the plan he had presented.

His idea was to use jet skis to get close to the swim platform, then while spraying the fools on board, they could launch one of the skies onto the platform, which led into where all the pleasure craft and 'big boy' toys were kept.

'It is sure to cause a lot of damage,' he assured his boss.

He jumped at the idea. 'You are a clever lad, now who is going to pilot the jet ski?' he asked.

Pedro jumped at the chance to gain favour. 'I will ride the assault ski, and I have chosen a couple of younger guys to ride the 'distraction skis'.

'Perfect, now go and get organised, let me know when you are ready.'

Pedro rushed off, excited with his promotion to team leader. *Antonio* turned to one of his cronies, who was standing to one side, 'Is everything ready?' he asked.

His crony nodded, waving his hands, which were missing a couple of fingers, the result of his previous mishaps while making 'explosive devices.' 'As soon as he engages the throttle lock, which he will have to do in order to keep it heading straight after he bales off, it will arm the explosive, then *Boom*!'

'Have you left enough time for the boys to get clear?' he asked.

He shrugged his shoulders. 'Should not be a problem, provided they don't hang around,' he replied.

Antonio nodded in satisfaction. He had decided to add some C4 explosive, which was hidden under the seat. Not too much, just enough to get their attention, he thought to himself, 'Just adding a little more bang for his buck,' he chuckled to himself, something he decided to omit telling *Pedro.*

Just as they were finishing their conversation, the young guy returned. 'All set for action,' he shouted, playing his new role to the max.

Antonio gave him a friendly pat on the shoulder. 'Good, now remember, act the part, they must believe you are just playing with the girls, or they won't let you approach.'

Pedro nodded, 'No problem, Señor, we have had plenty of practice.'

'Good, now go and make me proud.'

He scampered away as fast as he could, delighted with the opportunity to prove himself, but oblivious to the utter devastation that was about to unfolded.

56

Pedro and his compatriots roared off into the fray. Within moments, to the delight and screams of the 'jet set' aboard Rostov's yacht, they were spraying them with the water from their jet skis as they cavorted in front of the swim platform.

Pedro had set up between his mates that when he signalled they should back off as he made his final run, ready to pick him up when he bailed off. They continued for a time, enjoying their new assignment. At last, he nodded to his mates that he was ready. He turned, pointing his projectile at the swim platform aperture, then opened the throttle wide open, set the lock and with a big grin on his face, and headed straight for the unsuspecting victims. At the absolute last moment, just before the impact, he could see the looks of confusion on their faces as he did a graceful barrel roll backwards of his craft. He hit the water and immediately surfaced to see the results of his plan. He was greeted by the sight of a massive ball of flame, followed by a couple of ear-shattering explosions.

Luckily, he had the presence of mind to plunge under the surface, avoiding the fire ball that engulfed the panicked crowd which had thrown themselves overboard into the water to avoid the mayhem. Many of them were not so lucky.

When the jet-ski hit, it launched itself into the bowels of the ship. It impacted the bulkhead, where it shattered, followed by the detonation of the explosive. The first blast devastated the compartment, which housed all the pleasure craft and all of the fuel storage. The accumulation of the fumes that collected in the confined area provided the ingredients to create the secondary blast, which was so powerful it expanded the hull of the boat like a balloon. The reinforced upper deck protected the upper part of the boat, but the deck that separated the area from bottom of the ship was not as strong. It disintegrated, destroying the twin-drive shafts and steering gear, leaving them looking like strings of spaghetti. The pressure was so intense that many of the shafts' seals failed, and the ship began to take on water.

Pandemonium ensued. Not only on board, but the explosion and the resulting alarms which were activated created panic in the marina. The first reaction of the crowd was to duck for cover. But, as they realised the source of the explosion was on the giant yacht, which sat belching smoke and listing heavily to the starboard side, there was stampede of spectators rushing to see the damage and destruction. They were met by an exodus of screaming passengers and crew from the stricken ship, who decided the best course of action was to desert the ship. In their midst was a young couple completely naked, who must have been caught in a compromising position when this all went down. They were dragging a sheet behind them, which was achieving nothing but impeding their escape.

Later, spectators would say they saw Rostov Janko being carried off, surrounded by his henchmen who hurriedly pushed him into one of his *Escalades*, which were always parked at the marina. The others piled into the remaining vehicles and were seen speeding off in the direction of *Palma*. Within minutes the place was invaded by every type of emergency vehicle, headed up by the *'Bomberos'*, firemen, who were trying vainly to clear a path to the stricken vessel.

Out at sea another drama was unfolding.

57

On the fishing boat, *Antonio* and his crew stood in stunned silence. A few moment ago, they were looking on gleefully as they watched *Pedro* and his pals perform, waiting for him to implement his attack.

Focusing on him as he headed directly at the swim platform of the yacht, they watched the ski launch itself inside the hull, not sure what to expect. What they got was way beyond their expectations. As the first explosion happened, before they could react, all hell broke loose. In front of their disbelieving eyes, a massive burst of flames and smoke belched out of the side aperture. At the same time, the hull of the ship expanded like a balloon, causing the ship to shudder and lift out of the water, then come crashing down and at list heavily to port.

Antonio was the first to react, he turned looking for his explosive fella. '*Chapo!*' he roared over the pandemonium that had broken out.

The hapless guy rushed over, flapping his damaged hands in the air. 'Señor, before you say anything, that is not my fault, the amount of material I used could not have done that,' he cried. *Antonio* just pointed to the scene of utter devastation, unfolding in front of their eyes. 'Señor, there must have been other explosives on board,' he offered as explanation.

'What do you think it was, a battleship, why would they have explosives on board?' he ranted, as he could see that his plan had turned into an utter disaster. 'Come on, let's get the hell out of here before the navy get here!'

As the crew jumped into action, scrambling to get under way, *Chapo* spoke to the boss. 'What about *Pedro* and the boys, are we not picking them up?'

Antonio shrugged his shoulders, 'They have jet skis, and they can look after themselves,' he replied dismissively.

He was shocked, they were a part of the crew, and he felt a little responsible, seeing as he had hidden C4 under his seat! Thinking quickly, he said, 'Señor, do you think that is wise, if they are picked up by the authorities, they are sure to identify us?'

That got his attention. 'They would never betray me,' he replied, with not a lot of confidence. 'If you are sure, Señor,' Chapo added, then waited.

'*Joder*,' he screamed. 'Okay, tell the captain to pick them up,' he ordered. *Chapo* hurried off before he had time to change his mind.

Within minutes, they were treading their way through the myriad of craft that were aiding the people that were struggling and injured in the water. It was fortunate that they returned, as the force of the blast had rendered the other two riders unconscious. When they came along side, *Pedro* was struggling to get one of them to breathe. They jumped into action to first help their buddies aboard so that they could get medical attention. Shortly afterwards, the jet skis were hoisted aboard and hurriedly secured.

As they made their way out to sea, *Antonio* watched as this Faustian drama unfolded. Just as they rounded the bluff of *Torra Nova*, to his horror he saw a couple of navy patrol boats arrive.

'What more could go wrong?' he groaned to himself.

He had no idea!

58

By morning, word of what had happened had roared around the island like wildfire. *Vic* arrived early to the ranch with the news. They all gathered around as he described the mayhem down at *Puerto portals*.

'The place is surrounded by police; they have sealed off the access to the jetty connecting to the boat. From what I can understand, they are waiting for the army to come and check if this was just a terrible accident or sabotage.'

Des laughed. 'I think we know where that ball is going to fall, when you stir things up Bro, you sure do a good job,' pointing at Chaz, who had been silent up until to then.

'If this was that idiot *Antonio*, he has escalated things too far, this can only get ugly from here,' he cautioned, with a concerned look on his face.

'I could not agree more,' replied Bill. 'I suggest we take a drive to check out the situation. There was a clamber of agreement, with everybody keen to see a $600-million-yacht in pieces!

'Everybody needs to continue with what they are doing; this latest incident will only make things worse; we have to find a way out of this before it is too late. Des, it is most important we find out the significance of the caves.' Des nodded. '*Vic* you come with Bill and me, *Rob*, again we have to locate *Carlos*, also try find out the identity of the 'ice man,' referring to frozen Blondie. He also agreed, a bit upset not to be going to view all the excitement. 'Finally, *Meris*, I know it is very hard for you, but we really need for *Ricardo* to tell us everything he knows. I believe he is the only one that can help us.'

Meris stood for a moment, then nodded to Chaz, 'I will do all that I can.'

They drove as close as they could to the club, which was not all that close. The streets were jammed with emergency vehicles and all the onlookers, crowds of tourists anxious to get their monies' worth out of their holiday. When they finally made their way to the strip of bars and restaurants overlooking the marina, they were surrounded by a bustling hive of activity as the business's cashed in on the action. But the scene of utter devastation on the water was like a battle zone.

The entrance to the marina was partly blocked by tugs, which were using their powerful pumps to aid the struggling systems aboard the floundering ship. It was listing towards the starboard side, where there was a gaping hole where the remains of a swim platform used to be. Engineers were trying their best to seal the gap, but they were fighting a losing battle. The navy had reacted by creating a cordon around the yacht and the surround area to allow the injured to be removed. Fortunately, most of the blast had been contained by the hull of the boat, keeping injuries to the minimum.

Vic nudged them, 'Look, it's the '*Commandante de la Marina*',' pointing to a tall man, dressed in full uniform and surrounded with armed sailors. 'This is not good, he will not be happy with this happening on his watch, heads will roll. I will have to talk to the 'Chaps', they won't be happy.'

Chaz replied, 'I should imagine that the insurance company for that boat won't be that happy as well,' pointing at activity on the water.

Bill burst out laughing. 'You think that there was insurance on it? I would bet that it is registered in some land-locked country where the chance of locating the registered owner is slim or none. Remember the guys that can afford something like that value their privacy more. Anyway, the cost of salvaging her would probably cost more that the replacement.'

'So what happens to her?'

Bill pointed to the man surround by his sailors. 'It will be up to him, he is in command of all that happens in the waters surrounding the *Balearic* Islands. At a guess, after he concludes his investigation into the cause of the 'accident', he will have her towed out to deep water and scuttled.'

'Sink it, shit when I wanted to stir things up, I never expected something like this!' he gasped.

'Try to imagine what is going through that Russian's head now?' said Bill

He nodded. 'I wonder how *Antonio* could have planned something like this?'

59

Antonio was back at his fortress, surrounded by his worried crew. They were not rocket scientists, but even they knew this was way over the top, it was obvious that many were thinking of bailing out.

'Secure the property,' he ordered. 'Nobody leaves without my say so, prepare for some kind of response,' then turned to *Chapo* who was standing beside him, a worried look on his face. 'Explain to me how a small jet ski with, as you say, a small bit of C4 could destroy a ship of that size?' he asked.

The poor guy shrugged his shoulders. 'I am only making little car bombs, Señor. What happened here is a mystery to me,' he pleaded.

He dismissed him with a flick of his hand. Retreating to his study, he slumped into his chair and reached for his bowl of coke and proceeded to make two lines that would choke a horse. As they quickly took effect, he began to realise the gravity of the situation he was in. For sure the Russians would retaliate considering what had happened today. As usual he had not thought this through. He wished he had listened to *Carlo*s, and let things lie. But when the Irishman had brought him the news of the 'Blond guy' he could not control his temper. He had a feeling this time perhaps he had gone too far. As he sat there, repeatedly topping up his nose with white powder, there was a tap on the door.

'Señor,' a voice called from outside, 'it is *Carlos,* he wants to talk to you.'

'Put him on,' he roared, reaching for the phone, to discover there was nobody there. 'He is outside the gate, Señor. Will we let him in?'

He jumped to his feet. 'Let him in and bring him here,' he commanded.

Carlos pushed past the henchmen and launched at the door to his study open with a fierce kick. 'You have really screwed things up this time! Are you crazy, trying to sink Rostov's yacht? What did you think was going to happen, they would pack up everything and just go home? You have created an international incident that will have extreme consequences.'

Antonio put up his hand to stop the guards intervening, signalling them to get out. As soon as the door was closed, he indicated for C*arlo*s to sit down as he went to the bar to fetch a bottle of '*La Panto*.' one of the best Spanish brandies. 'Here have a drink and calm down.'

'How did it ever get to this?' he asked, rhetorically. 'All that was needed was to get the Irish out of the club, then this Russian appeared, and everything when to shit.'

'What I fail to understand is why they reacted the way they did. What prompted them to attack your villa and the restaurant? They could not have thought you would sabotage your own operation!'

Carlos snapped, as he could see his carefully laid plans slipping away. 'What on earth were you thinking of trying to sink his ship?'

Antonio slugged his drink. As he refilled it, he explained how his plan to disrupt Rostov and the Irish had got out of control. After he was finished putting the best spin on it he could, he slumped down in his chair to use his coke.

'Anybody that has any experience with explosives would have known the danger of a secondary explosion. What do think ships run on?'

'Fuel.'

'Which is a perfect ingredient for a big explosion. What on earth prompted you to do this when I specifically asked you to hold off?'

Antonio jumped to his feet. 'I will tell you; your Irish pal came and saw me to fill me in on what happened in the club and to make it known that they were not involved with the mishap.'

Carlos snapped to attention, 'You mean the blond one or the big one?'

'The big one with the scar,' he replied.

'What did he say?'

Antonio began to recover his composer as he continued. 'He told me who had destroyed the club,' he replied smugly.

A confused look crossed Carlos's face, 'How would he know?'

Antonio explained the conversation they had, leading up to his description of a mystery blond guy.'

He could not believe his ears. 'And based on the fact the guy was blond-haired, you decided it had to be Rostov and proceeded to bring this unmitigated disaster on us?'

This hurt *Antonio's* already damaged pride. He rose up in anger. 'Who else involved in this would look like the person Charles described, blond, pale skin, looking like a block of stone unless there are some other players in this mess? It had to be the Russian mob.'

There was silence for moment as *Carlos* digested this information. He realised that he had badly underestimated these Irish brothers, especially the big one. He was quite sure that the revealing of his German idiot's presence at the club was to achieve exactly what had happened. He had led *Antonio* by the nose and pointed him in Rostov and the Irish's direction. He would have to recover control of this situation, or he would never achieve his goal.

'You are right, perhaps I have been a bit judgemental, but I believe there is more to this story. Allow me to talk to this Charles, and get to bottom of what is going on. In the meantime, sit tight and remain in the safety of your home.'

Glad of the opportunity to shift some of the responsibility, he agreed. 'I will remain here until you contact me. What should we do in the meantime about the *Cabrons* back home?' knowing that as soon as word of the war that had started, all hell would break loose.

'Tell them there is somebody else interfering with our plans and that I am dealing with it. Whatever you do, don't mention anything about our Irish friends and their 'fabricated' Nordic bomber. If they think we have lost control, we are finished,' slicing his finger across his throat in a slashing motion.

It was not lost on *Antonio*, knowing full well the preferred method to '*Borrar*'—'to erase'—someone, which usually meant the loss of their head!

60

Carlos got up to leave, while at the same time telling his cocaine-addled buddy to 'stay cool' until he returned or called him. Leaving as quickly as he could, the trip back to his place back in *Palma* he seemed to be in a dreamlike state. He kept running the events of the last few day over and over in his head. Cursing himself again for allowing that idiot to convince it would be a good idea to sabotage the place, then to make matters worse allowing himself to be seen by of all people the Irishman. A cold shiver ran down his back, again 'the brothers,' he muttered, as he realised the one common denominator since all this craziness had started was them!

As he entered his place, a gremlin of a plan started to grow in his head, remembering his grandfather's words, 'The enemy of my enemy is my friend.' He picked up the phone and placed a call. 'This is *Carlos*, get word to Bruno I have information that is of benefit to both of us. Tell him to keep this to himself until we speak.' Then he hung up, poured a drink, and strolled out on to the balcony. As he surveyed the city, he mumbled to himself, 'Where are those clever shits hiding out?'

Fifteen minutes later, the phone rang, 'It's me,' the coarse voice said.

'Thanks for calling back so soon, we need to talk.'

Bruno scoffed, 'Are you crazy? You have just destroyed Janko's boat and fucked up our operation and you want to chat!'

Carlos smiled to himself. The fact he had called him so soon told him that he was concerned as well, so he decided to use the soft approach. 'Bruno, I can assure you I knew nothing about that crazy incident. I believe we are being played, meet me alone so we can try to work thing out before this gets completely out of control.' There was silence on the other end of the line, then, 'Where and when? It has to be in public and come alone, or I am gone,' he demanded. *Carlos* quickly arranged to meet him in a major shopping centre in the centre of *Palma*, later that morning.

He was seated at a coffee stand on the main floor of the complex when he spotted Bruno approaching. He stood to greet him, shaking his hand. 'Glad to get this chance to sort out this madness.' He too extended his hand, at the same time checking out his surroundings for any sign of a double cross. 'I am alone,' he assured him, 'let's walk.'

As they strolled around like a couple of shoppers, Bruno spoke first. 'It is not you guys I am worried about; I am more worried about what this mad brunch out of Russia will do. I am expecting a poison dart at any moment. If it is not them it will probably be the Israeli mob,' he cursed.

'Let's stop here,' *Carlos* said, pointing to a tavern, I think we both need a drink. After they had ordered drinks, *Carlos* was the first to speak. 'I have to ask, what prompted you guys to respond so dramatically after the accident in the club.'

'That was that crazy fuck, Janko. As soon as Chaz told him what you guys wanted him to do, and then the destruction of the club drove him over the edge, I tried to talk him out of it,' Bruno lied, 'but when Chaz told him he had nothing to do with it and had rejected you guys, he assumed you had taken things into your own hands.'

Carlos gasped, 'Chaz and you believe him, why would we destroy our own place? Even *De Sota* is not that crazy.' He then went on to tell him about the brothers' visit to *Antonio*, and his convincing him that Janko was behind the attack, avoiding mentioning Klaus. 'I told him not to react until I got to find out exactly had happened, but he is just as crazy as your boss.'

Bruno jumped in, 'He is not my boss, that crazy fuck has turned this into an international incident. If I don't see a way out real soon, I am gone!'

'Okay, calm down, the first thing we have to do is locate the brothers and find out what they're up to. In the meantime we have to keep a lid on this.'

Bruno looked at him strangely, 'You don't know where they are staying?'

'No, do you?'

'Yes, they are where they can't be touched. They are under the protection of Bill Heart, which means the London Mob. We have enough trouble without getting them offside!'

Carlos nodded. He had heard about this Bill Heart. He kept a low profile, but anybody in the know knew he was the sheriff of this island. As long as you did not disturb the tranquillity, you could continue your business. But when somebody pushed the unofficial rules, he stepped in. An example was of a high-flying businessman from Australia who decided to hide out on the Island. When the people he fleeced came after him, mainly the Australian Government, he faked an illness in the courts to avoid extradition, and with the corruption he was succeeding. The resulting publicity was too much for the 'Chaps', so he developed a real illness. The nurse that was attending him was replaced by one of Bill's choosing and within weeks he was on death's door for real. He was on the next airplane back to Australia where he spent his last days in misery.

Carlos didn't know if there was any truth to this, but the way things were going he was not going to bring anymore unwanted attention if he could help it. 'Bruno, keep your 'partner' from going off the deep end, until I can get my hands on those brothers and find out what they are up to. If we don't get control of this soon, the *Bruja* is going to step in. Remember she is still looking for someone to hang the death of her son on,' as the beginnings an idea began to take root.

'I will do what I can, but I think Rostov's time is running out. That yacht did not belong to him, he told me. Boris, or whatever is the name of the president, took it from another oligarch, and has threatened to return it. If he does not straighten things out with the Israeli crew.'

Carlos exploded, 'What are they doing getting involved in this?'

Bruno shrugged, 'I have no idea and I don't want to know. I only found out about them the other day, and if things keep going like this, I am off to my place in *Portugal*. It's much safer there, this mob are bat-shit crazy!'

He nodded in agreement. With his German connection, the last thing he needed was them getting interested in him.

They agreed to keep in touch while *Carlos* tried to figure out what they were up to. After Bruno left, he sat for a moment staring into nowhere.

'What are you up to, Chaz?' he wondered.

61

CHAZ

It was two days since the boat attack, and I was sitting at one of the bars overlooking the events that were taking place in front of the marina. That morning *El Comandante de la Marina* had taken the decision the scuttle the yacht. His investigation had discovered traces of C4, and all efforts to discover who the ship was registered to had failed, which was not surprising. He had decided in the interest of public safety, restoring traffic to the marina and, most importantly, to return the area to the holiday-makers who were paying his wages.

The place was packed with onlookers. I had decided to be here in case *Carlos* or any of the 'usual suspects' appeared. I needed to find out what that guy was up to, and I also had to decide how I could use the 'ice man' to our advantage. Bill was expected to be locating where Carlos was hanging out. So far he had located *Antonio* back at his hideout, bunkered down as if expecting an invasion. Which was not surprising considering the disaster he had created after I planted the seed about the blond guy. In my wildest dreams I did not think he would resort to blowing up the yacht.

Vincent was sitting beside me, sipping a bloody mary to help cure the hangover he had acquired with Bill last night as they swapped war stories. I had no idea just how involved Vin was with the London underworld. What really surprised me was how many times members of the Royal Family's names drifted into the conversation. Any reporter that could have recorded what was said would be looking at a Pulitzer Prize.

'When are they going to get on with it?' he asked *Victor*, our source of information.

'Any time now. They've decided to sink her in the deep-water surrounding *Cabrera*, a small uninhabited island. It will provide an artificial reef for fish and provide a tourist attraction for divers,' he told them.

'Enterprising fellas, these Spanish,' Vincent declared, as his drink started to take effect.

The tugs, tasked with the job of towing the crippled ship into position had connected their hawsers and proceeded to gently coach the heavily listing vessel away from the harbour wall. At the same time, the skeleton crew placed on board by the navy kept the pumps working at maximum power. Even though they had lagged the seals on the ruptured shafts as best as they could, they were barely able to maintain her afloat. Sluggishly, she got underway and started the short journey to her final resting place. Twenty minutes later, she was positioned, ready for her trip to the bottom.

'What happens now?' I asked.

Vic responded, 'The *Commandante* will be advised they are ready. He will issue the order to scuttle her, and the crew will open her bilge valves then return to their ship to watch her go down.'

With that a signal blast cut the air and we all watched in awe as the magnificent ship began to slip below the surface on her journey to the bottom of the ocean. We watched until she disappeared below the surface to her final resting place.

'Okay, enough of the show, let's get down to business. Where are we at with Des and his investigations?' Vince asked breaking the moment.

'I am going to catch up with him later as he says he has something to report, what are your plans?' I asked.

He was into his third drink by now and was a fully recharged QC. 'I think it is time I had a chat with my friend *Christina de la Vaga* and get her view on things.'

'Are you going to tell her about us?' I asked, a worried look on my face.

He laughed. 'A good lawyer never divulges his clients,' he replied.

'So we are your clients?' I asked.

'Don't be silly, you guys could never afford my fees. No, I have come to an arrangement with Bill and his 'Chaps' . They will cover my cost, but don't worry, you are covered under their attorney-client privilege.'

I nearly choked on my drink. 'You are charging for this?' I croaked.

He looked at me as if I had lost my mind. 'Of course, a good lawyer always finds a way for someone to pay. Something you guys should consider.'

I could have killed him. 'I am here because of our idiot brother, should I charge him?' I snapped.

'I don't think there would be any point, he is just like Dad in that regard. Never pay anybody,' he reminded me.

I finished my drink in silence, as I remembered why he was the successful brother.

62

At the same time as they were watching the sinking of the ship, on another large shipping vessel moored just offshore, an interested party was watching proceedings.

Viktor Vostok stood on the deck as he watched his precious yacht sink below the waves for the last time. Fresh from his unexpected release from Gulag and his restoration to favour with the 'boss man', he had flown on a private jet under the express orders to 'clean the mess up', something he was delighted to do. He had been met by a couple of tough-looking thugs from the Israeli crew, who without much conversation escorted him by helicopter to the waiting ship where he now stood surveying the demise of his boat.

'Where is he?' he asked the guy standing beside him. Uri was his name, and he was the one he had been 'advised' to use in the clean-up operation.

'He has gone to ground, but it won't take long to locate him,' he replied in his strong accent.

'Remember, no violence, the boss doesn't want an international incident. Locate him and any others that are involved in this disruption, then we will discuss the best course of action,' he said.

At the same time, Rostov Janko was trying frantically to arrange a quick exit, but word had quickly spread that he was out of favour and being around him could present a serious danger to your health. He could not contact Bruno, who had vanished from sight. The only one who had hung around was Mick Ryan, mainly because he was short of options. Since the episode at the villa and at the yacht with that prick Chaz, he had found himself on the outer with the Irish crew.

'Have you found him yet?' he said, referring to Bruno.

'Not a sign, but the word is that he is trying to resurrect a connection with the Columbians since *Antonio* has fallen out of favour, he thinks he can fill the gap.'

'Fucking turncoat, he is mistaken if he thinks he can avoid the fallout,' he roared. But he knew that if he succeeded in cutting a deal with the cartel, he would be well protected. They lapsed into silence, then he asked, 'Where is that Irishman that came to see me, he seems to know more about what is happening than anyone?'

Ryan almost exploded; his face flushed with rage. The main reason he had hung around to get a chance at revenge was that he hated Chaz with a passion. Chaz had humiliated him so many times that putting him in the ground would be the only thing that would satisfy him. 'They are living in luxury on a ranch in the outskirts of *Magaluf*. He is under the protection of the London underworld. Billy Heart is their unofficial representative over here.'

Rostov lost interest in the narrative, as all he could concentrate on was his survival. As for Mick, he had other ideas, first he had to find a way to get some fresh clout. He looked at the shaken Rostov and a germ of an idea crept into his crazed brain.

63

MICK RYAN

Mick Ryan was sitting in his hideout bar, which he only used when he felt the need, which was now. Whilst contemplating his next move over a couple of drinks, he felt a presence behind him. He turned, jumping to his feet in shock at the sight of some tough-looking Arab type, flanked by some Eastern-European dude.

'What do you want?' he asked, stepping back in terror, thinking his time was up.

'We just want to talk, don't be concerned,' the European said, indicating that they should take a seat. Something, from the look of the tough guy, was not open for discussion.

'I'm not afraid, I have friends,' he croaked.

'Exactly, and that is what we want to talk to you about, your 'friends', we are anxious to locate your boss Bruno and most importantly his associate Rostov Janko.'

Mick was a survivor, and his loyalty only reached as far as himself. 'If I help you, what's in it for me?' he asked.

This time the other guy spoke. 'If you assist us, there will be an opportunity for you to join us ... ' He left the sentence open, but the message was clear, and Mick did not hesitate.

'I can help. Bruno has gone on the run, anyway he was small time, I would have got rid of him if he had not split,' he lied.

Viktor Vostok smiled to himself, this guy was a small-time hustler. But he had something he wanted, his knowledge of how things worked around here. 'I am sure, but I am more interested in his Russian friend.'

'I can help you with that, he is well protected, because where he lives in the city is surrounded by official buildings. The police presence is over the top, due to recent outbreaks of violence.' Something he neglected to point out, he was part of it.

'That is our problem, you only have to follow instructions and you will be compensated,' the Israeli replied, indicating for him to sit down so they could discuss how he could save his skin.

64

DES

Des was sitting at *Ricardo's* meeting place in *Portals Ves*. After a lot of pressure from *Meris*, he had finally agreed to talk to him alone, something Des has insisted on.

'But he might not understand you,' *Maria* moaned, not wanting to miss out on the adventure.

Des laughed, 'Trust me, I've got it covered. If I have a problem I promise you are the first one I will call.' She reluctantly agreed on the proviso that he divulged everything that was said.

He knew his best chance to get anything out of this strange guy was to have him want to tell him what he knew, something Des discovered he had unique skill for. Convincing people to do things they normally would never consider, that was his 'thing.' So, when he saw his guy approaching he jumped to his feet and greeted him like a long-lost friend.

'*Ric*, can I call you that? Back home that is what friends do. Last time we started out on the wrong foot, but I would really like to be your friend, you see I realised we are the same!'

He looked at him, puzzled, '*Que*, you want to be my friend? I thought you wanted to question me?' he asked.

Des gave him a hearty slap, 'Remember our adventure in the cave, it was you and I that took care of things. That's when I knew we were cut from the same cloth.' Again '*Que*?' not understanding his slang. 'Sorry, I mean, we have both had struggles in our youth and have had to rely only on ourselves.' Looking him in the eyes, as if they had a lifelong connection, 'Like what happened to your son.'

This was when the magic started to happen. He sat down, while the waiter brought his usual coffee with a healthy dash of brandy. 'It's called a '*Carajillo*.'

'Make it the same for me then,' he indicated continuing the bonding process.

'*Maris* has told you what happened?' he asked.

Des nodded, 'Only that they were lost in the caves, and many blamed you. But *Maris* told me that she knew you were not responsible.'

'She was always the wise one, her sister *Monica* was the other side of the coin. It was *Monica* that convinced my son to adopt the 'cave life.' I told them it was not a life for a young couple, depending on adventurous treasure seekers or crazy's to scrape out a living. Do you know that I live in an old mobile home with no electricity or running water? That is no life for young people today.'

Des remained silent, allowing this fella to recover memories he had not brought to light for years. He signalled for another round, then *Ricardo* looked him in the eyes, 'I don't know why, but I trust you. Something I have not done for a long time. I have a story to tell you!'

65

THE STORY.

For as long as he could remember, people had been eking out a living from the caves and grottos that covered this volcanic island. Whether that be from smuggling, which still is one of its main purposes, or since the end of the war, treasure hunters. Or simply the curious who wanted to explore the abandoned sub pens. The *cavernicola's*, 'Cavemen', a slur nickname given to them by the Islanders, turned to this trend to make money. The problem for explorers was that the entrances to the sub pens had been through natural underwater entrances that led to the pens. These had been constructed prior to the outbreak of war. This was when *Franko* and Hitler were amigos. Later, due to Spain being neutral, all activities had to be conducted in secret, which is where the cavers came in. Only a few who knew that area, something they guarded religiously, as this was their main income to them.

After the war, all sort of rumours started to appear. Stories of vast treasure smuggled out of Germany by the Nazis to finance their escape. This led to a vast numbers of treasure hunters scouring the pens. As they took a breather and refilled their drinks, Des had to ask, 'Did they find any.'

Ricardo smiled. 'Not a thing, the pens had been picked clean. By who, nobody knows. Probably by the crews of the submarines in the dying months of the war.'

As time went by, a story surfaced of another pen that was constructed in secret using POWs shipped in from concentration camps. If this story was correct, they were left to die so as to keep its location secret. This place, if the story was to be believed, was one of the locations for Hitler to make his escape if the war failed.

'Is there any truth to this?' Des asked.

'If you had asked me a couple of months ago, I would have said no, but let me continue. Of course, none of the people making a living from this story were going to deny it. It was a good way to make some money, sadly some people believed the fable and paid the price.'

'Your son!' Des gasped.

He nodded his head sadly, 'Yes *Monica* got hold of the story and convinced him this was the answer to their prayers. I could not convince him otherwise, he was not the brightest I am afraid, and she was young and foolish,' he stopped, lost in thought.

Des was silent, feeling the pain of this poor guy, who then took a deep breath and continued his story. 'During the construction of the night club, they needed people that had knowledge of that area of the cave system. As a young man this was where I had operated.'

So he had been called on to help map the caves and the grotto involved in its function. This is when the story took a strange turn. He was approached a couple of months ago by a guy looking for his help. This was to be *Carlos*. He said that he had discovered who *Ricardo* was from old records of the club's construction, and that he had an equally fascinating story to relate. He believed he had information that would lead to the discovery of the 'lost' pen.

Des stopped him. 'What has this to do with the club?' he asked.

Ricardo, put up his hand, 'Please Señor, let me continue, this is very hard for me! *Carlos* had explained he knew of a secret room constructed by his grandfather, which he could only access from the sea. He wanted me to find an access from the area of the club to this room, so he could continue his search.'

Des could not contain himself. 'That is why he wanted the club closed!' he cried.

'Yes, I heard him talking about that in German. He thought I could not understand him. But I had many people from that part of the world come here over the years, and I picked up enough German to understand. He said there was too much activity there for him to continue his search in secret, so he had a plan to disrupt it for a while.'

'Blow it up?' Des cried.

'No Señor, he was very angry when that happened, he kept cursing some guy called Klaus for that.' Again, he continued, 'As you know I found access to the room, where he kept all his stuff, which was when I discovered the area where he believed the base was. I told him I could not help, he became very angry, showing me drawings and directions that he said would locate the place. I told him I knew of the area, and nobody ventured there. Those that tried never came back.'

Des realised at once, 'That is where your son went in search of the treasure!'

He nodded. 'And that is all I can tell you. After that I became afraid. I believed that he would have killed me, so I have kept out of sight.'

'So, this has been all over some ridiculous hunt for Hitler's bailout stash,' Des cursed. He turned to the sad old man. 'Thank you for your help, I believe you are right, he would have disposed of you. That guy in the cave we discovered, I believe did not drown. I am sure you would have been next; you should come and stay with *Maris* until this is all sorted out.'

He declined the offer, saying he was safe amongst his own. Des turned to leave when he felt a tug on his arm, 'Señor, you are a special man, I have not spoken to anyone about this before. I feel ashamed that I had not had the courage to go in search of my son and his lady, thank you.'

Des smiled, 'You did the right thing, no point in you dying also. Two people was enough, and all for a wild-goose chase.'

He pushed something into his hand, 'But Señor, it is true!'

66

Des had them all collected back to *El Rancho*, which he had decided to name it. *Meris* had demanded to know what he had found out. But Des, the last of the great showman, had insisted it was so important that they all had to be assembled. Everybody was there, even the two dogs who were sitting at Vincent's feet, much to his discomfort. Dawi was invited to join, and she decided to sit beside him, which included the hounds, so he quickly got over it.

'Okay, enough of the drama, get on with it,' Vin snapped, as one of the pups decided to lick his $1000 shoes. Des launched into the amazing story he had uncovered from *Ricardo*. When he was finished there was silence, then all hell broke loose.

'A notebook,' Vincent cried.

Chaz put his hand up for silence. 'I am sure you all have a hundred questions, especially you *Meris*, what I suggest is you each pick a time with Des alone to have them answered. I can assure you he is the perfect person to help you if he can.' A look of shock came across his brothers' faces, giving compliments was not a feature of our family.

Bill stepped in, 'I agree, what we have to do is focus on the problem at hand facing us now! Can we see this notebook?' he asked.

Des handed it to him, 'Not sure if it is of any use, I can't understand anything that is in it as it is in German.'

Bill took it, 'No problem, I have a friend that can translate it for us. In the meantime, we have the problem of the *Bruja*,' looking at Vince.

He nodded, 'Before I see her, I would like to know if there is any truth to this treasure yarn. Perhaps it is something I could use to our advantage.'

Bill nodded in agreement. 'I will have a translation to you later today. In the meantime you should lay low here, no point in them finding out you are involved at the moment.'

That suited Vin. As he glanced at Dawi sitting beside him, he moved a little closer, which provoked a low growl from the dogs. Des and Chaz grinned to themselves, seeing his discomfort.

'Over to you,' pointing at Chaz.

'Well, the way I see it, until these crazy people stop trying to destroy the whole Island, nobody's going to listen to us.'

'I agree,' Vin replied.

'So what is the plan?'

Vin thought for a moment before replying. 'First we have to locate *Carlos*, remember we still have his friend here. What you have is someone that could connect him to this, why don't you interrogate him?' Vince asked.

They looked at each other, realising they had forgot to tell him about the guy they had on ice. Bill replied, 'It is the guy we found in the cave, we have him in our freezer.'

Vin nearly fell off his chair. 'You have the dead body here!' he croaked.

Before he could continue, Chaz butted in, 'Leave that part of it to us brother, you stick to what you know. I've got it covered.'

He groaned. 'Now you are sounding like him,' pointing at Des, who was enjoying his brother's bickering. For a change he was not the butt of the argument.

Chaz continued, 'If you guys could get out there and see what you can find out, you blend in a lot better than we do,' looking at the Heart brothers. They nodded in agreement and headed off at once to start their search. 'Des, you and *Marie*, have done a great job, continue digging to see if you can find out anything more about this secret submarine base.'

They nodded, delighted with the compliment. Bill looked at him, 'What is your plan?'

He thought for a moment. 'As soon as we locate *Carlos*, I have a bit of a wild plan to force him to show his cards.'

As he began to explain his idea, Bill's face broke into a grin.

67

One week later and things had returned into a sort of normal as far as the tourists were concerned. There was still plenty of police presence, but a sort of calm had settled over the island. Not so back at *De Sota's* place.

Things were getting to boiling point back there. *Antonio* had word that he was on borrowed time with the cartel and *Carlos* was not returning his calls. His crew had only remained because the safest place for them was here. That wasn't going to last for long, they knew his mad act on the yacht could spell the end for him and the longer it went on the more likely they would need a new employer.

Things were not much better at Viktor Vostok's place. Rostov's new adversary was grilling Mick Ryan for information about Janko's movements. 'He has not left the apartment since the attack. He knows that you are looking for him. He is going on the attack, threatening to go to *Christina de la Vega* and expose everybody unless he can be guaranteed his safety.'

Vostok knew this would be a disaster, the 'boss' would not tolerate any publicity however remote. He turned to Uri, his Israeli sidekick. 'Make sure nobody draws any attention to us until we resolve this situation,' he ordered, 'And where is that sidekick of his you have been telling me about?'

'His name is *Carlos*, he seems to have had a falling out with *Antonio de Sota*, and word is he was not happy about the boat attack,' Mick replied.

'Find him, we need to talk,' Viktor ordered. Mick jumped to it, delighted to be accepted. At the same time Viktor continued to contemplate his next move.

Carlos's ears would have prickled up if he had heard that conversation. He was running around in circles trying to figure out how to get out of this mess. There was still no sign of Klaus, or what was left of him by now. Which concerned him, where the hell was he?

His search for the secret location had stalled. That weird guide *Ricardo* had vanished from the face of the earth. As soon as he had disclosed the area where the secret base was supposed to be located, his attitude had changed. He became very afraid and refused to give any more help.

Before he could deal with him, he disappeared. Since then, he had reached out to his family connection for another guide, but before he could continue, he had to get access to the caves again.

As they were all trying to figure out their next moves, the messages started to arrive.

68

THREE DAYS EARLIER

They were all gathered at the ranch at Bill's request. He had contacted a German guy, who was one of the 'Chaps' and he had agreed to come over and translate the notebook. There was great excitement as they greeted him. Herman Swartz was his name and his jovial nature quickly endeared him to everybody. After all the introductions were over and drinks were in hand, he launched into his presentation with great gusto.

'I think it is best if I paraphrase the translation. As the guy who wrote this was obviously a fanatic and a loyal supporter of Hitler and his disastrous regime,' he stated. 'He begins by saying how proud that he had been to be personally selected by the Führer himself, for this very secret mission. He had been tasked with setting up some of the escape routes specifically for Hitler.'

'Some?' questioned Bill. '

Yes, he refers to many others, but this book deals only with the one here on the Island.' He continued, 'It would seem that he was a keen scuba diver. Whilst stationed here for the construction of the main submarine bases. By accident he discovered an underwater entrance that led to, what he describes as an 'underwater cathedral' . When he reported his findings, he was immediately recalled to Berlin where he met for the first time his beloved leader. During this private meeting what was described to him was a plan for the survival of the Third Reich and the leader himself, in the event of the war turning against them. He goes into a lot of detail about the lengths they went to in order to keep its location secret, to the point that all the POWs that were used in its construction, and here I use his words,' he said, with disgust, 'were 'removed' permanently. He next describes the difficulty finding access from above ground, although most materials and workers could be transported by submarines. In order to function quickly they needed access to above ground. It would seem by chance he found one of the old '*Cavernicola*' who discovered an entrance.

He goes on to describe the access as 'Not for the faint-hearted', as they had lost quite a few traversing it, even as he says, 'Proper Germans'.' He said this taking a sip of his drink. 'And now it gets interesting. He goes on to describe stocking the place with all that would be needed for his onward journey to his final destination. He described all sorts of security devices to protect its 'precious cargo', which was hidden in a safe location.'

He stopped and put the notebook down. Des was the first to speak, 'Does it give directions?'

'Well perhaps, but this is where it gets difficult. At this point he begins to use a sort of code to communicate to whoever this was written for. It's as if he added this information much later, probably after the war and he realised that his leader didn't make it. He starts by saying, 'Where the great mouth of the cliff welcomes the mighty sea into its inner cathedral of grandeur. Go to where it takes its first taste and follow its flow.' It then goes on to describe a ('*Sendero*') a path, and he goes on to say, 'Follow the signs of the old ones, they will guide you to the chamber. But be warned do not venture from the chosen path, to do so will leave you to wander for eternity.''

'Is that all it says?' Des queried.

'No, the book is full of jottings, but they all relate to the original construction of the sub pens. There is a notation here describing how, when it was completed, the pathway from above ground was sealed. Leaving the sea as the only access available.'

'So, this secret entrance he is describing must have been discovered after,' Des jumped in again. In excitement, 'He describes the guys that helped build the original sub pens as 'the old guys' earlier, it must mean that he found one of them to help him find this pathway he is describing now!'

Vincent cleared his throat. 'I think at this point we can call a halt to this conversation and remember what we are trying to achieve. It would appear that now we have discovered the reason behind this fiasco, a search for some mystery treasure, driven by this *Carlos* guy, which from all accounts, is a rather small player. As we know, it was his idea to involve my brothers,' glancing at them with distain. 'But let's remember, our object is to find a way out for Des, who has his crime spree in Barcelona hanging over him. I should remind you that a crime that involves personal injury, which his did,' he emphasised, 'carries a twenty-year jail sentence.'

This brought silence, and finally Chaz spoke, 'So what is our next move?'

He replied, 'Now that I have enough information, it is time that I paid *Christina de la Vega* a visit to discuss how we can be of assistance to each other. While I attend to that, I believe it is time for you to implement your plan,' pointing at Chaz.

He turned to the Heart brothers. 'Are you sure you have located *Carlos?'*

Vic answered, 'Sure, it was no problem, remember nobody is that interested in him. He is just considered a fixer; he is hanging out at his apartment in *Palma*.'

Des jumped in, 'What about the treasure?'

Vincent answered. 'Do nothing. Our friend here,' pointing at the German 'Chap','has offered to translate the notebook. You can try, with the help of the family here to make sense of it,' he nodded, but as he turned away, a sly grin crossed his face.

Chaz stood. 'Okay, you all know the plan. You have your jobs, let's get to it,' as he turned to the brothers, 'Time to send the notes. Let the games begin!'

69

Mick Ryan was the first to receive the mysterious note. It was for Bruno, but seeing as he was on the missing list, he decided to use it to his advantage.

'I have something that will be of interest to you, a message for Bruno just arrived at the apartment,' he said excitedly, as he entered the safe house of Viktor Vostok, waving the message.

Uri grabbed it to read. As he finished, he turned to Vostok, 'You need to see this,' handing him the note.

He started to read aloud. 'If you want to find out who destroyed the club, come to the address below tomorrow night at the indicated time. No more than two people. Any sign of violence or argument and the answer will disappear. No exceptions. Apt 401 *Los Delfines, Palma Nova at* 10 pm. The door will be open, enter.'

As this was happening, Rostov Janko was just in the process of reading his message, which carried the exact same instructions. At first, his reaction was to discard it and focus on his escape. But he began to consider that if he could prove that he had nothing to do with what happened, perhaps he could dig himself out of this hole he found himself in. He picked up the note, reading it again, and began to consider who to bring.

Antonio de Sota also could not believe what he was reading. If he could show the cartel who destroyed the club, it might take their focus off him and give him a chance to get re-established. He took a deep breath to calm himself as he realised his first thought was to go in heavy-handed. But as he focused on the message, he realised this was not an option, and filled his nose with his product. No, he decided, better if I get to the bottom of this. If he could discover who killed *La Bruja*'s son, she would probably be grateful, something he could use to his advantage. So, the next question was who to bring? Where was that bastard, *Carlos*?

Carlos, in fact, was kicking the shit out of anything he could in rage. He re-read the message again and again. Who was behind this? At first, when he saw that the meeting was in the apartment that he had got for the Irish brothers he immediately suspected Chaz. But that made no sense? Why meet there of all places, and what was in it for them? All they wanted was to get home, not to get further involved. He realised his only option was to try to find out who was behind this and if he had any chance of finishing his quest.

It was this determination to get his prize that made him decide to attend.

70

Vostok and Uri were the first to arrive, or really, to case the place first. They had circled the apartment block and checked of any suspicious activist.

'They chose well this place in the centre of the tourist area; any funny business would attract too much attention,' Uri commented.

Viktor nodded. 'You are right, let's go and check it out, we still have a little time,' looking at his watch, It was 9.30 pm, dusk was falling, and a sprinkling of stars were beginning to appear. Uri parked the car a little distance from the block, but in sight of the entrance. They approached the main door, as a couple emerged. Uri grabbed the door, allowing them to pass, and the girl smiled and thanked him. He nodded and they entered. The lobby was deserted, they went into the elevator and pressed the button for the 4th floor. As they arrived, they stood to the sides to be prepared as the doors opened, but again they were alone.

Number 401 was facing to the front of the building on a corner. They approached the door, it was ajar, and light filtered from the apartment. They could hear the sounds of music coming from inside, and looked at each other in puzzlement. Viktor looked at his watch 9.45 pm, 'Might as well crash the party,' as he pushed the door gently. But before they could enter, the sound of the elevator stopped them. Uri quickly took up position to one side of the lift, as the doors slid open.

Antonio and *Carlos* stepped out to be greeted by the sight of Viktor standing in front of them. 'Who are you?' he asked.

Carlos glanced at *De Sota*. 'I could ask you the same question, and we live here, do you?' pointing at the apartment.

Viktor stepped aside, 'After you,' he offered.

Before things could escalate, the elevator pinged again to announce its arrival. They all moved to the side, as the doors slid open and out stepped Rostov and one of his henchmen. He stopped in surprise, looking at the assembled crew. When he caught sight of Viktor, he screamed, then turned and proceeded to smash his face into the closing door. As he turned back, clutching his bloody nose, it was obvious thing were going to explode.

'STOP!' roared C*arlo*s, 'Can't you see we have all been set up? I would imagine you all received a message instructing you to be at apartment 401 at this time as we did,' pointing at himself and *Antonio.* 'And if you did, you would have been told that any violence and it was all off. Now I suggest we all put away our grievances and find out who is leading us by the nose.' They all nodded in agreement. 'Now I have another question? Who are you?' he said, turning to Viktor.

Before he could answer, Rostov burst out, 'He has been sent to kill me,' he cried. *Carlos* shrugged his shoulders, then looked at Viktor and Uri. 'I believe this is something that can be settled later.'

Viktor nodded, 'Let's get on with it.'

Uri gently pushed the door open. In front of them was a short hallway leading into the main room where the light and sound was coming from. He held up his hand for them to wait until he cleared the room, then he crept along the hall until he could see if it was clear. He stepped inside, then stopped, then he held up his hand indicating for them come.

'You have to see this for yourself,' he croaked as he moved to give them room. What greeted them stopped them cold.

There sitting on a chair in the centre of the room was a blond guy in a rubber wetsuit, with a note pinned to his chest.

71

'Is he dead?' gasped *Antonio*.

He was the first to break the silence. There was a bit of mumbling amongst them, then finally Uri took the initiative to go and check. He checked for a pulse, then gave him a brief examination. He stepped back wiping his hands on a piece of cloth he picked up.

'He is dead alright, cold as the devil's heart, and what's more he has been dead for a long time. Someone's been keeping him on ice,' he told them.

'How do you know that?' *Antonio* asked.

He looked at him with a cold stare, 'Because that is my job.'

That was enough to cause him to drop back behind *Carlos*.

'Does anybody know who he is?' Viktor asked.

They all shook their heads, *Carlos* could hardly breath as he looked at his idiot mate Klaus, sitting there dead as a dodo. He managed to shake his head but started to perspire from every pore in his body. He was sure someone would notice at any second, but he was saved by the sound of the lift approaching. Uri took charge, indicating for everyone to stay quiet, while signalling for Rostov's sidekick to follow him.

They took their position just inside the door, waiting to see if anybody would approach. They could hear the sound of heavy steps in the hallway. They came to a stop in front of the door of 401. There was silence for a moment, then the door was pushed open,and someone stepped in. Before he could react they grabbed him and propelled him into the room, where he fell in a heap.

As he sat down there were a couple of gasps from *Antonio* and Rostov. 'YOU!' screamed *Antonio*, who looked in need of a nose full of 'blow.'

There was silence as the guy sat up and looked around. 'What are you lot doing here?' asked a dazed Chaz.

Then everybody started to talk at once, each trying to figure out what was going on when an almighty yell stopped them in their tracks.

'IT'S HIM!' Chaz pointed at poor dead Klaus in the chair.

It was lucky nobody was looking in *Carlos's* direction as he flopped back against the wall. 'What is this fucker up to?' he thought, as he slid down to the floor, seeing all his plans disappearing in front of his eyes.

At the same time, all attention was directed towards Chaz. *Antonio* saw his chance to claw his way out of this mess. 'Do you mean this is the blond guy you saw sabotage the club?'

Chaz nodded feverishly. 'That's him, I will never forget the face of the guy that tried to kill me,' heavily overacting his distress. Then he pointed at the corpse. 'Have you read the note?' he asked. They looked confused, and he pointed again, 'The note pinned to his chest!'

Viktor turned and glared at Uri. He shrugged his shoulders, 'You only asked me to check if he was dead.'

'Get the note and read it,' Viktor snarled.

Uri went over and grabbed the note in anger, 'It says, 'Play the tape'.'

He looked around and discovered an old reel-to-reel recorder by his side. He brought it over and handed it to Viktor who placed it on the table in front of where he was sitting.

'I suggest we all gather around and listen to this. I for one am very anxious to find out what is going on here and who is behind all this,' waving his arms around indicating the whole elaborate setup.

They gathered around, with the exception of *Carlos* who remained squatting, his face the colour of chalk as Viktor pressed the PLAY button.

72

CHAZ

I gently slid back against the wall and observed my plan developing in front of my eyes.

The night before, *Roberto* and I had transported our defrosted friend to the apartment and set him up in all his glory. Bringing him inside presented a bit of a problem as this was a fairly busy block. Plus, we had to leave him in the wetsuit. We were afraid that if we took him out, he might flow all over the place. It had taken 24 hours sitting in front of a furnace to thaw him out enough to move his limbs.

It was Des that came up with the idea. 'Remember when we used to bring Da home, his arms over our shoulders. He never knew that his feet were not touching the ground. He used to peddle all the way home,' he laughed.

So that's what we did. Rob and I put a big tarp on him and then brought him upstairs, as if he was a mate that had a bit too much to drink, which in his case was true.

We stepped back to survey our handiwork, 'Well if this does not get things moving, I am not sure what will. Have you put the note and tape where they can see them?' I asked.

'They would have to be blind not to!'

When I found myself in the middle of the floor surrounded by angry faces, I quickly figured they had not heard the tape. I could have been killed as soon as I came in. How could these clowns have missed it? Rostov looked like he had aged 10 years since I last clapped eyes on him. He was still dressed in standard Russian oligarch getup designer gear. Based only on the price and with no regard for taste, which brought me to his clone sitting opposite him. I had no idea who he was, but it was obvious they were not friends. And his bodyguard, I heard him call him,

Uri. He was dressed in a black t-shirt, and the same colour jeans, with the usual bulging muscles to suit.

Antonio was definitely the worst for wear, his usual impeccable attire was in disarray. His French-silk shirt and linen slacks were grubby and his $1000 loafers had scuff marks on them, plus his nose had traces of his product on it.

My eyes settled on *Carlos*, the one this presentation was really arranged for. He refused to make eye contact, while trying to maintain some composure. He was dressed much the same as Uri, only a little less threatening. He did not look nearly as tough as he had back in Dublin all that time ago. I could not believe it was only a few weeks since I had stumbled into his mess. I glanced down at myself; I couldn't talk. I was wearing the same two colours I always wore, black and grey, top or bottom did not matter. 'Suits your personality', as my father would say. I preferred to call it 'incognito' the way a lot of Dublin men dressed. I believe we prefer to let our actions define us not our clothes!

I snapped back to the present as the voice from the tape broke the silence.

73

A heavy Spanish accent broke the silence, as *Roberto* began to speak. We had decided it was better to use someone that could not be recognised.

'I represent a group of people that has invested a lot of time in maintaining calm and stability on this Island. The recent outbreak of violence will no longer be tolerated. For this reason you have been invited here to give you one chance to redeem yourselves. You all know Chaz Savage. His purpose here is to identify the fella sitting in the seat as the one he encountered sabotaging the club. He does not know his identity. That is your task. He is to be released unharmed and can leave now if he desires.'

They all looked at Chaz. He shrugged, indicating he would stay. The tape continued, 'What is required of you is that all hostilities stop at once. You have one week to deliver the identity of those behind the death of *Christina de la Vega's* son and his companion. Failure to do this will result in steps being taken to resolve the matter. This will have international repercussions. If you are wondering why we have not undertaken this task, any official investigation could bring unwanted attention to *Señora De la Vega*, so insure you tread carefully. This is your first and only warning!' as the tape clicked off.

Viktor was the first to speak, 'Who is this guy?' pointing at Chaz.

He decided to act first, 'Who the hell are you? I know these guys, but who are you and your buddy?'

Viktor ignored him, turning to Rostov, 'Do you know him?'

He proceeded by telling him the story which Chaz had fed him, 'This is all on them, Viktor, they started all of this!' he ranted.

Chaz began to realise that this new player had been sent from the mother country to clean up Rostov's mess. How he had found out about the meeting was a mystery to him, so he decided to bail out before they started to ask too many questions.

'Well, whoever you are, I can't say it has been a pleasure, and that goes for the lot of you, I am out of here.'

Carlos erupted. 'You are just going to take his word that the damage was done by this guy,' pointing at Klaus's rapidly decaying body. 'How does he know it is the same guy? Look at him, he looks like something out of Madame Tussauds, he could be anybody.'

Chaz pushed away from the wall and made his way across to the 'ice man', stepping in close and staring at the mask-like face. He then turned and said, 'I would agree, if not for this,' pointing at his cheek. There was a small tattoo of a swastika, which stood out starkly against his porcelain-coloured flesh. As they all crowded around to check it out, he made his way towards the door. As he passed, Carlos he whispered, 'I will be in contact, soon,' closing the door behind him as he left.

Viktor took charge. Directing his conversation in the direction of Rostov,'If there is any truth in this we need to identify this guy as soon possible. So, it is in both of our interests to unveil whoever is behind this. If we do this, it will satisfy all the interested parties and allow things to return to normal. Are we in agreement?'

Rostov nodded his head vigorously. *Antonio* looked to *Carlos* for guidance, with no avail. He was transfixed, switching his glances from the door to the assembled group. As the fight-or-flight response set in, leaning heavily towards flight.

Fortunately for him all attention was directed to Uri who was busy cutting the fingers off the corpse. 'What are you doing?' screamed *Antonio* in horror.

'Perhaps you would prefer to take a photo and ask if anybody recognised him?' Uri asked, sarcastically. 'It's for his fingerprints, the skin will have to be rehydrated in order to get reliable prints,' he added.

'How long will that take' *Carlo*s asked.

He shrugged, 'No more than a couple of days, then if he is in the system we will have a name.'

Carlos now knew how long he had to dig himself out and rescue his mission. Viktor started to speak again, breaking into his thoughts.

'We will use our resources to obtain his identity. I suggest we meet again in two days' time to consider our next move. Until then we are all facing the same enemy, so put all disputes aside until we resolve this situation, agreed?' Again, addressing Rostov, who was only too glad to agree.

Antonio also nodded his agreement. 'What about him?' he asked, pointing at the fella sitting in the chair, less his fingers and smelling pretty bad.

Viktor for first time addressed him directly. 'Your town, your problem.'

Antonio looked at *Carlos*, then replied, 'No problem, we will take care of it.'

74

They completed their grizzly task two hours later. *Carlos* had decided the best thing was to give him a burial at sea. The first thing they had to do was get him out of the apartment without being noticed. *Antonio* discovered a tarpaulin ‘conveniently’ hidden behind the chair that the poor chap was rotting away in.

He and decided to wrap him in it, as by this time with the humid climate he was really getting on the nose. Both were retching badly by the time they had him rolled up in a long bundle.

Their struggle down the stairs and into the car drew a lot of strange stares from passers-by, but the angry look on their faces soon deflected any unwanted attention.

An hour later they had loaded him *into Antonio's* speedboat, where they took him out into deep waters. *Carlos* secured him with some old chains he had found. As he tipped him over the side, he muttered to himself, ‘I hope that’s the last time I have to do this to you.’

‘What did you say?’ *Antonio* asked.

‘Nothing, just saying glad to see you go,’ he replied.

Back at *Antonio's* place, the conversation started to get awkward for *Carlos.* ‘You will have to reach out to your contacts in the police. As soon as you get the fingerprints, we need to be the first to question whoever is behind this,’ *De Sota* demanded.

Carlos knew he would have to keep this coke-addled lunatic under control until he could figure out whoever was behind this and pulling the Irishman’s strings. Never for a moment considering that it could have been Chaz who was the architect of this scheme. Big mistake.

‘As soon as they recover the prints, I will see if they are in the system,’ something he already knew. Of course, they were. The idiot had travelled on his real name and would be simple to identify. This would soon lead straight back to him. He had to buy some time. 'In the meantime, while I get to the bottom of this, can you stay put for your own safety?'

He was shocked to hear this. 'What do you mean, they agreed to lie low until we get this sorted.'

Carlos shook his head. 'Did you not see that the Russian dude only addressed Rostov? He has another agenda, and I don't think we are included, remember you just destroyed their $600-million yacht.'

De Sota went white in the face. 'I will stay here until you return with news,' heading to the pile of white powder sitting on his desk.

'Good idea,' *Carlos* said as he headed out, wondering when he would be contacted.

At the same time, a similar conversation had been carried out at Viktor's palatial villa that he had rented. Uri was in the process of getting the prints recovered, while Vostok was issuing instructions to Mick Ryan to locate where Chaz was hanging out. '

Whoever is directing him, will be likely to contact him to find what happened.'

'That's easy,' he replied.

Explaining who he was living with and therefore under the protection of someone who was considered untouchable. Viktor scoffed at the idea that anybody was as he said, 'untouchable.' But when Ryan outlined exactly who William Heart represented, he quickly changed his mind. He knew from experience it was very unwise to mess with those crazy Londoners. They put some of the Russian mafia heavies to shame.

'Okay, what I want you to do is keep an eye on their movements, just in case you spot anything unusual, can you handle that?' he snapped.

Mick, only too happy to oblige, jumped into action. 'I am on it; can I borrow a car?'

Viktor threw him the keys to one of the Range Rovers he had rented. 'Report back as soon as you learn anything, do you understand?'

He nodded vigorously as he sprinted out.

75

Chaz arrived back at the ranch, anxious to fill them in on the success of their plan.

When he told them about the new players, Bill's reaction was instant. 'You boys get to the bottom of who these guys are,' he instructed his sons.

Chaz added, 'They almost certainty are some sort of clean-up crew sent to sort out Rostov. I reckon somehow they got a hold of Bruno's invitation, might be worth checking that lead out.'

They nodded as they headed for the door. Bill reminding them to keep a low profile. 'We don't want to show our hand just yet,' as they gave him the thumbs up.

'When will you contact *Carlos*?' Des asked.

'I will let him stew for a day or two, no doubt the others will be doing their best to discover just who their frozen friend was, which considering the Russian influence should not take long.'

'What do you think he will do?' he asked again.

Chaz glanced at Bill, then with a grin replied. 'Hopefully what I want him to do!'

Des jumped in, 'Perhaps we can help with that. With Herman's help, we have translated the notebook completely and a few interesting things have emerged. I will let him explain,' handing over to their translator.

'I would begin by saying this is only my, or should I say our,' indicating Des and *Marie*, 'our interpretation of what he was trying to convey.' He could see the puzzled look on their faces, and hurried to explain. 'You see, based on the different styles and use of the complicated-sentence structures of the German language, it would appear that this had been written over a period of time and by different people.'

'So, there were others involved in this?' they asked.

'That's just it, the answer is no, the same person wrote all of this.'

'Now I am completely confused,' replied Bill.

'Allow me to explain. By analysing the handwriting, which because of my work as a linguist professor and studying of old documents, I was able to satisfy myself that the same person wrote the notations. But not in the same mind.' Before they could interject, he continued. 'In simple terms he was losing his mind, probably dementia or some other degenerative-brain disease.'

Des could not contain himself. 'We were trying to figure out why, if *Carlos* had the directions to the treasure (he could not help himself calling it that) he needed all this help. Plus how did he not notice the missing notebook?'

He answered, before anybody asked. 'We reckon there are many different books and who knows what else.'

'Okay, how do you know that?' This time it was Chaz. Des directed the conversation back to Herman. 'When people start to have mental deteriorations, especially someone as fanatical as he was, they would have tried to record as much as possible. The problem is that after time, they forget what they have recorded and start all over again, but each time little differently. Plus, as we see in this book, the worse he got the more he used 'old German'. Which would have made it nearly impossible for a person without an in-depth knowledge,' pushing his chest out.

'They could not be sure what message he was trying to relay.'

'*Carlos* can't be sure which the proper instruction are!' Des cried.

'This is perhaps something I can use. Remember we have to force him into getting the police in Barcelona off Des's back, then we bring them all down, and for that it is over to Vincent,' pointing at his brother. 'I have arranged a meeting with this lovely lady, *Señora de la Vega*. Des If you could discover if there is even a shred of truth in this story, other than an old notebook written by some crazy, would give me some leverage.'

'Funny you should say that, *Maria* and I have a meeting this afternoon with *Ricardo* on that very subject!'

76

DES

Maria loaded the dogs into the rear of the Range Rover, then hopped into the passenger seat as they headed to their rendezvous with *Ricardo*. She had arranged to meet at his usual spot, his bar in *Portals* Ves. At first he was reluctant, not wanting to get further involved. She felt it was because it was dragging up too many bad memories. But when she explained that they had translated the notebook and it perhaps held some answers for him, he quickly agreed. They decided to meet mid-afternoon. By then the lunch crowd would have dispersed and they would have the place to themselves.

As they pulled away from '*El Rancho'* with the dogs bouncing around with excitement, they failed to see the car pull in behind them and began to follow.

Ricardo was sitting at his usual spot by the bar. He had a glass of red wine in front of him, and when he spotted them approaching he picked it up and indicated a table on the fringe of the beach. They made their greetings, then while Des went to get some drinks *Maria* began to fill him on the translation. By the time he returned with a bottle of wine and some glasses, she had got to the point where in the book it seemed to confirm the existence of the secret sub pens.

'So, does it explain how to get to it?'

Des chimed in. 'Well, that's just it, it does in a sort of way, and this is where you come in.' As he began pouring the drinks, he went on to explain how the message was a bit garbled, as he quoted the description of the entrance.

'A mouth God to follow old signs, what does all that mean?' he asked.

Des smiled and leaned in. 'The first part I can help with, the second part is where you come in.' Before he could react, Des continued. 'Remember, when he was describing his path, the night club that everybody is so interested in, did not exist.'

Ricardo's eyes opened as if a light had gone on. 'The entrance to the grotto!' he exclaimed.

Des clapped him on the back. 'Exactly, and I believe I know where the 'Path' begins. I have seen the inlet, and at the rear are some heavy doors, probably used as a storage area. I believe it is somewhere behind there.'

'So how do you know which one?' he asked.

'This is where you come in again. In the notebook he says to look for the 'old signs.' Don't forget he probably used some old '*Cavernicola*' and I think he is referring to his markings.'

'How does that help?' he asked.

'Because you and I are going to find it, and you are going to help recognise these signs.

He jumped up in horror. 'Are you crazy? You know what happens to those that look for the place, no way am I going to help you,' slamming his hand down, spilling the drinks.

Des calmly sorted the glasses, then turned to *Maria*. 'Would you mind getting us some refills?' he asked, giving her a wink, indicating he would like some time alone with *Ricardo*. When they were alone, he leaned in, looking him straight in the eyes. 'Let me ask you a question. If there was even a slight chance that we did discover this path, that opens up the possibility that we could find some indication of what happened to *Monica* and your son, what was his name?'

'*Diego*,' he whispered.

'*Diego*. If that was to happen, can't you see how knowing what happened to them would give you closure. Perhaps this would allow you to get on with your life. If not for you, consider *Meris*, not knowing what became of her sister. It is all right to be afraid; I am afraid almost all the time, but I won't let it deprive me of anything. It is there to protect, not to freeze you. In any case, it is up to you. I am going whatever, and here are the drinks,' he announced, as *Maria* returned with a fresh bottle in hand.

She sat down, sensing something had happened. 'So, what's happening?' she asked.

Des said nothing, just fixed *Ricardo* with a stare and waited. There was a tense silence, then he broke the silence. 'Pour the drinks, it looks like we are going to need them.'

Des jumped up with delight, 'I never doubted for a moment,' grasping his hand, pumping it until he had to pull it free.

'I might need that arm, if we are to have any chance of any success.' A rare smile crossed his face.

'So, when are you going?' *Maria* asked.

'No time like the present, there is only a couple of guards around the club at night, we will be able to slip in from the seaside in your small boat. I will meet you back here in an hour, I need to get some equipment before we head out,' he said as they made their way back to the car.

In the undergrowth, Mick Ryan was also hurrying back, anxious to tell his boss what he had overheard. He was just pressing the key to open the door when for a millisecond he felt a presence behind him. Then it felt like a huge weight had fell on him from a great height, as his world dissolved into darkness.

77

Mick Ryan could hear the sound of voices as he slowly began to regain consciousness. As he slowly opened his eyes, at first he thought he had gone blind. Then he realised he had something over his head. He started to struggle, realising he was tied to the chair he was sitting in.

'Stop wasting what little time you have got left,' he heard a familiar voice.

'Chaz,' he gasped, through his head covering. 'Let me out. I can't breathe,' he implored.

'If you can speak, you can breathe, for how much longer, depends on you,' came another voice, one he did not recognise. Bill had got in on the act. With that, the cover was ripped off his head. He struggled to clear his vision as the bright light focused on his face blinded him.

'Here is how this goes,' Bill continued. 'You will be asked some questions. Now your first reaction will be to lie, because that's the type of low life you are. So let me explain, every time you lie, and we will know. As some questions we already know the answer too, this is what will happen.' A hand appeared out of the dazzling light, clutching a lump hammer, which came down with a massive crunch inches to his exposed toes. He gave an involuntary scream, thinking he had been hit. 'So now you know what to expect, let's begin. Where is Bruno?'

'He has done a runner to Portugal as far as I know.'

The hammer appeared again but remained poised for a moment then retreated. 'How did this Uri guy and his Russian mate get the message we sent?'

'I was staying at his place when it arrived, they grabbed me and forced me to give it to them.'

'The hammer appeared again. 'Wrong answer,' as it came down on his big toe, he nearly swallowed his tongue as he tried to scream and vomit at the same time. 'That was only a love tap, one more wrong answer and you won't be walking again for a long time, though maybe that won't matter,' he added menacingly .

'All right!' he screamed again. Then proceeded to fill them in on how he had become involved with these new players, and how they had asked him to keep an eye on Chaz.

'Next question, and remember we know what was said. Repeat what you overheard, and don't leave anything out,' as the hammer menaced again.

'I could not hear very well from where I was,' he pleaded frantically. The silence prompted him to continue. From his babbling they perceived that all he had discovered was that they were looking for some hidden room that had something of value inside.

They left him there to stew while they discussed what to do with this wrinkle. 'We can't let him go, if we do he will run straight to the Russians,' Des lamented.

'What do you suggest, get rid of him?' Bill asked, in a matter-of-fact way, which brought chills to Chaz and Des's backs. Luckily Vincent was off somewhere with his new companion Dawi.

Chaz put his hand up, 'I can take care of both problems, and first we have to get him to pass on the information to his employers.'

'What?' whispered the others.

'Listen, we need *Carlos* under as much stress as possible. If we add this bunch into the hunt, it could force him to reach out. Remember, he has to believe he needs our help.'

'How do we do that?' Bill asked.

'We get him to make a phone call, as if under pressure. Give them what he believes he heard, then as soon as they begin to question him, he will be cut off.'

Bill grinned, 'I don't think that being under pressure will be a problem, but that still does not explain what we do with him after?'

Chaz gave him a clap on the back, 'Leave that to me, I will have to borrow your boat,' he added.

They returned to Mick, who by this time was bathed in sweat from fear and the intense heat of the lights. Chaz appeared at his side and began to explain what he was to say on the call. 'Any deviation will result in further pain,' indicating the hammer poised above his already swollen foot. He nearly swallowed his tongue, trying to agree as quickly as possible. Chaz placed the phone close beside him, 'It is on speaker, so remember we can hear both sides of the conversation.'

Mick gave them the number to dial. It started to ring and was answered quickly. 'Hello?' It was Uri. Chaz indicated for him to start speaking. He could not have been better; he hardly took a breath as he quickly related his news. When he finished, Uri asked him to hold on for Viktor, but Chaz cut him off abruptly.

'Did I do alright?' he pleaded. But the next thing that happened was the hood was thrust over his head again, then silence. A couple of minutes later he felt himself being lifted out of the chair and carried somewhere. He could hear the sound of doors being opened and closed, then he was suddenly bundled into what he assumed was the booth of a car.

'Open your mouth to make a sound and we will put something in it you would not like, got that?'

Before he could even try to reply the lid came down sealing him in. He felt the car in motion, and in what seemed to be an eternity, it finally came to a stop. He heard the doors open, then the lid popped. He was again lifted out. As they were carrying him, be began to hear the sound of the sea and could smell the pungent seaweed. He began to cry like a baby.

'If you don't stay quiet I will have to shut you up,' he heard a voice he recognised; it was Des.

He was lifted into a bobbing boat, then almost at once it sprang into life and headed off at great speed. After what seemed to be a couple of hours, they came to a stop. He was lifted upright, and he could feel somebody putting a heavy jacket on him, guiding his arms into the openings. He began to cry again.

'You are going to drown me; you know I can't swim,' he blubbered.

The hood was snatched off his head. He blinked furiously to clear his eyes, as he looked around all he could see was open water. Before he could say anything, Chaz stepped in front of him and began to speak.

'There are certain people who wanted you gone permanently, but I persuaded them to give you another option. In this direction is *Minorca,*' pointing into the distance. 'The ocean current will deliver you there in a couple of hours, hopefully for your sake it is a sandy beach. If you have any sense at all you will head anywhere but back to *Palma*. If I, or any of my family see you again, it won't be a life jacket you will be wearing but something much heavier. Am I clear?'

He nodded. 'But I can't swim,' he moaned.

'Something I have been advising you to learn, remember?' as they threw him over the side.

As they headed back, Des pointed, 'Look!'

There was the figure of Mick bobbing along in the current frantically paddling, trying the reach the sanctuary of the Island. 'Will he make it?' he asked.

Chaz laughed, looking at the figure of the forlorn Mick Ryan vanishing into the distance. 'Bill assured me that it works; he has used this method before.'

78

Uri slammed the phone down. 'Prick,' he muttered as he went to give Viktor the new information.

'Secret hiding place, something of value, what was he talking about?'

Uri shrugged. 'I don't know, he was terrified. I was asking him for more information, but he got cut off, it sounded like he was in big trouble.'

Viktor slumped down into a chair. It had seemed like he had got a 'get out of jail free card' when the boss had given him the opportunity to reprieve himself. All he had to do was get rid of Rostov and tidy things up over here and he could go home a free man.

'Buried treasure, this is getting worse by the minute,' he ranted. 'Do you think there is any truth to this tale?' he asked Uri.

He shrugged his shoulders. 'I don't know, but it could explain why the club got blown up, it would give whoever was looking for it some privacy,' he speculated.

Viktor jumped up and started pacing, massaging his temples. He stopped, turning to Uri. 'Arrange a meeting with these idiots we are dealing with, someone must know what he was talking about.'

Uri got to work contacting the rest of the crew. The first was Rostov, who sounded just as confused as they were, but was delighted at the opportunity of anything that would take the focus off him, so a meeting was arranged.

Next was *Antonio*, who in typical style started to rant and rave. 'That sounds crazy. If there was anything of value I would have been told.'

Uri shut him up. 'Well, Viktor wants everybody together to discuss this new devolvement. Get your sidekick *Carlos* and meet us,' telling him where. He had decided to use the apartment where they had met the frozen Klaus Becker. *Antonio* had told them it was rented under a false name for the next month, so they agreed to get together later that evening.

When *Carlos* answered the phone, the last thing he expected was *Antonio's* first words. This might be 'All about some hidden treasure,' he yelled into the phone. He almost collapsed, as he tried to regain his composure.

'What are you talking about?' he spluttered.

Antonio went on to explain about the call from Mick Ryan and his disappearance. As he related the story, he could not believe how Desmond, who he did not credit with much importance, could have found out about the sub base.

'Who was he talking to?' *Carlos* asked, his voice starting to crack.

'What's wrong with you, did you not hear me, just some old Spanish guy. I told you he was scared shitless. According to this guy, Uri, he wasn't making a lot of sense, then he was cut off. He reckons he is done for, from the sounds of it.'

Carlos couldn't speak, how did they know about the Spanish guy *Ricardo*? But he discounted that, he was petrified at the mention of looking for the place, plus he had never spoken about what he was looking for in front of him.

*Antoni*o broke the silence. 'Are you still there? What the hell is wrong with you, are you sick?'

'No, just a bit of a head cold, I will see you there tonight. In the meantime I will see what I can find out,' he lied, anxious to get off the phone so he could get a stiff drink.

As he sat nursing his drink, he wondered how things had got so screwed up and more importantly how he could rescue the situation. Remembering Chaz's parting words, he reached for the phone.

Later that evening they all gathered in apartment 401. *Antonio* was the first to arrive, closely followed by Rostov. 'Is it true, is this all about some treasure hunt?' he asked.

Antonio shrugged. 'I find it hard to believe. Stories of things left over from the war have been circulating for years, it is only avid conspiracy nuts that believe this stuff,' he scoffed.

With that Viktor arrived with Uri in tow. ‘Where is your friend?’ he snapped at *Antonio*.

That got his back up. ‘Who put you in charge?’

Uri stepped in. ‘Do you have a problem with that?’ he asked, menacingly.

But before things got out of hand *Carlos* arrived, looking flustered. ‘Sorry to be late, I was trying to find out if there was any truth to this story.’

‘Well, what did you find out?’ Viktor interjected.

‘Nothing of value, there are plenty of tales of such things, but nobody has ever discovered anything. The submarine bases were picked clean before the end of the war. Other than that, nothing,’ he replied.

‘Have you discovered the identity of our friend?’ pointing to the chair he used to occupy.

Antonio spoke, ‘I have reached out to my contacts and should have his details tomorrow.’

Carlos could not contain himself. ‘Who have you been speaking to? I am the one with contacts in the police,’ he snapped.

Antonio, glared at him. ‘Remember your position, I expected you to have found out already. I have my own sources, perhaps they are better than yours?’

Again, Viktor stepped in. ‘I believe that matter will be resolved even earlier, we have reached out at the highest level. I am confident I will have that information within hours. But the old sayings are often the best, ‘There is no smoke without fire.’ We had a body in a wetsuit put here for us to find, and now one of these Irishmen is asking about some hidden stash. We have to assume that whoever they are they need us involved.’

Rostov spoke for the first time. ‘So, what do they want?’

‘Maybe the same as us, the identity of the mystery man. So until we have that information, I suggest we continue as planned, with no distractions.’ Looking at *Antonio* and a stricken *Carlo*s, ‘Until then, we wait.’

As he and Uri left, they were leaving three very confused and scared guys, each for a different reason.

79

DES

Dusk was just about to set when Des and *Maria* left to meet with *Ricardo*. He had loaded some things he had borrowed from Bill's extensive stock of diving equipment into the back of the Range Rover. Quickly followed by the dogs, which *Maria* insisted accompany them. 'They are part of the family,' she insisted. Des had tried to dissuade her. But he had enough experience to know there was no point in arguing with a woman that had made up her mind. So, Lobo and Bear, took up their positions in the back, happily licking *Maria's* hand as she scratched their ears.

They had arranged to meet *Ricardo* at a little inlet close to *Portals Ves*, just after dark. He was waiting patiently when they arrived. He looked like a different man. He had his shoulders pushed back, with his back straight, and his long-grey hair pulled back in a ponytail. He seemed to have lost ten years.

Without wasting any time, they loaded the equipment into the dingy, then they and the dogs jumped in as they pushed off.

The journey to the entrance to the grotto only took a few minutes. As they suspected, it was deserted. They moored the boat alongside the deserted restaurant close to the cave entrance. Des and *Ricardo* carried the equipment, while *Maria* and the dogs led the way with the strong flash lamps they had brought to illuminate their descent into the caves.

The huge entrance was a black hole. As *Maria* shone the light into the dark depths, they could see the destruction the flooding had done to this magnificent structure. Des pointed to a huge pile of rubble below, where the disc jockey used to perform. 'That is where I had to drag Chaz out of. I thought he was dead,' he remembered with a shudder. 'Over there,' he pointed to where large gates sealed the entrance which would be where the book referred to. 'We are in luck, somebody forgot to lock up,' he grinned, shining a torch up under his chin, giving him a ghoulish look.

Maria gave him a slap. 'You will frighten the dogs,' as he pushed open one of the doors and shone his light inside. They could see this had been a storeroom, and somebody had picked it clean already.

'Be careful where you step, it can be very slippery,' warned *Ricardo.*

'There,' said Des. Indicating numerous openings all-around the back of the cave, he quickly made his way over, avoiding the stalactites that still remained on the floor. When they got near they could see most had been blocked by piling used crates in front. 'Okay, your turn *Ric*,' deciding to shorten his name. 'According to the book, in order to find the entrance, we have to follow the 'old signs'.'

He nodded, 'We all have our own methods to mark our tracks. Some use very complicated ways, most just use simple signs.'

'So, we look for any markings that seem to be manmade?' *Maria* asked.

'Yes,' he replied, 'anything that seems out of the ordinary.'

'Nothing ordinary about any of this' muttered Des, as they started to search for clues.

Over the next couple of hours, they moved crates and obstacles in their search, with no success. 'I have not seen anything that looks like what we are looking for,' *Ric* said dejectedly, as he stood with Des.

After searching all the possible openings, they had not seen anything that looked like a sign and were just about to call it a night when a yell from *Maria* made them jump. 'Look here, hurry up, I may have found something,' she cried.

They hurried over to where she was down on her knees in front of a smaller aperture. They bent down to look at what she had discovered but could not see anything. The confused expression on their faces prompted her to show them what she had discovered.

'Watch out,' she said as she pointed to a steady stream of water that was cascading down one side of the opening.

They still could not see anything until she put her hand up to deflect the flow. There in front of their eyes was a crudely carved arrow.

Ric reacted first. 'God! I have seen that sign before, a very long time ago, it is the sign of one of the old timers, this must be it.'

Des gave *Maria* a big hug, which brought a huge blush to her face. They started to clear away some debris from the entrance and shone the light down into the darkness. They could see as it descended that it opened up considerably.

Suddenly, Des yelped, 'There!' pointing the light to where the tunnel started to curve. There, clear as day was another arrow. 'This has be it, let's get ready.'

Maria jumped up in shock. 'You are not thinking of going down there?'

He grinned in the half-light. 'For sure, we have not come this far without checking it out. Don't worry I have *Ricardo* with me. If it looks too dangerous we will turn back.'

'Well, I am coming with you,' she demanded.

'Listen, you are our safety net. If by any chance we didn't return, you can go for help.'

She could not argue with his logic, so reluctantly she agreed. 'All right, but you are taking the dogs with you.'

He knew there was no point in arguing, so he nodded in agreement. 'Let's get ready'.

80

They crouched in front of the entrance; Des turned to his companion. 'Ready?' ad he gave the thumbs up. Des blew a kiss to the anxious *Maria.* They started their journey, followed closely by the dogs, who were enjoying all the new smells and tastes they could explore. *Ric* led the way, cautioning Des to not step out of the path he was following.

'It is very dangerous in these caves, many hidden obstacles, one slip and you could find yourself trapped by falling rocks, or injured,' he said.

They proceeded down the narrow path, lit by the powerful lamps they held. At the next arrow *Ric* stopped to contemplate their next move. In the direction it was pointing it opened to a much larger tunnel. They could see by the undisturbed dust on the ground, nobody had been down this way in a long time. Signalling for them to carry on, he reached into his backpack and took out a short stick with a small red flag.

'This is important. If we were to lose light, our only chance would be to find these markers,' and drove it into the ground with his heel, then nodded. 'Let's go.'

When they arrived at the end of the passage they shone their light into the darkness. They were greeted by a massive cathedral-like chamber. Shining the lamps upwards, the light danced off the hundreds of stalagmites in their myriad of colours reflected by the different minerals that had helped form this wonder of nature.

'Now that's something you don't see every day,' quipped Des in wonderment.

Ric nodded in agreement, as he shone his light around the walls looking for their way out. 'There,' he said, pointing at a number of openings dotted around the walls. 'Before we move on. Remember from now on as soon as we move out of this chamber, any misstep and we could be lost in here forever!' he warned.

Des nodded soberly. This was completely out of his comfort zone. They moved around, carefully avoiding the stalactites rising from the ground. These were directly opposite the ones above. The drops of water that carried the material that formed them was how the ones below were formed, *Ric* informed him. The dogs seemed to instinctively know to avoid the obstacles as their night vision was far superior to humans and did not have to rely on the direct light to find their way. So they just carried on sniffing as they went, seemingly not bothered at being deep underground.

At each entrance *Ric* would stop and carefully search for a sign of some kind. As they moved on to the next, Des marked each one with an X to indicate that it had been checked. It was slow and tedious work, something that was not to Des's temperament. On the other hand, his intrepid guide seemed to have found a new lease of life, buoyed be the opportunity to finally rid the worry that had consumed him for years.

They were now about three quarters of the way around and were examining an unusual opening. 'Notice anything unusual?' he asked. Des shook his head. 'Look closer, see the chisel marks on the walls, this opening has been enlarged,' as be begun a careful examination. He was just about to give up on this one when he exclaimed, 'Look at this!' He indicated something scribbled into the wall. It was partly filled with dust and grit but as he carefully dusted it, something began to appear. They gasped, as they recognised what they were looking at.

'A Swastika, this has to be it!' Des cried, clapping him on the back.

They gathered their equipment and headed into the darkness. The path was different than before, seemingly manmade in places. Each time they came to a junction they would find the same markings indicting which path to take. At the first junction *Ric* pointed to the entrance they had emerged from. 'Notice anything?' he asked. Des shrugged. 'No markings. Whoever made this path did not want anyone to know how to get out. They must have done something like I am doing,' as he pegged another flag at the entrance.

Des nodded. 'Remember in the book he referred to the 'disposing of the workers,' and shuddered at the horror of what they were uncovering.

After passing through at least six different junctions they entered a large circular cave. Standing inside they looked around but there was no sign of another exit. Then Des noticed the dogs drinking from a pool in one corner. He carefully wandered over to see what was going on.

'Check this out,' waving *Ric* over. 'Look,' shining his light into the water. In the dull glow, they could just make out the outline of some steps descending into the depths. 'This has to be it, it must have flooded at some time. I am going to check it out,' as he stripped his backpack, shirt and shoes off.

Ric looked on in horror. 'It is too dangerous. If you get into trouble I can't do anything. I can't swim!'

Des grinned. 'Then I better not get into trouble, I am just going to drop in to see what I can find out.' Then he proceeded to descend into the darkness.

After what seemed like an age he resurfaced. 'Well, this is the entrance. I can see the swastika on the wall. I don't know how far it goes, so I am going to use one of Bill's mini breathers.'

Ric eyed the facemask with a small air bottle attached. 'Will there be enough air?'

'Sure, I will watch the time. There is enough air for fifteen minutes, twenty in a pinch.' He prepared himself, but before he set off, he turned to his pal and the dogs, who looked ready to plunge in also. 'Hold the dogs, and if by any chance I don't come back, just go and get help. I will be fine.'

He waved goodbye and vanished out of sight.

81

The light from his torch cut through the darkness as he swam along the tunnel, taking care not to brush off on the side. He did not think there were any predators in the water, but did not want to leave any blood trail, just in case. As he proceeded deeper, he kept checking his time. As it approached six minutes he started to get concerned. He had taken lessons while he was helping 'The Shoe' with his operation. He cursed him under his breath. Swimming in total darkness with only fifteen minutes of air was not covered in the classes he had taken.

He was just about to abort when he detected something glinting in the beam of light. It was a metal ramp, which ascended. He quickly paddled forward and crawled upwards. His head broke water and his first thought was to turn off his air, to preserve it for the return journey. He then carefully climbed out, placed his equipment safely to one side, then shone his light around.

He could not believe what he was seeing. He was standing in a Second World War submarine pen. Exactly as described in the notebook. He looked around in wonderment, trying to take everything in.

He could see the dry dock, which would have been used to service and unload the boat. It was empty. All around were the remains of the equipment and lots of empty containers. It looked like the place was stripped bare, probably by whoever was the last to use this place. As he panned the light, something caught his eye—bones littering the floor.

He nearly dropped his lamp in shock. He carefully approached, not wanting to walk on somebody's remains. His first thought was he had discovered *Ricardo's* son and his girlfriend. But he quickly realised it was not them. First of all there way too many bones. These had to be the remains of the construction crew, left to perish down here. He shuddered as he continued with his search. Suddenly he stopped as his light played over a large-concrete structure about the size of a large-double garage. In the centre was a solid-steel door. He moved in for closer inspection. He could see it was designed to be very secure. The door was set inside another steel frame, no hinges were visible but at one side was some kind of primitive keypad. But instead of buttons it had a series of wheels inset with a dial surrounding them with letters on them. At once he recognised it, the famous Enigma machine used by the Nazis during the war.

He had found it, this had to be the hoard! He was about to set off back, when he realised that there was no way of knowing if there was anything inside. He could hear Chaz's voice saying, 'It does not matter, and we only needed to find the place!' But he let his curiosity get the better of him. As he inspected the building he could see it was made of reinforced concrete, which was beginning to crumble in places. But would still need some serious equipment to get inside. He decided as a last resort to climb up on top. As he clambered up, he could see that due to the steady accumulation of water up here it was much more eroded. He poked around directing his torch in all corners of the roof, then spotted something curious, water moving slowly in the centre. He pulled out a hefty knife he had found at Bill's and started to prod to where the water he thought was heading. To his surprise, it sank into the hilt. The roof at this point had eroded to the point that water was starting to leak through. As he started to dig furiously he realised that someone had done a repair job here sometime in the past. Very soon a hole appeared. This gave him renewed energy. He soon had a hole big enough for to poke his head in and look straight down. It was full of crates of all shape and sizes. This had to be what they were looking for. He kept chipping away until he could squeeze his shoulders through. As he poked his arm in, first holding the light, he pushed his himself inside the roof. He began to pan the light when he felt himself falling.

He tumbled inside and landed on top of a pile of crates. He sat up, checked nothing was broken, then decided, 'In for penny in for a pound,' as he dropped down to the floor.

Ricardo was just about ready to go for help when he saw the glow of a light approaching in the water. Just then, Des surfaced. 'You are alive!' he cried, helping him out.

Des stood shaking the water out of his mop of golden hair. A huge smile appeared on his face as he grabbed *Ric* and began to dance around with him, much to the delight of the dogs.

He yelled at the top of his lungs, 'We found IT!'

82

'Are you crazy? You went looking for the place alone?' yelled Chaz.

Des, *Maria,* and *Ric* sat calmly, smiling at the crew assembled around them. 'I was not alone,' pointing at his companions. 'In any case, we found it,' he yelled, hugging *Maria* while at the same time clapping *Ric* on the back. The dogs who were sitting at their feet got into the action by joining in yelping at all the excitement.

Des had called them together as soon as they returned. Bombarded with questions, he launched into a detailed description of their discovery, culminating in their reuniting with *Maria* in the main cave. 'I was never so relieved to see you guys emerge for that place,' patting the dogs to include them.

They all started to ask questions at once. Chaz put his hand up. 'Well since you all returned safely, I guess the big question is, was there anything inside that place you took a head dive into?' he asked.

Des took a deep breath. 'Well, when I fell to the floor, my first reaction was to get back out. But when I realised I could use the crates to climb out. I decided to have a poke around. Everything was packed into crates, all the labels were in German, and I did not want to disturb anything. Most of them were sealed tight but a few I could see inside the gaps in the wood frame,' he paused. 'Those were stacked full of what I can only assume were gold bars.' He paused, waiting for the response.

'Are you sure it was gold?' Vincent asked.

Des looked at him. 'Well why would anybody got to the trouble of constructing that place with all that security, to hide fake gold?'

'Go on,' Chaz urged.

'The place was packed, I barely had room to squeeze between all the crates and boxes. But from the shape of some of them, I would guess they held paintings. In fact I would say everything held something of great value. If this hoard was to give Hitler and his cronies funds to start the Fourth Reich, he would not need to invade any country. He could just buy a couple of smaller ones no problem and have plenty left over for the good life.'

He then explained how he climbed out and covered the opening with some slabs he found lying around. After that, his return swim to *Ric* was uneventful. Then using *Ric's* unique road map he had laid, they made their safe return to the main cave and home.

'This is excellent news; it give us more ammunition, for me to negotiate with the lady herself, *Christina de la Vaga*,' said Vince.

Des jumped in again, 'Oh, something I forgot to mention. The place is wired with explosives; anybody tries to break into that store house will bring the whole place down on their heads,' he added, as if an afterthought.

'What!' Vince gasped.

Des went on to explain about the weird-locking mechanism on the door. 'When I was inside the room, I gave a thought of just going out the door, but when I examined the lock from the inside I could see it was connected to a complicated switch system. If I was to take a guess, anybody who did not know the correct code would blow themselves up, and the treasure along with them.'

'Are you sure about the explosives?' Chaz asked.

He nodded. 'When I climbed out on the roof, I could see wires leading up to the surrounding walls. I climbed up and could see enough C4 to bury the place. Any sort of forced entry would spell disaster.'

Bill stepped in, 'Well, I am glad you made it out safe and sound, but what do we do now?'

Vincent responded first. 'With this information, I have something to bargain with. I know you have said the objective is to clear his name,' pointing at Des. 'Perhaps I can influence her ladyship to intervene on our behalf.'

Des jumped up. 'But I thought that this is what we wanted to force *Carlos* to do?'

Both Chaz and Vince looked at him as if he was retarded. 'Do you really believe we can trust that to him?' Vince said.

Chaz replied, 'I agree with Vince. If he could get her to intervene, I would have a lot more faith in that than any promise from *Carlo*s. Don't forget he probably killed that Klaus guy, and he was probably his friend,' he added.

Bill nodded in agreement. 'With friends like that, who would need enemies,' which brought a dry chuckle from his sons.

'So, we are finished with *Carlo*s?' Des asked.

It was Chaz who replied. 'In no way, I intend to teach him and all his cronies that they crossed paths with the wrong people.' He said this with such conviction, all the laughter stopped, as the atmosphere became very tense. Realising he had said a bit too much, he continued. 'Plus, let's not forget he is probably the only one that will have the combination to open the strong hold without blowing the place up,' he added.

Des could not help himself. 'Hopefully,' he mumbled.

'Leave him to me, but I will need your assistance,' pointing at Des.

'Okay, then it is agreed Vincent will tackle the authorities, Chaz and Des will work on *Carlos*. So, what do we do?' Bill asked.

As Chaz revealed his plan, it brought a few gasps. 'Will that work?' Bill asked.

He grinned. 'I will answer that when it is all over!'

83

THE PLAN, PHASE 1

Carlos had received the worst news possible. His family connection had contacted him. Their concern was the absence of any contact from Klaus Becker, compounded by the fact that inquiries were being made regarding the identity of someone that sounded a lot like him. He had done his best to calm them, explaining that Klaus was on a special job for him and would be out of touch for a few days. He assured them he would have him make contact as soon as he returned.

As he sat there, he knew that had bought him a few days at the most. If only he had discovered the access to the treasure he would at least be in a position to bargain. He cursed under his breath. A loud banging on the door shocked him to his senses. His first thought was they had discovered Klaus's identity and had come to share the news with him or to exact revenge. As he peered through the spy hole, to his complete surprise, standing there were the two Irish brothers! He stood in shock, trying to make sense of what was happening.

'Open up *Carlos*, we know you are in there. I told you we had to talk; it is in both of our interests,' Chaz shouted.

After a couple of seconds, he slowly opened the door to peek out. 'Are you armed?' he asked, holding his own gun firmly behind his back.

They both did a slow spin. 'Guns are not really our thing, now can we get on with this, time is wasting. Which incidentally is something you don't have a lot of. Have they identified Klaus yet?' he asked.

He whipped the door open. 'Come in, what are you doing mentioning that name out loud?' he hissed. A lot of his usual confidence and calm had disappeared.

Des gave him a playful push. 'Don't worry, we are all friends here.' But the look in his eyes said otherwise.

Carlos retreated into the main room. 'What do you want?'

'Well, for a start, you can put the gun you are hiding behind you back away. We are here to give you some great news.'

'What?' he asked nervously. Chaz glanced at his brother, he shrugged, then turned to *Carlos*. 'I found the place you are looking for.'

'Not possible. You have no idea where to look or what you are looking for,' he snapped.

'Show him,' Chaz requested.

With that, Des spoke, 'You are looking for Hitler's loot, and before you ask,' producing the notebook and waving it in his face.

'How, did you get that?' he gasped. 'Sit down and put the gun away, or we are out of here. We will take our chances with the authorities; I am sure they will be very interested in all of this.'

He quickly sat, as he tried to process this news. He began to see that if this was true, it could be his salvation. 'Where did you find that?' pointing at his grandfather's notebook.

'You remember when you were trying to dispose of your friend?' *Carlos* was about to deny it when he realised that ship had sailed. 'Well by coincidence, some people witnessed you making a run for it in your boat. Sadly for you, you were recognised. But luckily for you, they are friends of ours,' pointing at his brother. 'They found this close to where your pal was sitting. What a great story, did you know the author?'

The shock of hearing this prompted him to respond without thinking. 'He was my grandfather.'

'Did you know him before his mind began to fail?' Des continued.

'How do you know all this information?' he gasped, unable to understand what he was hearing.

Chaz took over. 'Listen, that is not important right now. What you need to focus on is how we can help each other. We can lead you there. Can you open the lock?' he asked.

Carlos began to relax a bit, perhaps he could continue to use these guys.

He did not know how they had stumbled on to his operation. But as luck would have it, if it was true and they could lead him to his prize, he would play along.

'Yes I can, that notebook you found was one of many in which he recorded his plans for the resurrection of his beloved Third Reich. Sadly, as you deducted, as his mind started to fail him his writings became more garbled. Often they repeated themselves and often with conflicting information. Fortunately, the code for the lock was safely recorded, with all of the safety instructions,' he added ominously. 'This was recorded just after its construction. So, I can open it safely, now what do you want?'

'That's easy,' replied Chaz. 'What we always wanted, Des cleared of all charges, and satisfying the authorities about the Club incident, not to mention the death of the guys. We don't care who gets the blame, so long as we are not implicated.'

Feeling more confident, he replied, 'As far as the Barcelona incident, that I can fix. The other could prove to be a bit more problematic.'

Again, Chaz stepped in. 'We can help with that. I don't know why your pal decided to wreck the club and we don't care. But that is something you can use?'

He nodded, 'How?'

'You bring the other players in on the deal!'

'What! Are you crazy? Those '*gilpollas*' will try to steal the lot!'

'Of course, I would expect nothing less. But listen, you have a very small window of opportunity. They will have the identity of your dead friend very soon and won't take long to put two and two together. If you're dead, the treasure is not much good to you.'

He nodded, 'Okay, what's your plan?'

'Listen up,' he began to explain. 'You contact them at once, sound excited and urgent, tell them you have discovered the identity of the dead guy, and that you have some exciting news. Don't let them question you over the phone. Arrange a meeting, then this is what you will tell them,' as he outlined the details of phase one!

After he had made the call, they left his place headed back to the *El Rancho*, which everybody had begun to call it now.

'Can we trust him?' Des asked.

'As far as carrying out the meeting with his pals, I believe so.'

'Will he try and double cross them?'

'Absolutely,' he replied.

'Will he do the same to us?'

Chaz looked at his brother. 'We better hope so!'

84

PHASE 2.

They had all gathered as *Carlos* had requested, using the same location as before. When they arrived, they found him already there, with a bottle of *La Panto* open on the table, surrounded by four glasses.

'Come in gentlemen, I believe I have some exciting news.'

'How did you discover who the frozen guy was? The prints have only been available since this morning?' Uri asked.

'Relax, have a drink, I will explain everything,' as he launched into the story he and the Irish brothers had prepared. He went on to explain how one of his contacts in the police had recognised the description he had given. 'As it happens, this guy heads up the terrorist watch list, and this guy, our 'Mr X', is on it! He came here from Argentina a few weeks ago supposedly on business. But his close connection to the remnants of the Nazi party that took up residents there sent up a red flag. This is where it gets interesting. After they lost sight of him they decided to raid his apartment. They found numerous books and letters that indicated that he was in fact here to search for lost Nazi treasure!' The place erupted, as they bombarded him with questions. He put up his hand for silence. 'I will answer all your questions, but if we are to capitalise on this information, we have to act quickly.'

'Why is that?' Viktor asked.

'Well, because the information they discovered was obtained by 'illegal search'. They are keeping it under the carpet. He has agreed to pass them on to me if we will cut him in. But we have to act quickly, he says he can't contain it forever. Which to me means if we don't do it he will give it to somebody else.'

They sat around the table drinking as *Carlos* answered their questions. No mention was made of the Savage brothers. The agreement was that their names would be kept out of it. Chaz had warned him if he failed, they would vanish, and everything would go to the authorities.

The Irish clowns had believed him. In any case, when he got what he wanted, he would take care of the pair of them, and all of this mob too.

He looked at his excited partners. 'His name was Klaus Becker,' and he went on to create a back story that would hold water long enough for him to complete his plan. 'He is, or I should say, 'was' a fanatical follower of the Nazi party. And part of a group bent on restoring it to its former glory. This information was given to me by my colleague. The material they collected is in German, so far all he could make out is that it is something of great value. I have arranged for someone I trust to translate it, and we should have the information later tonight,' which was an easy promise, as it was himself. So, it was arranged to meet back there the following morning to continue their plans. 'One thing, stop all enquiries about our mystery benefactor, the less attention we bring to him the better.'

They all nodded agreement, as they left to make their own plans. With the same intention, *Carlos* phoned Chaz to report how the meeting had progressed. Then they continued to discuss the next part of the charade.

'So, when do we go to inspect your find?' he inquired, barely able to control his emotions.

'Before that happens, my brothers have to be cleared, not just for what happened in Barcelona, but all the shit that happened over here as well.'

'How would you like me to achieve that?'

'I don't want to tell you how to do your job, but if it was me I would shift the blame to someone else.'

There was a puzzled silence on the other end of the line. Chaz imagined his slippery mind trying to figure a way to convince these dumb Irish that he intended to fix their problem, but not in the way they believed.

Then he hit upon the solution. 'Would you have any objections in that being some of the other players?'

Chaz scoffed. 'I wouldn't care if it was the King of Spain, so long as our names are out of it.'

'Okay, I know you have some very 'influential' friends. If you have them reach out by this time tomorrow to their contacts, all mention of Des will disappear from the records and be replaced with our own *Antonio de Sota*. As to events here, I have plans for them which will include them being found responsible for the death of *De la Vega's* son and his companion. Is that agreeable?' he asked.

'If what you say happens tomorrow, you can get your crew ready go treasure hunting. Remember they must all accompany you,' Chaz warned.

'I would not have it any other way,' he assured him.

Before he could hang up, the voice on the other and end said, 'Oh, also be prepared to get wet!'

85

They were all assembled the next morning for the translation of the notebook, as *Carlos* prepared to launch into his 'modified' version of what it disclosed.

He began by explaining that it contained details of a plan to hide enough funds for the escape of Hitler and his entourage, also enough to fund the return of his beloved party. There was a chorus of questions. He put a hand up for silence. 'Let me finish, then we can discuss our next move,' as he continued with his story. 'It would seem whoever wrote this was the person who orchestrated the plan. But when Hitler committed suicide, he became very disillusioned and decided to keep the information to himself. Perhaps he intended to keep it for his own designs. But somehow it had fallen into the hands of this Klaus fella.'

Viktor spoke first. 'How does this help us? We know nothing about searching for this stash, how do we know if this place really exists?'

Rostov jumped in, 'If it was true, finding something left over from the Nazis would make the boss very happy,' thinking of his own skin.

Uri shut them up. 'Before you start deciding who gets what. we still have to find it!'

'But It has been found,' laughed *Carlos*, waving a piece of paper around. 'Before he got himself killed, he found an old cave guy who followed the clues in this notebook which led him to the location,' and then went on to describe how it led to the secret submarine pen and, as he paused for effect, then described the giant storeroom.

'Did he discover anything inside?' Uri asked, now that he could see that there was a strong possibility of some truth to this story.

'No, and for good reason, it is sealed by a solid-steel door!'

'So, can we follow the clues?' *Antonio* asked, quite happy to let his man handle things, firmly believing he was acting for both of them.

Carlos nodded, 'Good question, hopefully we won't have to. I have some local people out looking for this guy, they are a very tight group, I am confident I will find him. So I suggest we get ready to make a trip underground. Until then, everybody, keep your heads down and wait for my word and be prepared to move as soon as we find this guy.'

The feeling in the room was electric, believing that this wild story was a possibility, rich for life! They began to fantasise about how they would spend their fortune.

Carlos agreed to contact them later that day, or as soon as he found the '*Cavernicola*', his guide to their fortune.

When they left, he began his prepared explanation for *Antonio*. He followed the outline of the story Chaz had laid out for him. He began by explaining how the Savage brothers in their hunt for the mysterious Blond Bomber, had come across a mysterious old guy with a strange tale. He told of the discovery of a guy who sounded a lot like 'Blondie'. They had discovered him drowned in one of the caves. What made it more interesting, he told them that a few days previously the same guy had got him to retrace an old map, which he described as a small book. It described a difficult path which led to this submarine place. He had assured them he could retrace his steps and had agreed to lead them.

'So why do we need those *Conos?'* referring to the Russians.

'Because the boys insisted that someone takes the fall for the troubles they are in, which is why they approached me.'

'So, the set up with the guy's body was all their idea!' he yelped.

'I don't believe that pair could have come up with such a plan, remember they are only here a couple of weeks. No, I believe there is somebody else pulling the strings.'

'So, what do we do?' *Antonio* blustered.

'Nothing, we follow their plan, I am sure the others will be hatching their own ways to gain the upper hand. It won't matter, as soon as we discover the location, I have something up my sleeve,' he added slyly. 'Don't concern yourself with that, the only thing you have to worry about is if you can swim!'

Rostov was pacing back and forth in Viktor's place. 'Don't you see, this is the way out for all of us? We can satisfy the boss by producing Nazi treasure. It would be a huge feather in his cap, to flaunt in the faces of his Western foes. Plus, I am sure there will be enough left over to buy as many yachts as you want Viktor,' ignoring Uri in the conversation.

'Calm down my friend,' he replied with a smile on his face. 'All that you say has merit, but we must first find the goods, then get control of the situation, agreed?'

Rostov nodded his head vigorously, 'Sure, sure, whatever you say. I will head back to my place to prepare,' grabbing his things as he headed out the door.

Uri turned to look at Viktor with a quizzed expression. He shrugged his shoulders, 'Don't concern yourself. He will go in with us, but he won't be coming out!'

86

Des, Chaz, and Vincent had called everybody together to go over final plans.

After the filled them in on the meeting, and how *Carlos* played along. Bill was the first to speak 'I hope you don't trust that guy; I would bet the bank that he killed the frozen guy and was probably responsible for the other two that got crushed.' He was now completely invested in the scheme; those guys had disrupted his carefully crafted lifestyle. Now it was time for payback.

Chaz nodded. 'I would be surprised if he did not try something, but at the moment he need us to point the way to the trove. Did you check out if he followed through on his promise?' he asked.

'It sure looks like it,' he replied. 'They could find no mention of the affair on the records, but all his pals are bent, it could switch back if he wanted it to.'

'Yes, no doubt about that. But if things go as planned it won't matter. A bigger problem is predicting how the Russians will react, they are a strange bunch.'

Bill stepped in again, 'The 'Chaps' put out the feelers. That Uri guy is one bad dude. His name is Uri Pavel, supposedly originally from the Ukraine, where he was mixed up with the separatist movement. Apparently his methods were too brutal even for them. He next popped up in Israel, where he connected to a gang which had ties to the Russian mob. It would seem that Viktor has brought him along here to do the 'wet work'. As to Rostov, what he does, your guess is as good as mine. I would say what ever happens, he is living on borrowed time.'

'Which leaves us with *Antonio,*' Des added.

Chaz answered, 'He will be predictable, whatever *Carlos* does he will follow.'

'So, if all goes to plan,' glancing at Vincent, who nodded his head, 'I will have news for you before you decide to begin.'

'Well, what ever happens we are a go in two days' time, any longer and we risk of it blowing up in our faces increases. These guys will all have their own agendas. The longer we give them to plan, the more chances for things to go wrong.'

'What do you want us to do?' *Rob* asked.

'You guys have done enough, from now on it is up to us,' indicating his brothers. 'Before you object Bill, it is important that none of you are implicated. Anyway, if it goes wrong who is going to bail us out?' Then seeing the reluctance on his face, 'Don't worry, there is plenty you guys can do behind the scenes. A few days and I hope we can put all of this behind us.'

'What about the treasure?' Des asked.

Vincent answered, 'That is our best tool to bargain with. Whatever happens, whoever tries to cash in on that I believe is doomed to failure. It has too much history, all it can bring is trouble. Focus on the objective, clear your name, and get rid of these assholes for good.'

Just then Dawi arrived to announce dinner was served. 'Hope this is not the Last Supper,' Bill grumbled, as they made their way outside to eat.

87

CHAZ

I had got them all to meet at the apartment for the last time to go over the final details before we headed into the caves.

Observing this eclectic bunch of crooks chatting like old friends about to go on a fun trip, I realised that, different as they were, they all spoke a common language: money. How else could you get a Colombian drug dealer, two Russian failed oligarchs and a crazy Israeli hit man together in the same boat? Add to that the secretive *Carlos*, whose role in all of this was still to be fully explained. I could not have cared less what their plans were with regard to the loot as long as we all came out of this in one piece.

I had explained to Des and *Ricardo* their roles in all of this. '*Ricardo*, you will have to stay out of sight until they have gone through the flooded tunnel. We don't want *Carlo*s to know you are involved. Can you go first and mark the way for Des?'

He was not convinced this was a good idea. 'It is very easy to miss a sign in the caves, remember he has no experience down there,' he cautioned.

This was certainly a concern, but it was Des that came up with a bright idea. 'Let's use the dogs, *Ric* can leave a trail of something they will recognise, that way I will have back up.'

I had to agree it sounded feasible. So, it was agreed he would go down before the others and leave a trail of beef fat smeared on the walls for them to follow.

'*Antonio* will lose it when he sees the dogs,' Des sniggered.

'Good, anything to keep them off balance until this is over, but be prepared for anything,' I cautioned.

'So, what do you want me to do when we are inside?' Des asked.

'That depends on how *Carlos* decides to play it, remember he is running his own game. Plus he is the only one that can open the strong room without blowing the whole place up. Let's not forget, it is one thing to find the goods, it is another thing to figure out how to get anything out.'

'Well, what do we do?' he asked.

'Nothing, if they behave like I expect the one thing each will have in mind is to remove the other players and later recover the prize.'

'What should I do?' he asked.

I looked at him. 'What we do best, ad lib!'

I returned my thoughts to the players in the room, who were in deep conversation. I got their attention, with a discreet cough. 'Let's get to it. Tonight, at dusk we will meet at the sea entrance to *Cap Falco*, in the deserted restaurant. Please dress suitably for what you are about to do.' Directing my attention to the Russian dudes, dressed in suits, they nodded in agreement.

'Who will lead us?' *Antonio* asked.

'My brother, Des. He is the only one amongst you who knows the way, so I should remind you his safety is of paramount importance. Get lost down there and you will spend what is left of your short life in darkness, understood?' The look on their faces indicted that they got the message, and I went over the final instructions. 'This will not be a walk on the beach at moonlight. It is a difficult route, so be prepared to rough it, leave your egos outside. Follow his instructions if you want to get out of this. Understood?'

They all acknowledge their agreement, not that I believed them. The best thing we had in our favour was, as much as I did not trust them, they felt the same way about each other. I was counting that would work in our favour. They filed out with hearty encouragement all around. It was amazing how the thought of riches for life can make strange bed fellas.

As I closed the door behind them, I thought to myself, *Now to the hard part!*

88

THE CAVE

Des was waiting for the crew to arrive. He had arrived just as the sun was slipping under the horizon, and the evening shades of dusk cast an eerie shadow over the grotto entrance. As a cold breath of wind sent a shiver through his body, he hoped this was not a bad omen.

The sound of an approaching speedboat snapped him back to his senses. The dogs began to growl softly, sensing his tension. He scratched them behind their ears to reassure them as the boat slipped alongside the moorings provided for the guests of the restaurant.

Uri was the first out, busily securing the boat. *Antonio* who had provided the vessel was driving with *Carlos* acting as co-pilot. They all disembarked and unloaded massive amounts of equipment. Des looked at the pile of stuff, then at the assembled group of misfits.

'I don't know what all this stuff is, but you won't be bringing any of it. I have all the equipment we need for this trip. What you have to focus on is listening to my instructions, that's if you want to survive this journey …'

A shrill scream stopped him as everybody looked at a terrified *De Sota* quivering in the boat. 'What are those doing here?' pointing at the canines.

'They are here to keep me company, they go everywhere with me. Don't worry, they won't touch you. Unless I tell them,' he added.

'Enough of this, let's get on with it,' growled Viktor, who looked slightly ridiculous dressed in a bad copy of Indiana Jones in *Raiders of the lost Ark*. Rostov was not much better; his only concession was to change his designer shoes for sneakers and substitute his suit coat for a leather jacket and baseball cap. He looked like an American tourist in Africa.

Des pointed to separate backpacks for each of them. Alongside them were their separate lamps. 'Guard them with your life, no light and you will spend what is left of your life wandering in total darkness.' They all gripped their lifeline a little firmer, as the thought of being lost underground sobered them up very quickly.

'Okay, also we have this,' showing them a fine nylon rope with clips spaced along for them to attach to their belts. 'Until we get there we all depend on each other, just to remind you we are a team!' he said sarcastically, as they entered into the labyrinth.

The darkness enveloped them like a damp shroud as they entered, the feeling was so oppressive they could not switch their torches on quickly enough.

In single file Des guided them through the first narrow tunnel, leading into the large grotto. When they shone their torches around, the light reflecting off the stalagmites and stalactites created a spectacular light show. The lights danced around in a multitude of colours, illuminating the space around them so that even these hardened criminals could only look around in wonder.

'Over here,' he indicated, following the carefully disguised clues *Ric* had left for him to follow. 'Watch your step, if you stab yourself on the sharp protrusions I am told that the ensuing infection will probably kill you.' He then pointed to the cave entrance they had to follow. 'From here on, there will be many twists and turns, so remain very vigilant. If you lose contact or become separated you will become disorientated in minutes, so keep your line firmly connected at all times,' he cautioned as they entered the eerie gloom of the cave.

For the next hour they traversed through the multiple different paths and obstacles, once even Des missed a clue and had to retrace his steps to pick up the trail again.

'Are you sure you know where you are going?' *Carlos* asked, as they went deeper and deeper into this underground maze.

'If you want to get out of this, you better hope so or you are all doomed.' Then finally they arrived at the chamber. Where the flooded path commenced, he called a halt. 'Okay, we stop here to prepare for the next obstacle,' pointing at the dark pool of water in the far corner of the cave.

There was silence for a moment, then a chorus of voices broke out in panic. 'You don't expect us to go in there, do you?' Rostov asked in terror. 'I can't swim!'

Des turned to address them. 'I don't expect you to do anything that I have not already done, and remember, when I entered I had no idea where it would lead me. At least you will be following in my footsteps.'

There was a buzz of conversation amongst them, finally it was Uri that took charge. 'Enough,' he roared. 'Let's get on with this. How do we negotiate the water?' he asked, turning to Des.

'We use these,' producing the facemask breathers he had used before. 'Get into whatever you want to swim in, it is about a six-minute trip. So, breath slowly as the air in these small tanks barely have enough capacity for the return journey.'

'Count me out,' Rostov chipped in, 'And me,' added *Antonio*, 'my swimming is only good enough for a hot tub.'

Des shrugged, 'Suit yourselves, but if you were thinking of making a bolt for it, it will be last thing you will do. Anyway you will have them for company,' pointing at the dogs, which prompted a whimper from their previous owner!

While this discussion was going on, the others prepared for their dive. Viktor stripped down to his underwear. 'Not a pretty sight,' Des muttered under his breath. At the same time, *Carlos* and Uri, who were obviously competent divers, had prepared quickly. Des checked that Viktor understood how to use his mask. He had scuba diver training in his compulsory army training and seemed confident enough.

'Just remember, small breaths, if you want to come back,' he warned.

Viktor shrugged him off. 'Don't concern yourself with me, just get us to where we are going,' striding to the edge of the submerged path.

'You lead off,' Des pointed to Uri, 'I will take up the rear in case anybody gets into trouble,' he nodded and began to descend into the darkness. He was followed by Viktor, then *Carlos* and finally by Des.

The darkness enveloped them until they lit their torches, which were of little help as the murky water acted like fog, reflecting the light back at them. Des indicated to them to deflect the light with their hand so as to point it towards the roof or the floor. Uri caught on pretty quickly and set a steady pace. As predicted, just after six minutes they could see the light reflecting off the opening. One by one they clambered out of the water. They stood together and shone their lights around, frozen to the spot at what appeared in front of them.

The eerie sight of a deserted submarine base untouched since the end of the war greeted them. As they panned around, in front of them were the bones of the unfortunate construction workers scattered around like some dystopian scene. Then they locked their gaze on a massive structure with solid-steel gates, which brought a gasp from them.

The treasure!

89

Again, it was Uri that took the initiative. 'What are we waiting for?' As he picked his way over the debris to the gates of the strongroom, the others followed, all focused on the prize at hand.

'How do we open it?' Viktor asked, standing there in his shorts. With his mask perched on top of his head, looking like some sort of circus clown.

'Not so fast,' *Carlos* interjected. 'There are a couple of things we need to discuss before we come to that. According to this,' waving to the notebook in his hand, 'there is a series of numbers that have to be introduced into the locking mechanism. Any error will result in the safety devices being activated.'

'Safety devices?' queried Uri.

'Once opened, there are a number of safeguards to ensure somebody is not being coerced into opening it. Failure to implement the safeguards will result in being activated. By that it would seem explosives were planted, which would bring this place down, burying everything us included. So, if any of you were thinking of keeping it all for yourselves. I have memorised the steps and removed them as insurance.'

Viktor stepped in, 'We are all in this now, I am sure there will be enough for everybody, are we all agreed?'

There were mumblings of agreement all round. So, Des stepped in. 'Can we get on with this? I don't know about any of you but all I want to do is get out of this place in one piece and not end up like this lot,' indicating the bones scattered around the floor. He turned to *Carlos*, 'Get on with it, or we will have to order in takeaway!'

Nodding, *Carlos* crouched in front to the intricate mechanism of the lock. There were four circular metal wheels inserted into a solid plate with symbols surrounding the dials. He took a deep breath and slowly started to move the wheel on the extreme top right. Whispering, mostly to himself he started to rotate the wheel. 'Four positions on the top right.'

Then slowly moving the device until an audible click could be heard, he continued to rotate it again to the right until another click. He then reversed the rotation back past to the first markers. Again, a click, then finally again to the right.

He took a deep breath and wiped his brow. 'One down three to go.'

He continued by moving to the bottom left, again repeating the instructions to himself, 'Bottom left three positions,' as he carefully rotated the wheels, first clockwise and then twice anticlockwise. Each time waiting for an audible click. Now he moved to the bottom right, again repeating the process, this time with five rotations. Finally, top left. This time only two rotations. After the first one they all focused on the safe door, not knowing what to expect. Turning the wheel for the final time, it engaged and the familiar sound could be heard.

There was silence for a moment, then all manner of noises began to emanate from the doors and the surrounding frame. Devices that had not moved since the end of the war effortlessly commenced their task. A testament to German engineering, the solely mechanical devices began to release the locks securing the doors. Then, like a giant blue whale emptying its lungs with a blast of air, the doors began to slide open. *Carlos* jumped back to avoid the massive doors, standing in awe with the others as the interior beckoned.

Viktor was the first to react, stepping forward to enter. They all followed, taking in the incredible sight. Rows of crates, some of which were immediately recognised as gold bullion. There was narrow passageways down both sides that they could just squeeze through. On the sides were containers that on inspection appeared to hold paintings, no doubt stolen from museums and homes of wealthy Jews. *Carlos* gave a startled cry as he prised open a smaller chest. Peering in they could see it was packed with jewellery of every description. Moving on, opening boxes and containers, each one containing items of extreme value, from bearer bonds to all types of precious metals and stones.

'Enough to have set him up for life,' Des mused.

Viktor raised his eyebrows. 'Yes, enough to do anything he desired, perhaps enough for him to give the whole war thing another go?'

'Good job he never got to then,' he replied.

After they had poked around to satisfy their curiosity they headed outside. 'Well, we have to decide what our next move is,' *Carlos* said as they gathered at the entrance. The lamps that had been secured around to illuminate the front of the storeroom cast dark shadows around the vast empty space that once was a military base.

'That has already been taken care of,' came the voice of Uri, as he stepped out of the gloom, pointing a Glock 17 clutched firmly in his hand.

Des froze on the spot. At the same time *Carlos* let out a scream. 'Are you crazy, we have to plan how to get this stuff out of here?' pointing frantically at the exposed treasure.

Viktor took charge. 'You are a fool. Did you believe you could just walk out of here with any of this stuff, it is all tainted. Proceeds of criminal acts. Everything here will have to be dealt with great care. If word of this was to get out, every country in Europe would want their share. Not to mention the descendants of the Jewish families that were stripped of everything. No, this operation will require the support of powerful people. People with political connections,' referring to his beloved leader.

'You still need me. I am the only one that knows how to safely secure this place,' waving at the open door of the safe room. 'And just in case you think now that the door is open, you are safe, there are things that have to happen in a prescribed time or the whole place goes *BOOM!*'

Uri looked to *Viktor,* who gave a nod of his head. 'Okay, perhaps you may be of use for the moment, but unfortunately for you Mr Irishman, your usefulness is at an end,' indicating for Uri who was pointing the barrel of the gun at Des's head.

90

Des stood frozen, staring at the hole where death was about to be delivered. It looked so big he felt he could crawl inside. In his short life he had found himself in lots of sticky situations, but never anything like this. It seemed to him what they say is true—in moments like this your life flashes before your eyes.

He braced himself. It was as if time had slowed down to a snail's pace. In the peripherals of his vision, he could see the coal-black eyes of Uri as his finger began to tighten. Behind his back, the darkness seemed to take on a shape, which at the same time as he depressed the trigger, enveloped him, sending him crashing to the floor.

Des felt the pressure of the air around his ear, as the bullet missed him by a hair's breadth passing over his shoulder, hitting *Viktor* in the temple, taking out part of his skull and brain, along with his face mask and air bottle he had perched there. His body poised for a microsecond then slumped to the floor like a net of fish.

Before Des could get over the fact he was still alive he saw the big shadow begin to stand, then started to take shape. The figure beneath threw the tarpaulin he had used for disguising off and grabbed the gun that Uri had dropped. It was Chaz!

Within seconds, Uri lay unconscious on the ground, a blow to the head from the hunk of wood that Chaz had in his hand. Des looked up, fixing his brother with a shocked look.

'You took your time.'

91

24 HOURS EARLIER

Ricardo led Chaz down the labyrinth until they reached the water part of the entrance. 'This is where you go on alone, I am not fond of the water.'

Chaz nodded and he donned his breather mask, checking that it was working. 'If you can, let Des know I will be in position,' as he descended into the darkness.

He had decided that since they had no idea what these guys could be planning, there was no way he was going to leave his brother in their clutches in some abandoned cave. So, he found himself swimming in darkness, his light barely piercing the murky depths. As he broke surface he wasted no time in exploring this strange environment, finally settling down in a secluded corner for the long wait.

The sound of voices and movement brought him out of his troubled half sleep. For the next couple of hours, he listened and through glimpse of light from their lamps he could see them open the storeroom and disappear inside. After what seemed like an age they reappeared. That's when things took a turn for the worst. Uri produced a gun!

Stunned, he was unsure what to do. But when he turned the gun on his brother, he launched into action, grabbing a hunk of wood lying on the ground. He crept forward as silently as he could in the darkness, then with all his considerable strength smacked him as hard as he could, milliseconds before the gun discharged.

'A gun!' he cried. 'Did you not search them before you came down here?'

'Oh, I am sure they would have let me pat them down, no problem,' he replied sarcastically. Then his gaze moved to the lifeless body of Viktor.

Des stooped down to lift the mask away from his destroyed face. At that moment, whilst there attention was riveted on the gruesome sight, Uri regained his senses. Looking around, he spotted the shattered remains of his boss, realising that without his gun he was outnumbered, so he decided to make a dash for it. Grabbing a breather from where they had discarded them, he plunged into the pool to make his escape.

The splash as he hit the water alerted them. 'Quick, go after him! The others are waiting on the other side of the water, and they will get away. I will take care of him,' Des yelled, pointing at *Carlos*.

At the same time, he threw the mask he had retrieved from the stricken guy on the floor to Chaz who, without hesitation, went in hot pursuit of Uri.

92

He cautiously surfaced on the other side, unsure what to expect. He lifted his head above the water enough to look around. From the glow of a lamp lying on the ground inside the chamber he could make out the shape of somebody lying on the floor. Climbing out he cautiously crawled over to whoever was lying there. It was *Ricardo*! He quickly began to check for signs of life. To his immense relief, *Ricardo* immediately began to groan. As he struggled to sit upright, he helped him into a comfortable position, checking him for signs of damage.

'Are you hurt?' he asked.

He shook his head, 'No, just a bump where that '*Cono*' Uri hit me with something,' as he massaged his head, then explained why he was here. 'When you went in last night, I decided to hang around, just in case you needed a hand.'

Chaz looked around suddenly, 'The dogs?' he asked in alarm. Ric put his hand up to reassure him. 'When I heard them coming I hid in another chamber, the dogs must have picked up my scent, because they arrived to greet me! Later, I decided to go back to check thing out, I told them to stay put. When I got here, Uri was standing there dripping wet. He was with that Russian dude and *Antonio*, when they saw me. Before I could act, Uri jumped me and clobbered me with something. The next thing I remember is you sitting beside me.'

Chaz shone the lamp light around the place, it was deserted. 'They must have tried to make their way out,' shining to the tunnel they had entered from.

'Impossible, they don't know my signs they will get lost for sure.'

Chaz shook his head. ' Uri is clever, he brought this in,' waving the gun, he had retrieved and kept with him. 'They would have had a plan in case they needed to make their own way out. I am going after them, and they are not getting away with this shit!'

Jumping up, he looked around for any signs to where they went. He quickly found their tracks leading into the way they had come. 'Is this the only light you have?' he asked.

Ricardo shook his head. 'Take it, I have another stashed nearby. Hold on and I will come with you,' as he struggled to his feet.

'No, you need to recover, besides, Des should be coming through soon and he will probably have company. Better you stay and lend him a hand.'

Then without another word, he turned and darted into the darkness.

* * *

Back in the sub pen, Des watched his brother disappear into the water. Then he turned to face *Carlos*. 'Finally, it comes down to this. Remember back in Dublin when you were playing the 'hard man' in front of my brother. I bet you never in your wildest dreams thought you would find yourself in your magical Treasure cave, dream child of your fucked-up grandfather.'

Carlos let out a blood-curdling scream, launching himself at Des, swinging his ham-like forearm and fist, aiming to take Des's head off.

It never arrived. Before he made contact, Des planted his size 13 boot between Carlos's legs, crushing his privates. He collapsed like a dead body; the shriek that emanated from his mouth could have woken *Viktor's* corpse. But he was made of stern stuff and pushed himself off the ground to slam into Des, carrying them to the ground. *Carlos* was used to intimidating people, and when he had to resort to violence his size and strength usually finished it quickly. But he had picked the wrong one! Des had been dealing with this type for a long time. As soon as they were down he delivered a couple of elbow strikes to his forehead, resulting in a huge gash opening up, blinding *Carlos* with his own blood. As he pushed away, he followed up with a stunning blow to the kidney, the most painful body blow you can give, sending him stumbling back towards the door of the room.

'You are coming with me, even if I have to carry you or you swim, your choice.'

The expression on Des's face said it all. The frustrations of the last weeks finally came to a head as he enacted his revenge. For the first time fear crossed *Carlos's* face. 'You are crazy, what about all this. We can share it!' he screamed.

He shrugged, 'Too hard to carry, let's go,' he replied.

Carlos lurched to his feet in rage, stumbling back against the door. Suddenly it began to ratchet, as it started to close. *Carlos's* face turned from rage to abject terror.

'NOOOO!' he screamed. He launched himself at the door wrapping his arms around the edge in a futile attempt to stop it.

'What's wrong?' Des yelled.

'The mechanisms have to be reset before it closes,' was the frantic reply.

A cold realisation swept over Des. 'So, let's go and reset it,' he called.

But *Carlos* seemed to not hear as he tried vainly to stop its steady progress. Bracing his feet against the surrounding frame with his body half in and half out, he refused to give in. Finally, he gave a desperate croak as the door pinned him in the jam.

Much to Des's horror, *Carlos* was no match for the powerful motors that powered the door. With a gruesome squelch he watched as *Carlos* separated at about shoulder level. The lower half of his body slid down the frame leaving a vivid blood stain as it settled on the ground. Then with a final thump the door settled into its frame. There was silence for a moment then all hell broke loose. All kinds of strange sounds began to emanate from around the deserted submarine base. Des had no doubt what was about to happen.

He made a dash to the pool, grabbing a kit bag, breather and was just about to grab a lamp, when a huge pressure blast plunged him into the water and darkness.

93

CHAZ

As soon as I entered the tunnel I could see that this was the way they had gone. I continued to follow their tracks until I reached the first intersection. Much to my surprise, the trail went directly to the correct exit. I carried on, carefully looking out for some kind of trap. I figured a guy like Uri would not be happy to have been foiled in his plan by what he would consider an amateur. Plus, the fact it had resulted in him killing his pal.

Following the signs *Ricardo* had left, it was obvious that they were following some kind of trail. I knew they could recognise his markings, so I had to assume he had figured out his own method to find their way.

Suddenly, the whole place trembled and shook. My first thought was that it was an earthquake, but then a thunderous explosion followed. Before I had time to react, the entrance where I was standing began to shake violently as a massive blast of air, dust and rubble punched me in the back, propelling me out and covering me in debris. I must have blacked out for a moment. As I shook my head to try to clear my vision through the glare of the lamp that had flown from my hand, I could see the shape of somebody stoop down and pick up the gun which I had also lost.

'So, kind of you to return this, it is my favourite,' Uri said, pointing it at my head. 'It would seem your brother failed to prevent *Carlos* from blowing the place up. No problem, in fact it will help things. Now that the treasure is buried, and as soon as I dispose of you, its location will remain our secret,' indicating *De Sota* and Rostov standing behind him.

'Time to join your brother.' Fixing me with a cold smile of revenge, he began to pull the trigger

'NOOOO!' came a terrorised scream from *Antonio*. He paused, but still kept the gun firmly pointed at me. I realised there was nothing I could do.

He was professional enough to keep sufficient distance between us, so I had no chance of rushing him.

He fixed *De Sota* with a withering stare. 'What?'

'If you discharge a gun in here while this place is unstable, you could bring the whole place down, you will kill us all,' he pleaded.

He continued to keep his eyes fixed firmly on me. 'It seems you will see daylight again, but try anything and I won't hesitate, risk or not,' he warned me, indicating for me to get up. I stood shaking the dust off, pointing at the light.

He nodded, allowing me to retrieve it.'Okay, you lead off,' and before the thought could even enter my mind, he added, 'In case you are thinking of leading us in the wrong direction, I have this,' holding a small handheld device aloft. 'When we entered, did you think I would leave our return trip in your hands? I placed digital markers all along the route, invisible to the naked eye, but with this it is easy,' indicating the small screen with a small arrow pointing the direction.

We continued, me leading, followed closely by Uri. *Antonio* stuck closely by him, probably afraid he would be left here to die. Rostov just limped along behind, head down, not having a clue what they had in store for him. By his expression, he did not expect a great outcome.

Finally, we reached the last grotto where the entrance to the ruined night club lay. I had been racking my brains as to how I was going to make a final attempt to save my skin. But he was ready for any attempt on my part.

We made our way to the final tunnel that connected us to the outside. 'Lead on Irishman, I know you want to try something, it is what I would do. By all means try, I will give you a sporting chance, you never know you might make it,' he mocked.

You could hear the pleasure in his voice, knowing he was in control and held all the cards. I led the way, four to five paces in front of them, knowing whatever the outcome I was going to try something.

I emerged into the half-light reflecting off the inside marina. 'Keep moving to the water's edge,' Uri instructed.

I took a step forward, preparing to launch an attack, expecting a bullet to put my light out. Suddenly, the place burst into blinding white light.

For a second I wondered if I was dead, and this was the light at the end of the tunnel I'd been told about. Then a deafening voice broke the silence, enhanced by a loudspeaker. 'Stand where you are, put your hands in the air.' The authority in the voice left me in no doubt that to not comply would be a very bad idea.

I stuck my hands up, staring into the blinding glare, unable to see anything. I turned to see Uri emerge with his gun pointed to the lights. 'Drop the gun!' the voice demanded.

He continued to point it menacingly. 'Is this another of your tricks Irishman?' he sneered.

Before I could open my mouth a withering burst of machine gun fire hit Uri full in the torso, shredding him almost in half. What was left of him slumped to the ground like a butchered cow.

'The rest of you step forward,' the voice instructed.

The two remaining guys stepped forward to flank me, staring at the remains of Uri in horror. Then the lights were turned away, and I could see the place was full of soldiers with guns pointed at us. An imposing figure emerged, obviously a high-ranking one by the uniform he was wearing. Then from my peripheral vision I saw a familiar figure step alongside him and point at me.

'Not that one, he is with us. In fact, he is my brother,' declared Vincent Savage QC.

94

As Des hit the water, his survival instincts cut in. His primeval part of his brain did everything possible to keep him alive, forcing him back to consciousness. He clutched the face mask and somehow in his confused state managed to get it on his face, grabbing the mouthpiece and sucking in sweet-tasting air.

As he regained his senses, he realised that he had no light. He had no idea how he was going to navigate the way without it. He had no choice; no way was he going back. Using the walls for guidance he worked his way along, checking the ceiling height for orientation. It was slow going and time was against him. He had no idea how much air he had left. Under normal circumstances he had done this trip in around six minutes. He had no watch, but he was sure it was taking longer than that.

Being immersed in total blackness, his spatial awareness was also altered, and he knew he could be swimming up and down or even backward without being aware of it. He felt he had been going forever when, to his dismay, he could feel his air beginning to falter.

Trying not to panic, he began to conserve what was left by breathing shallow and holding as long as he could. But this only lasted a short time. Finally, it gave out. Sucking his last breath, he resigned himself to his fate. As he sank towards the floor, he imagined he saw a flash of light. Finally, he had no choice but to exhale.

He was just about to fill his lungs with water when someone grabbed him, thrusting a mouthpiece in his face. Sucking in life-giving breaths his rescuer shone a light in his face. It was *Ricardo*! The guy that was afraid of water. He was signalling frantically for the air, realising they were buddy breathing. Des passed it over, as *Ric* urged him to follow. Fortunately, the end was only a short distance away. Clambering out, Des dragged himself out, pulling his kit bag which was attached to his belt.

Then collapsed on the ground, but he had made it; he was alive!

He jumped up and grabbed his life saver in a bear hug. 'You saved me; how did you know to come looking?' he asked, as *Ric* struggled to release his grip, it was making him embarrassed.

'When the explosion came and the whole place nearly came down, I knew I had to go and see if you were still alive. I was not going to leave anybody else down here,' he said with a glimpse of a tear in his eye.

Des sat up abruptly 'Where is Chaz?' with concern in his voice.

'He went after the others,' replied *Ric*. He explained what had happened, with him being knocked out by Uri, then Chaz pursuing them. 'He instructed me to wait for you, but when the explosions came I thought the whole place was coming down. Then when you didn't appear, I finally worked up the courage to search for you.'

'It's a good job you did, another few moments and I would've been a goner.' Again, giving his rescuer a hug, increasing the poor guy's discomfort.

They checked what equipment that remained. Food and water would not be a problem, but they were concerned about how much charge they had left in the couple of lanterns they had left. Then *Ricardo* reacted.

'The dogs!' he cried, jumping up and rushing down one of the passages.

Des followed in hot pursuit, not sure where they were going, but not wanting to lose contact with the only one that knew the way out of this death trap. A couple of minutes later they entered another chamber to be greeted by two very happy dogs. After the usual greeting of licks and jumping up, almost bowling them over, Des shone the lamp at *Ric*.

'Okay, let's get the hell out of here before it comes down on our head!'

Returning back to the entry point, *Ric* pointed at the entrance that the others had taken. Des nodded, 'Lead on,' he instructed, shining his light to assist. The four of them headed off following the trail that he had left. Everything was going fine until they entered one of the caves that had multiple exits. *Ric* pulled up sharply.

'What's wrong?' Des asked.

Instead of replying, he just shone the light at a solid wall of rock. The exit had collapsed. They were trapped!

95

VINCENT

Chaz stood in total shock at what had just happened. 'How?' he spluttered.

Vince took him aside as the soldiers took care of the other pair. 'It's like this … '

TWO DAYS AGO

Vincent was ushered into a luxurious living room, in what could only be described as a mansion. He was in the home of *Christina De la Vaga*. A few strategic calls to some influential friends in the Spanish Royal Family had resulted in this audience with the reclusive and powerful *Señora*.

Seated beside an ornate fireplace sat a beautiful woman that could only have been the person he was here to see. At first appearance to Vincent, she reminded him of the film actress Salma Hayek.

She rose to greet him, extending her hand. She was tall and used her height to present herself with the dignity and power her position dictated. Her pleasant but cool greeting, indicated to him, that this meeting was only made possible by his connections.

'Thank you so much for your time. I will endeavour to illustrate to you how, what I present, could be the solution to the recent tragedy that has befallen you.' Pausing to indicate his condolences.

She waved her hand in irritation. 'Speak plainly, I have little time for this,' indicating that his time was limited.

He squared his shoulders and 'Vince' became Vincent Savage QC. 'Very well, what if I could present to you a plan that would bring to justice those that have been responsible for the destruction of the historic landmark, '*Cap Falco*', as well as all of the recent criminal wars and the damage they have caused to your valuable tourist industry? And of course, the death of your son and his companion,' pausing for effect. 'But most of all. To provide you with the location of a treasure trove of artefacts stolen by the Nazis. Enough for you to obtain any amount of favours from the countries you return them to.'

He could see he had her undivided attention. 'And what would you want in return for this information?' she asked.

'Our request is very simple: my clients, who have been drawn into this mess, are by being blackmailed. All we ask is this matter be resolved with the relevant authorities involved.'

She smiled, 'I would assume the 'authorities' involved are Spanish?'

'Correct,' he replied.

'Let's say for a moment I believe you, what proof do you have that any of this is true?'

'No more than I would ask. At the moment we have the advantage, one of my clients has found the location of the treasure with his own eyes, and together we have devised a plan that will deliver the culprits and the location. All that will be required of you is to collect the spoils.'

'Do you drink wine, Vincent? May I call you that?' she inquired as she ushered him to the seat opposed her.

'But of course, and what should I call you?'

A beautiful, cheeky smile crossed her face. 'When there are others around you should call me '*Señora de la Vaga'*, but since we appear to be about to become *amigos* you can call me *Christina.*'

The wine arrived. 'Should I guess where it came from?' he joked, as they sipped.

'You can try, but I should warn you, it came from one of my vineyards.'

He coughed. 'Okay, *Christina*, here is the plan.'

96

'So, this is what I came up with,' indicating the armed response he had arranged with *de la Vega* and her Commandante and close friend. 'I rushed back but you had already vanished, and nobody knew where you had got to.'

Chaz steadied himself on his brother's shoulder as he explained how he had decided to hide out in order to back up Des, and what had happened down in the cave.

'So, Des and *Carlos* are still down there?' he gasped. Chaz nodded as he started coughing violently again. 'Can we get a medic over here,' he yelled, as his brother struggled for breath.

As soon as help arrived, Vincent rushed away to inform the Commandante and the rescue teams that his other brother was trapped in the collapse.

The next few hours were a flurry of activity. *Antonio* and Rostov were transported to a navy vessel for transportation under heavy guard to prison in *Palma*. At the same time, the rescue squad were attempting to work out a strategy to rescue those trapped in the explosion. Chaz had recovered enough to explain, through an interpreter, how they had marked the path. Suddenly, he had a brainwave.

Remembering Uri's contraption that he had used to mark his path, he rushed over to the remains of his body, which had been covered with a ground sheet. He searched his pockets frantically, ignoring the bloody state of his body. 'Got it,' he cried rushing over to the bomb squad. 'He used this to mark his way to the cave. This should show you the way,' thrusting the device into the guy's hand.

After he explained to them its function, they got their communication specialists to look at it. After he examined it carefully, he explained through the interpreter that they believed, if it was still functioning, he should be able to locate the place it led too.

An agonising few hours crept by, with Vince and Chaz constantly inquiring for any news. Finally, the Commandante took them aside to explain what was happening.

'The device is working, and we have been able to triangulate the location of the cave, but please don't get your hopes up yet. All attempts to find access has failed. All the access points have been blocked by the explosion. The engineers are attempting to dig their way through, but as you can imagine they have to proceed with caution for fear of causing a further collapse. Please take your brother home and be with your friends, you cannot be of help here. In fact, you are a distraction to the operation.'

They were smart enough to see that their continuous questioning was only impeding the rescue operation. 'He is right, let's get back to Bill's, the others will be beside themselves worrying about what is happening.' Chaz nodded in reluctant agreement. A grateful Commandante arranged transport back the ranch.

When the army vehicle pulled up and the weary and dusty pair emerged, they were greeted by Bill and company, delighted to see them back safe and sound. Leading them inside, they clustered around bombarding them with questions about how their plan had gone. Suddenly, a loud cry quietened everybody down.

'Where are Des and *Ricardo?' Maria* yelled. Suddenly, the rest of the family realised they were missing too.

'Let's go inside and we will fill you in with what we know at this time,' Vince instructed. He and Chaz filed inside, followed by a stunned family, especially *Maria.* She was clinging to her dad for moral support, afraid of the news to come.

After they all gathered around, *Meris* attended to Chaz's cuts and bruises. He began to explain what had happened in the cave. Bill already knew of his plan to hide out and be ready to help Des should he needed any help.

'They were going to shoot him?' *Maria* cried again, collapsing into tears. Chaz continued, explaining how he had disarmed Uri and in the confusion had escaped.

'Des urged me to give chase, assuring me he could take care of *Carlos.*

When I emerged on the other side of the water barrier I found *Ricardo.* He had been knocked out and the other three had made off. He was fine,' he assured *Meris,* who looked at him in concern. 'He was just a bit dazed. I decided to take chase. *Ric* said he wanted to wait with the dogs for Des, so I continued. I don't know how long after that, it seemed only a short time and the explosion took place.'

He had to pause as this piece of news was too much for them. Vince put up his hand for calm. 'Please, everything possible is been done. Thanks to our plan to have the military there, they were able to mount a rescue operation almost at once.' Then, he went on to explain how Chaz's discovery of the tracking device had enabled the signal's unit to identify the exact location of the cave. 'At the moment access is blocked. They have assured us they will keep us informed regularly,' he explained in the most confident voice he could muster, in spite of his doubts.

Chaz continued. 'Well, when I regained consciousness I discovered Uri with his gun recovered. I had no choice but to follow his instructions. That's when I discovered he had that tracking device. When we emerged, his intention was to shoot me. However, thanks to my brother here and him bringing most of the Spanish Navy, it turned out to be Uri who ended up getting shot.'

The rest of the night was spent in low discussion, with copious amounts of coffee, served by Dawi, who continually came over to comfort Vince. They received numerous updates from the rescue site, but still no sign of a way through. Even more worrying was the absence of any signs of life, by way of banging or some other kind of signal. *Maria* was inconsolable, curled up in a ball in her mother's lap. Bill and his boys sat with Chaz and Vince, doing their best to keep their spirits up.

Dawn came with no news. Breakfast was served outside but hardly a thing was touched. It was one of those blistering hot summer days, not a cloud in the sky, a solid dome of brilliant blue overhead. None of this helped to lift the mood. When midday arrived and there was still no news, a grim reality was beginning to sink in.

Bill was approaching his sons to suggest going down to the site and try to help, instead of waiting here, when he stopped suddenly. 'Listen, do you're here that?' he asked.

Chaz lifted his head then suddenly jumped-up screaming, 'Yes I hear it, dogs,' he replied.

Everybody's attention was drawn to the commotion. Then to their amazement they were greeted by the sight of Bear and Lobo loping up the driveway, ears flopping, tongues hanging out in joy at being back with their family. They were only getting over the shock of the return of the dogs when, looking to the end of the driveway, they could see a dusty guy clambering out of the back of an open truck and helping his companion out. It was Des and *Ricardo*!

Maria was the first to react, wrenching herself free from her mother's embrace. She raced down the driveway, throwing herself on top of a very tired Desmond. They collapsed on the ground with her squeals of joy ringing in everybody's ears.

Chaos of joy erupted. They were almost carried back to the house where after a frantic period of time, basked in the delight at their miraculous return. Bill called for some calm.

'Can we give these guys a chance to catch their breath, and also to see if they need any medical attention before you badger them to death?'

At once *Meris* took charge. 'He is correct,' as she stepped in, clearing a space for her to examine the boys.

Des put his hand up. 'Listen we are okay, just very tired. Other than a few bruises we are fine, but I think I can speak for *Ric* by saying we would kill for a couple of beers!'

Suddenly everybody relaxed, the tension of the last twenty hours was broken. The girls were fussing over the boys while the others went in search of beer, not only for the returned heroes but also for themselves.

Finally, when calm returned and the realisation that the guys had somehow returned safe and sound, they begged for the story of their miraculous escape.

97

TWENTY HOURS PREVIOUSLY

Des shuffled over to *Ricardo*, in the dim light. 'No chance this way, I guess?' he asked.

He shook his head. 'It is completely blocked this way, we will have to try to find another way out,' he replied, without much conviction.

'What do you suggest?'

He shrugged his shoulders. 'I have no idea,' then he reacted suddenly. 'The dogs, they are our best chance.' In all the confusion of the last couple of hours he had completely forgotten their presence. Returning to where they had started, he indicated to the dogs a path leading into the darkness. 'This way,' shining the light to lead the way.

After a short journey, the sound of the dogs getting excited on returning to familiar scents was music to their ears. After the usual exuberance, Des asked, 'What now?'

Ric thought for a moment, then responded. 'Well, the route back to where we entered is totally blocked, our only chance is to hope we can find an alternative way out.'

'Do you think the dogs can help?' he asked.

'We have to hope so. Dogs have a built-in survival instinct. But if we follow them, there is always the possibility we could become totally lost,' he replied.

'Well, seeing as we are trapped anyway, I say, what have we got to lose?'

Again, *Ric* shrugged 'Nothing but our lives I suppose.'

Des went over to his pals, ruffling their ears. 'Well boys, I guess it is up to you, can you find the way home?' he asked. Their ears pricked up at the sound of the word 'Home' they started to dance around excitedly.

'Looks like they agree with us *Ric*,' as he jumped to his feet. Gathering what equipment they had, Des put his knapsack on his back, picked up his torch, while *Ric* did the same. 'Okay, let's go home,' he yelled, as the dogs scampered around waiting for his signal to go. Again, he looked at them shining the light around. 'Seek, find home,' he ordered.

They immediately started to sniff around as Des pointed at the numerous directions they could take, any of which he knew could lead them to their doom. Finally, Bear lifted his head and shot into one of the entrances followed by Lobo in hot pursuit.

'Come on, if we lose sight of them we are buggered,' Des cried, rushing after them, shining his light for them to follow. 'A dead end,' he groaned as they caught the dogs, finding them again sniffing around in all directions.

Retracing their steps, it was Bear again that seemed to find something that encouraged him to take off down another path. This went on for some time, going up and down blind passageways. After some hours, they stopped to rest.

'We are hopelessly lost,' *Ricardo* lamented.

'Here, drink some water, it will keep up your strength. It's not as good as beer, but I promise if we get out of here I will buy the first round.'

This brought a smile to *Ric's* face. Slugging some water, he struggled to his feet. 'Well then we better get out of here soon, so I can hold you to that,' as he urged their guides to continue their search for salvation.

They lost count of how many times they had traversed up and down different passageways. By now they had all blurred into the same, repeated again and again. A feeling of hopelessness began to creep over Des. Mumbling to himself, 'I have really screwed it up this time,' just as Lobo dropped something at his feet. He stooped to pick it up. He could not believe his eyes.

At first he thought it was some type of small animal, then he realised it was a small fluffy object. He recognised it at once. It was the rabbit's foot keyring *Maria* had given him for good luck.

'Look, at this,' he called to his exhausted friend.

Examining it *Ric* asked, ‘Do you know what it is?’

‘If I am right, it is our salvation. *Maria* gave it to me for luck when you took us to *Carlos*’s hideout. I must have dropped it when we discovered ‘Blondie’ floating there dead.’ He turned to the dogs again, holding the rabbit’s foot key ring he indicated to them. ‘Show us the way,’ waving it in front of their noses.

With a yelp they took off with the lads in hot pursuit, their energy restored with the hope of escaping their underground tomb. A few minutes later they entered a familiar place. It was where he had discovered the notebook. They hugged themselves with joy, then Des proceeded to roll on the ground sharing his happiness with their trusty guides.

After that it was an easy task for *Ricardo* to lead them to his usual entrance to the cave system. Emerging into the early morning, the feeling of the sun beating down from a clear blue sky was like being born again. Making their way to the road, they flagged down an early morning farmer heading back from the market. He gladly offered them a lift back to ‘*El Rancho*’ after they explained their ordeal.

Seated in the back of his truck with the dogs seated happily alongside them, the drive back felt like they were in the finest limousine.

98

'I had better tell the Commandante of your escape,' Vince said, as he called the rescue team with the good news.

While he was doing that Chaz asked, 'What happened to Carlos?' When Des told them of his fate and how he had been crushed, just before the explosion, Chaz added, 'So, Uri killed his boss, C*arlos* got crushed trying to save his beloved treasure, then Uri committed suicide trying to defeat the Spanish Navy singlehandedly. Sound about right?'

'What happened to the other pair?' he asked.

'In custody, awaiting their fate,' Bill replied. 'So it sounds like your plan worked out, too bad it is going to take an army to retrieve the treasure now. At least you are all safe, that's the main thing.'

Suddenly Des sat bolt upright in his chair. 'I forgot, where is my backpack?' Searching around franticly, 'I know I had it with me,' jumping up to search.

'It's here,' *Roberto* called, holding it aloft in his hand. 'You dropped it outside,' handing it to him.

'Come here everybody, especially the Heart family and you,' pointing at *Ricardo* as he gathered them, indicating for them to sit down. 'I have something to tell you,' and began to speak in a serious voice. 'When I discovered the treasure that first time, and when I was poking around inside, I discovered something I believed was important. I decided to take it out with me. Not sure what was going to happen, I put in my backpack and hid it, intending to pick it up whenever we got everything sorted out. So when I made a dash for it before the bomb exploded, I grabbed it. What I found, I believe, could be of great importance to the *Emanuel* family. That was you maiden name, correct *Meris*?'

She nodded, not sure what was going on. With that Des reached inside the backpack and pulled out a leather pouch. 'I think this is for both of you,' handing it to *Meri*s.

She gasped as she saw what was scratched on the flap leather pouch '*Familia Emanuel.*' Hands trembling, she opened the pouch and pulled out something wrapped in plastic. Unwrapping it, she opened the piece of paper inside. As she began to read, her eyes filled with tears.

Handing the letter to *Ric*, she looked up and gasped, 'They are alive.'

Bill rushed over, first to comfort his wife and find out what she was talking about. At the same moment, *Ricardo* reacted, handing the letter back to *Meri*s, and embracing her as they wept uncontrollably.

'It's in Spanish, here you read it,' Bill said in frustration at his inability to understand it fully .

He handed it to *Maria* who had joined in the crying. Wiping her eyes, she steadied herself. Translating, she began to read, 'To the Family *Emanuel*, and my father. We are writing this in the hope you can find it in your hearts to forgive us. All I can say in our defence is that the thought of not being able to spend our lives together was too hard to bear. So, we set off in search of treasure, never believing we would. Then we fell upon this by chance. We have taken only enough to give us a chance to begin a new life together. A friend of mine and his wife are leaving on a ship for Australia. We have decided to join them. If you decide that you can forgive us, we will begin our life in a place called Adelaide. If this is not to be, we understand and know that you will always keep a place in our hearts. Yours forever, *Monica Emanuel* and Diego Suarez, soon to be married.'

She handed the letter back to her mother. As they clustered around, they absorbed the information that there was every chance they were alive and well. Vince, Des, and Chaz, moved aside to let them enjoy the moment.

'I need a drink,' Vince declared, grabbing a bottle of *Solera Gran Reserva* and three glasses. Filling them he raised a toast, 'To Des, who never stops surprising me.'

Chaz added, 'And to making a few quid, because I see long flights in the future,' nodding in the direction of their adopted family.

A sly smile crossed Des's face. Standing up, in his loudest voice he called for attention. 'I have not finished my story.'

They all looked in his direction as he made his way to the table in the centre of the group. 'But, as you know, they say a picture paints a thousand words,' as he reached into his backpack again and pulled out what looked like a small football. It was a cloth pouch, which he upended onto the centre of the table.

A glittering array of what looked like polished glass heaped in the centre of the table. Waving his hand, he cried, 'I give you diamonds!'

99

Bill broke the silence, eyeing the mound of glittering stones. 'What are you going to do with these?'

As he inspected them carefull,. Des immediately replied, 'Not 'me', 'us!' Sweeping his hand all around the room, 'This is for everybody here. Without you guys, I doubt we,' indicating his brothers, 'would have survived. I know I speak for them when I say we consider you family. So, what do we do with them?'

Maria burst out laughing, 'I guess you don't know everything about my father. He is one of the leading dealers of precious stones in London. He even sits on the chair of the Diamond Bruges there. So, I think you have the 'What do we do?' covered,' pointing at her dad, who was engrossed in the pile in front of him.

'Well, Bill, have we done okay?' Vincent inquired, also inspecting their new riches.

Bill paused with some stones in his hand, then answered, 'From what I have seen so far, this is one of the finest collection of cut and uncut stones I have ever seen. Whoever put this together selected only the very best. Lord knows what the pile he was choosing from was like.'

Des could not contain himself. 'Are we rich?' he asked

All eyes turned to Bill. 'Well, let me put it this way, if we were to release all of these stones at once there is enough wealth here to put a big ripple through the market. So, yes you are rich, in fact we are all rich,' he laughed. 'But hold on, that depends on what you consider 'rich.' I reckon a better answer is to say, worrying where the money will come from for your next adventure. This would be taken care of that for the foreseeable future! So, a toast to the Savage brothers!'

All sorts of conversation broke out in this happy group. It was quickly agreed that Bill and Vincent would take charge of the diamonds and the plans to turn them into hard cash.

But before Bill could collect them up, *Maris* butted in. 'Before you do that, I have a suggestion. What do you think of the idea that Dad should choose a stone for each of us here? To be used, not for sale, but as a memento of the amazing thing that has happened?'

Pointing to include *Ricardo*, Bill said, 'It was Des's inquisitive nature and his initiative that has brought us hope of reuniting our family. So, for that reason this decision should be his.'

Without hesitation, Des turned to Bill. 'Great idea, I say do it!'

With nods of agreement all around they dutifully lined up to receive their stone. Ladies went first on Des's instructions. That held up proceedings for some time as Bill's choice did not exactly suit them. This did not worry the boys who were on their second bottle of *Solera Gran Reserva* brandy.

Ricardo was still getting over the shock of discovering he was a wealthy man. 'What are you going to buy first?' Des asked him. By this time, he was nicely merry, the guys had never seen him so happy. 'I will probably get a new motor for my boat,' he declared.

They collapsed in glee. Des said, 'You will be able to buy a fleet if you want.'

He shrugged, 'Only need one boat,' as he filled his glass again.

Finally, the ladies were satisfied with their choice, and it moved onto the guys, that only took moments as they gladly accepted Bill's pick. Des examined his. 'Out of curiosity, give me a ballpark figure what this is worth,' holding up the sparkling object.

Bill took it back and examined it. 'Somewhere between 25 and 35,' he replied. Des looked disappointed. 'I thought it would be more.'

Bill grinned. 'That would be 25,000 euros,' he added.

The place erupted in laughter as the celebrations continued late into the night.

100

CHAZ

It was a week after the 'cave collapse' and the rescue of some adventurers that were trapped in the caves. This, along with the news of the capture of the people behind the destruction of the '*Cap Falco*' and the recent crime wave that had swept the island, caused the press to descend on the island from all over Spain and other parts of the world, hungry for headlines.

Señora Christina de le Vaga was lauded for her initiative in using informants to bring down the gangs that had been disrupting the tranquillity of their beautiful island. No mention was made of any treasure.

The rest of the week was a blur. As statements had to be provided to the authorities, this is where Vincent stepped up. Thanks to his arrangement with *Christina*, a meeting had been convening at her house. Vince instructed us to keep our mouths shut and let him do the talking. I was perfectly happy with that.

When we arrived, we were ushered into a huge living room. By the actions of Vince, I could tell he was familiar with his surroundings. There were already a few people there.

I recognised the tough-looking gent in uniform, it was the Commandante from the battle and rescue, which seemed like a lifetime ago. He nodded in recognition; I quickly gave a small wave back.

Vince had also insisted that Bill accompany us, as he had a vested interest in the outcome of this meeting. Vincent had explained that an agreement had been reached between himself and *de la Vega* that they should convene, so as to decide how their stories should be presented.

Señora de la Vaga started proceedings. 'Perhaps introductions all around, to start.' Beginning with herself, then she moved to the Commandante

'*Edwardo de la Vaga,'* he answered with a smile.

She smiled back. '*MI Primo*'. My cousin, it pays to keep things in the family, don't you think,' with a sly jab at Vincent.

Vincent then began to explain the events that had brought them to this point. When he came to the part where *Carlos* had blackmailed them by hiding Des's involvement in the tourist-map scam, *Edwardo* interrupted, 'You are speaking about *Carlos Castillo?'*

Vince looked to me and Des for confirmation. Des acknowledged with a nod of his head. 'What you are describing is impossible, especially by a small-time grifter like him. That is something that could be covered up only by somebody at the highest level,' he explained.

Bill jumped in, 'Then how, when we forced him to get Des's name removed from the investigation, when I checked, his name was not there. In fact my source could not even find a file on it?'

Edwardo frowned, 'Excuse me for a moment.'

As he stepped out of the room, *Christina* spoke. 'Whilst my cousin is away, perhaps we can discuss the 'find'?'

Vince agreed. 'As you will have surmised, these are not only my clients but also kinfolk,' indicating me and Des. She smiled. Vince continued, 'Des is the brave sole. With the help of a friend of Bill's family, he discovered the treasure. He is the only one that has actually been inside the strong room, it is best if he describes what he saw.'

Des stepped forward, feeling very uncomfortable, but a stunning smile from this beautiful woman set him at ease. 'I did not have a lot of time, but I can confirm that the main crates are loaded with gold bullion. All around the sides of the room were crates, of all shapes and sizes. Those that I could open were crammed with valuables of all kinds. I could see through the gaps in the packing that the slim ones were paintings. But to tell the truth, it would take months to go through everything there. It was packed so tightly I could barely move,' he added for effect, as he swelled his chest, loving the attention.

Desmond the Treasure Hunter, I thought to myself with a smile.

At that point *Edwardo* entered the room, a smile on his face. Everybody's attention went to him, as he began to address me and Des.

'If I am to understand it, this guy *Carlos* convinced Des that he had evidence implicating him in an accident involving some young man of importance, due to some dubious tourist maps.' I was about to speak, but he held his hand up to continue. 'Then he flew to Dublin and convinced you that he needed your 'special talents', bringing you here for his harebrained scheme. Resulting in you nearly getting killed in his botched attempt to get the club temporally closed, correct?'

Before either of us could respond, he again continued. 'Would it interest you to know that the so-called investigation into the 'incident' was resolved the following day? It would seem that under interrogation the young punk involved confessed to have been in that area trying to score some drugs, something he had a record for. If not for his father's influence he would have gone to jail for wasting our time. The whole thing was closed the next day.'

Des blurted out. 'But what about the maps?'

The Commandante fixed him with a stare. 'If I had a euro for every crazy scheme that came across our desks, I would be a rich man. Never even reported.'

It was Bill who spoke next. 'So, when he said he had cleared Des's name from the records, he never had to do a thing, there was nothing there.' *Edwardo* nodded in agreement. Bill turned back to us. 'You got played!' he roared, bursting into laughter.

I could not believe my ears, all that had happened could have been avoided, if Des had bothered to verify what *Carlos* had told him. As they all erupted in laughter, I could not help myself, I burst out, 'Well, if we had not gone to the night club that night, I would never have seen the guy that blew the place up, and we would never have learned about the treasure.'

Edwardo raised his hand for silence 'What guy?' he asked.

I then realised we had not got to the point in the story where I had encountered 'Blondie', so I filled him in up to the point they discovered his body.

'Another body!' Was *Edwardo's* reaction.

Vince took over, explaining how we discovered the notebook and used the frozen corpse to implement their scam, when he disclosed this name, it brought an immediate reaction.

'Klaus Becker, we had been monitoring his movements, until he dropped out of sight. What happened to his corpse?' he asked.

Vince shrugged his shoulders, looking to me for an answer. 'I instructed *Carlos* and *Antonio* to dispose of him, I believe he 'Sleeps with the fishes', using a Godfather quote.'

'Well, that explains his disappearance and what he was up to with *Carlos*. We had all of you under surveillance, trying to figure out what the hell you lot were up to.'

I was the first to react. 'You were watching us?'

Edwardo grinned. 'We had our eyes on everybody, but nobody could figure out what two Irishmen with no gang affiliations were doing in the middle of this mess. Speaking for myself, I would never have believed you guys were the ones stirring the whole thing up.'

Des jumped in, 'Don't blame my brothers or anyone else, this is all my fault,' he pleaded.

It was *Christina* that spoke next. 'Blame you? On the contrary. If not for you and your friends, none of this would have come to light, and this treasure would probably have been lost for ever. We owe you a debt of gratitude.'

'So does this mean that I am in then clear?' he asked, nervously.

She glanced at her cousin, who answered. 'Clear as the driven snow. In fact you are all heroes in our eyes, but for all of your sake I think we should keep you and your friend's involvement in this low key.'

'Could not agree more' Vince replied. 'Now with your permission we should get down to the question of your 'find.' Is that okay *Christina* … sorry, *Señora de la Vaga*'?'

This slip brought a smile to her cousin's face. She nodded, 'I believe, considering the circumstances we can dispense with formalities, please continue.'

At this point he became Vincent QC again. 'Considering the origin of this find, I would suggest that it be treated with the upmost discretion. With that in mind, perhaps if you were to permit myself and a select panel, to include William Heart, who like you has the same desire to maintain peace and tranquillity here on the Island.' Pausing for effect, he added, 'The gold presents no problem as it can be made untraceable. Our idea regarding the paintings, is they perhaps could be used by you as bargaining chips with the original owners, where providence can be established.'

At this point she interrupted. 'How do we explain their appearance without drawing attention to the rest of the find?'

'What we have discussed as a plan,' nodding in Bills direction, 'is whenever you gain access to the cave again, we 'discover' an ancient burial site of Spanish origin and have it declared 'protected' from that point. The only people that will be granted access will be archaeologists of our choice, ensuring you have complete control of the find.'

She looked to *Edwardo* for his reaction. 'I can see you have given this a lot of thought, what you are suggesting makes a lot of sense. And from your point of view,' speaking to her cousin, 'it will provide you with a buffer. The only question I have is how do we account for the paintings or works of art?'

'Good question, this is where Bill and his associates come in. As art dealers they can make 'discoveries' in all sorts of locations. Allowing you to repatriate them with their original owners, which will probably be most of the museums in Europe. I am sure you will be able to use this to your advantage?'

Christina nodded in agreement. 'It would appear, *Edwardo*, that the treasure problem is in good hands. How goes the search for a way in?'

He smiled, glancing at Chaz. 'Thanks to Chaz finding the tracking device the Israeli had on him, we have been able to pinpoint the location exactly. With the help of that, divers have been able to locate the underwater entrance. It was partially collapsed but they were able to get inside. Work has already commenced in opening an entrance from the night club. Fortunately, the building that houses the treasure is buried from prying eyes, which is what Vincent has just suggested,' he replied.

'Which just leaves the matter of the crazy Nazis back in Argentina. They are going to wonder what has happened to *Carlos* and Klaus, and are likely to continue their search?' Vince queried.

Again, *Edwardo* replied, 'I will take care of that. As I said, we have been monitoring there movements and their association with the *Castillo* Family. I will be visiting them to let them know that their friends' remains have been discovered in a cave. Which had apparently been caused by their futile search on a wild-goose chase. A notebook discovered by their bodies spoke of some lost marine base, clearly the writings of some lunatic. I will be warning them any further attempts to continue this crazy endeavour would be dealt with most severely. With most of the repercussions falling on this family. They are already skating on thin ice, we won't have any more interference from that quarter,' he assured them.

Christina spoke, 'Well Vincent, if you agree, I believe we have addressed all of the pertinent issues, and can move on to then next issue?'

He looked confused. 'What other issue?'

'What you all would like to drink?' she cried in her delightful accent, as she rang a bell to attract the help.

101

THE FIESTA.

Three weeks had passed and the clamour for news had died down. Things had returned to normal on the Island. It was still a blur for all back at the ranch. There had been numerous meetings between Vince, Bill, and different members of *Christina's* inner circle.

Antonio had been charged with the destruction of the club and the deaths of *Christina's* son and his pal. While he was awaiting his arraignments, there was some concern of what he would say in open court. Sadly, for him he had an accident in prison, where he slipped in the showers, cutting his throat on a shiv.

The only comment from the *Guardia de Saville*, was that they were saddened that he had avoided the firing squad. As for Rostov, he was seen being escorted onto a private jet back to the motherland, provided by his beloved leader.

What happened to him was anybody's guess. But knowing *Christina*, his silence would have been assured by the late-night conversations had with the officials over there. The last thing they needed was more bad publicity.

It was decided that a proper celebration was needed. '*El Rancho'* was the obvious choice. The family pulled out all the stops. It was promising to be the event of the year from all accounts. Now that their relationship with *Señora de la Vaga* had become known, they had become the most popular people on the island. The guest list was the who's who, of Spanish dignitaries and some royalty.

Bill and Vincent had formed a partnership to deal with their windfall. He had invited a lot of the top 'Chaps' from the London crew. It was going to be some eclectic bunch, seeing as we had decided to fly Ma and Da over. They could not believe they had flown in by private jet.

We had decided to book then in to '*Palma Riad*', a quiet adult hotel in Palma. The shock would have been too much, having them at the ranch. Not for them, but for the Hearts!

Dad's first comment when he arrived was to advise Vincent that the company that owned the jet would not last long. 'There was more staff on the plane than passengers, we were waited on hand and foot. We were the only paying passengers. That gobshite will be broke in a month, if he keeps that up!'

Vince tried to explain, but he was wasting his time. Da would not have a bar of it. Vincent threw his hands in the air and walked off. 'Never listens,' he complained, as Des and I collapsed in laughter.

The day of the *Fiesta* arrived. From midday there was a steady stream of every conceivable luxury vehicle arriving, disgorging the guests. Dawi had pulled out all the stops. Awaiting their arrival was a team of waiters with champagne and a selection of the finest wines to greet them. In the area beside the pool, tables had been set up with all types of nibbles. While the chef was to one side basting some beasts on spits. There was beef and lamb, along with rows of chickens, roasting. Bill had arranged for a local band to provide the music. The theme was to be 'relaxed casual' and the Spanish certainly knew how to do that!

Soon, with glass in hand, everybody was getting into the swing of things. Suddenly the sound of an approaching helicopter got everybody's attention. As it circled to land on the lawn in front of the main house, the guests poured out in anticipation of its arrival.

As it settled on the ground and the rotor began to spool down, the door opened and one of the staff rushed forward to lower the steps. *Christina De la Vega* stepped out and descended to the lawn, followed by her cousin, the Commandante. She was dressed in western-style denims, with a pure-white, Mexican-style blouse, off the shoulders. Her hair was hanging loose in thick waves of dark-brown hair, complementing her dark complexion.

She commanded immediate attention, her elegance and poise left no doubt of her position. Bill hurried forward to accompany her inside, shielding her from too much attention. He did not have to worry. Her cousin, followed closely at her side and was quite capable of handling anything. It was obvious she was comfortable in this setting.

Walking inside, the first people she ran into was me and Des. She went directly to Des. 'My handsome hero, lovely to see you again,' giving him a hug and a traditional kiss on each cheek. She could not have failed to notice the glare she received from *Mari*a, who clutched firmly to his arm.

She turned to me. 'You have that dangerous look that attracts the ladies, how is it you are unaccompanied?'

Choking with embarrassment, before I could say anything, Dad who was standing beside me, cut in. 'That's what I keep telling him, he is not getting any younger. Tell me, are you attached yourself?' he asked.

Edwardo nearly swallowed his tongue. But *Christina*, seemed perfectly comfortable with his directness. 'Sadly, my husband has passed,' she replied.

'No point in wasting your life, a beautiful woman like you,. Come on, you and I need to have a chat,' as he took her hand, leading her over to the drink table before anybody could rush to her rescue. She looked over her shoulder, with a big grin, indicating she was perfectly happy been treated like a 'normal' woman. As they walked off, with him clutching her hand we could hear him ask, 'So, what's your name? Mine is the same as that 'single' son of mine, Charles,' he said pointedly, as he gave me a glare as if to say he was doing all the groundwork for me.

'He doesn't take after me, of course,' we heard him add, as he placed a drink in her hand. I looked at my father, from the worst part of Dublin and this regal lady of cultured bearing standing there like two long-lost friends. I realised in that moment that truth was stranger than fiction.

The *Fiesta* was in full swing when *Edwardo* grabbed me. 'Th*e Señora* has some information for you and the group, in private,' he informed us.

So we all gathered in Bill's study. When she had their attention, she said, 'I have some great news for you, but first, Desmond, where is the guide that helped you?'

'He is outside, his name is *Ricardo.* Will I bring him in?' She nodded. He went to get him. When they returned and was introduced, she shook his hand and asked him to sit down. 'I am going to speak to him is Spanish for a moment.' Then started to speak and I could see the tears welling up in his eyes. As she finished, she leaned in and gave him a hug, then continued to speak to us. 'I have been told the amazing story of the possibility that your family may still be alive. I have just promised I will use all our resources to try and locate where they went.'

Meris jumped up and ran to give her a hug. They embraced for a short time, then as she sat Christina continued, 'Now to the matter at hand. *Edwardo,* would you like to continue?'

Taking the floor, 'We have great news. We have broken through to the cave system and located the strongroom. As suggested, it is now a protected site and our team of 'specialists' have begun removing the treasure. To date we have only scratched the surface. The amount of gold we have recovered is staggering, not to mention the works of art and precious stones. As soon as you are ready Bill and Vincent, we will proceed with your plans,' he paused. 'To that end, *Señora de la Vaga* has something to say,' and handed the proceedings back to her.

'Although the arrangement I entered into with Vincent in the beginning did not include any division of the find, I feel in all fairness you all should be rewarded. To that end, Desmond, and *Ricardo*, today the sum of five hundred thousand euros each will be deposited in an account of your choice. As to the rest, we will begin with a payment of one-hundred thousand each. Of course, as the true amount is realised this matter will be revisited.'

There were gasps all round. 'Finally, we will add one hundred thousand euro to the search for your missing family. Now if I may suggest, there is a magnificent party awaiting us outside, and I can tell you, it is seldom I get a chance to let my hair down.'

As we filed out, I was gripped from behind. It was *Christina.* 'I wish to speak to you in private,' she said in a stern voice. Nervously I followed her to some seats. 'Can you bring drinks for us; I think we will need them.'

I had no idea where this was going, but I agreed, I certainly needed one! Handing her a glass of wine, she began. 'Your father suggested that I speak to you. But before I begin, I have a question: are you gay?'

I nearly choked! Before I came to this Island, I had never been asked that. Now I found myself being questioned for the second time, this time by the gay guy's mother! I spluttered my drink in shock.

She smiled. 'That's what I thought, but as you know I have had to deal with that with my son and had to be sure. Do you find me attractive?' was her next question. Again, I was struck dumb.

'Your father was right, impossible to get you to reveal your feelings. He said I would have to initiate things. So, I propose that we begin to meet socially, does this meet with your approval?' Somehow, I managed to nod my head like a simpleton. 'Good, then its settled, let's re-join the party.'

As we stood I spoke, 'I do.'

She turned to look at me. 'I do think you are attractive, but you are so much out of my league.' She smiled and reached in and kissed me, my legs started to tremble as I kissed her back. We separated and started to walk back outside. She whispered, 'I think your father was wrong about that.'

I stopped. 'What?'

'He said he didn't think you would be a great lover!' then striding off with a flick of her magnificent hips.

Forget about the money, it was so long since I had felt anything like this. I was over the moon. I rushed over to Dad. 'What did you say to her?'

He turned from one of the Spanish ladies at his side, 'I guess you are talking about *Chris*?' he asked.

His familiarity amazed me; he had only met her a short time ago. 'I just told her what a slow mover you were. I could tell she was interested.'

'How could you know that?' I asked. He just turned back to the lady, muttering, 'He can't be a son of mine.' As he began to chatter away to the woman who did not speak a word of English yet, seemed to be hanging on to his every word.

Ma was in her element. She had surrounded herself with *Meris, Maria* and of course Dawi. Holding court and filling them in with stories about her crazy sons. Of course, the plans to locate *Meris's* sister and *Ric*'s son was a top discussion. I could see that our two families, would from this point, be permanently bound. Looking at how Des and *Maria* behaved and seeing the effect Dawi had on Vincent, I began to feel for the first time my brothers could be getting their act together. Not that I could talk, as I found myself gravitating in the direction of *Christina* as often as I could. Where she would flirt with me with a glance of her incredible eyes. I could see I was not going anywhere anytime soon.

When it came time for *Christina* to depart, we accompanied her to the chopper. At the steps she leaned into me, whispering, 'Please come over to my house tomorrow night, I would like to continue our discussion,' giving me a playful pinch on my arm.

I stood, dumfounded, as her chopper disappeared into the evening sky. 'What was that about?' a voice came from my side. It was Vince.

'Nothing, she was just saying that we should arrange a meeting to discuss how we wanted our reward.'

He looked troubled. 'I feel a little bad, considering we have already been rewarded.'

Des, who was on the other side jumped in, 'Remember, she does not know that, if we refused it would look suspicious.'

I looked at him, 'Do you really think that she believed you were inside with all that loot, and the only thing you took was a leather pouch with a letter in it!' as we walked off, leaving him speechless.

'Does she know anything?' a worried Vince asked.

'No, but I am sure she knows enough about human nature that he was not going to leave empty-handed.'

I headed inside to catch up on my drinking.

?

EPILOGUE

The three of us sat outside as the party was winding down. Bill was inside surrounded by all the 'Chaps' deep in discussion as how best to capitalise on his newfound position. We had sent Ma and Da back to their hotel, with the promise to see them tomorrow.

We sat gazing at the clear night sky, with more stars than I could count. As the glow of the cooking fires cast light over our beautiful surroundings, so far removed from the family home back in Ireland, I raised a glass.

'A toast, to us, 'The Savages'.'

As we clinked glasses, I could see Des grinning from ear to ear. 'What are you so happy about?' I asked.

He turned to Vince and me, sticking his chest out proudly. 'I told you I had it covered!'

Watch out for the next Savage Brothers adventure!

www.ingramcontent.com/pod-product-compliance
Lightning Source LLC
Chambersburg PA
CBHW070843250626
47159CB00003B/905

* 9 7 8 0 6 4 5 5 0 7 2 9 4 *